The Gathering

THE GATHERING

Douglas Renwick

The Gathering Copyright © by Douglas Renwick. All Rights Reserved.

Author's Note

All the characters within this novel are fictitious, and any resemblance to actual persons is purely coincidental. While their beliefs and opinions are from my imagination, I do not necessarily share their views or their conclusions.

The novel is set in 2020. However, the technical, medical and statistical information on which it is based is real and current. Readers are urged to check for themselves any facts which they may find hard to accept. I struggled with some of them.

Douglas Renwick
December, 2018

'O death, where is thy sting? O grave, where is thy victory?'
1 Corinthians 15, Verse 55 KJV

'When Jacob finished charging his sons, he drew his feet into the bed and breathed his last, and was gathered to his people.'
Genesis 49, Verse 33 KJV

1

Ben counted the rings. He'd allowed himself ten, to give Fate a chance to play her hand. Not that he really believed in such things; you don't if you're a 34-year-old successful deputy hedge fund manager. That's all about analysing factors and trends and calculating risk and probability.

Concerning matters of the heart, though, Ben reluctantly conceded that there might be a fickle finger at your shoulder to point you in a certain direction – if you're not careful. That's what happened twelve years ago, when he was at uni. When Anna, the blonde blue-eyed ballet-dancing bombshell with a gorgeous smile and a wicked laugh pirouetted her way into his life.

Perhaps that finger failed him when he took the job in Hong Kong, leaving her behind to complete her degree course – and be snapped up by his mate, George. Or rather ex-mate. Not George's fault, though. All the time Ben and Anna were an item, George was careful not to muscle in. But does a blokey friendship bonded on the rugby field survive when a best mate marries the girl you should have married? Ben broke off all contact – and he guessed that George was happy with that. For Ben, it was the only way he could handle the loss of two good friends and cope with the ache of knowing you have made one of life's big mistakes.

At the time, it seemed the logical thing to do. To go east, young man, and take the job and earn some serious dosh for a year, then return and marry Anna and eventually buy her parents' house and keep bees and chickens and rear children – lots of them, to make up for the fact that neither Anna nor he had any siblings. That was the dream.

The reality, at the time, was that neither he nor Anna was ready to settle down. Ben was a restless twenty-two-year-old; Anna a year younger, a feminist and would-be God-botherer, if only she could find him – or rather her. And they clashed: there were arguments, disagreements and differing viewpoints.

But looking back, Ben appreciated that that's what you get when two undergrads, a natural scientist and an economist, both intellectually competitive, meet and fall in love. He did not share Anna's beliefs – the God thing, the life hereafter and all that – and he did not approve of her weekend retreats, the meditation and chanting and God knows what which went on this country house or that village hall, as Anna searched for something which he couldn't get to grips with, let alone provide.

He was as bad, almost, in that he would bang on for hours about how the world should be run, not by loonie lefties – or by elite ultra-right wingers – but by sane people who understood the laws of macro-economics and how money was the measure of man's achievements and the store of his efforts, rather than filthy lucre and the focus of man's greed.

For Anna, money was Mammon. She served the god she was struggling to find and despised money and the lust which went with it. She could afford to, being the only child of wealthy parents. Ben was the only child of a successful self-made shop-fitter from Sunderland, and he had learned through the example of his parents how hard work and diligence paid off.

Some might have said that they were totally incompatible. Different backgrounds, conflicting philosophies and few shared interests. Others might have said that Ben was punching above his weight, looks-wise, what with his nose remodelled by a rugby boot and a mild case of perichondrial hematoma affecting his right ear from the days before he wore a scrum-cap.

Anna was fine-boned with a slender jaw and a perfect skin which tanned naturally to a wonderful honey-tone which few blondes manage to achieve; light on her feet, dainty. In comparison, Ben was solid, broad-shouldered, slim hipped and had – according to Anna – a six-pack to die for. His skin was fair and freckly and, despite its light covering of hair over much of it, susceptible to sunburn.

Her blue eyes were deep enough to swim in, while his hazel ones twinkled below a male brow. But he had a kind face, square-jawed with a ready smile which revealed strong straight teeth, despite years playing the ruffians' game.

Anna was a true beauty. Character-wise, her friends would describe her as fun, feisty but inclined to be strident. The less generous ones, perhaps those who were jealous of her physical attributes, would admit she was prone to tantrums.

Ben was the opposite. Easy-going, practical, and – according to those who knew him well – he rarely got cross or grumpy, let alone lost his temper. Perhaps that's why, they wondered, he was able to handle Anna so well when she lost hers.

Rows between them were rare, but when they did happen they were short-lived. To mutual friends, of which they had many, it was a classic case of opposites attracting each other. It wasn't a case of whether Anna and Ben would tie the knot; just when.

Children: that's what they both were at the time, up at Cambridge. Kids trying to be adults. But Ben reckoned he'd mellowed somewhat over the past ten years; he'd grown up. And he wondered if Anna had done the same.

Thirteen rings.

Why the hell am I doing this? Having tapped in the number, he'd sort-of hoped to hear that continuous tone indicating that the line no longer existed. When he'd heard the very British double brrr-brrr ringing in that farmhouse in rural Kent, his darling Anna danced into his imagination and he heard the tinkle of her laughter. He knew exactly why he was hanging on, and what he was hoping for.

It didn't surprise him there was no answerphone or voicemail service. Not a techy sort of house; more of a homestead, locked into the late twentieth century. Perhaps a cordless phone, which had not been replaced in its charging station, ringing behind a sofa or from underneath the Sunday papers on the table in the study. Or in the kitchen, behind the mixing bowl on the pine table.

Seventeen rings, then they stopped. Ben heard a click and a female voice.

"Hello?"

"Hi, is that Mrs Black?"

"Speaking." A soft voice, hardly audible. Ben pressed his mobile closer to his ear.

"Hi Linda, it's Ben. Ben Bellamy." He smiled as he

pictured Anna's mum. Short black wavy hair, high cheekbones and full red lips. Large blue-grey eyes and the little laughter lines at their outer corners. And a dancer's body, just like her daughter's.

He heard a sigh followed by the sound of the phone being put down, perhaps on a table top, gently.

"Linda? Are you still there?... Linda?..."

"Hello, Ben. Arthur here. What a pleasant surprise! Where are you?"

"Hi Arthur. London, staying in one of those awful airport hotels, just for a couple of days until I get my bearings. I flew in from Hong Kong last night. On sabbatical, would you believe it, after ten years. How are you both? Still golfing?"

"We're... OK, but no golf these days. We gave it up a few years ago. I've got a few problems, and Linda's, umm, doing all right... And you? Hale and hearty? Married?"

Ben had fond memories of both Arthur and Linda. He hit it off with the pair of them when Anna brought him down to Uplands to meet them for the first time. After his own parents had emigrated to South Africa, the farmhouse had become a second home, and Anna's mum and dad made a special fuss of him, treating him almost as if he were their own son. Or son-in-law-to-be, perhaps. And he had always been ready to lend a hand, load the dishwasher or feed the chickens or repair the fence or mow the lawn.

When in the summer of 2010 he had announced he'd accepted a job in Hong Kong, they seemed desperately disappointed, especially when their daughter made it clear that she would continue her course and would not, thank-you-very-much, be trailing in his wake across to the far side of the world.

"Fine thanks, Arthur. And no, not married. Fancy free! No ties... And, er, the rest of the family?" Ben couldn't bring himself to mention Anna by name. He knew she was married – to best mate George – and the grapevine had told him they had started a family, with twin girls.

"Ben... Look, is there any way we could meet? Could you come down here? We'd love to see you, and, and..." Arthur's voice trailed away.

"Sure thing! Love to. I could train it down tomorrow and be there by lunchtime. Perhaps I could take you both out to lunch. At the Jolly Farmer?"

"That would be fine. Wonderful. Arrive at any time. It would be so good to see you. And have a chat."

Ben heard the line go dead. Something wasn't quite right. It was unlike Arthur to end a call so suddenly. Then his thoughts turned to Anna, and he wondered if she might be there the following morning. He hoped so. But his heart sank at the prospect of George also being there with her, and with their children, little versions of Anna made with George's kind help.

As the almost empty train barreled its way through the southern suburbs of London that Monday morning in March, Ben wondered how he would handle the situation. He considered the two possibilities and reckoned the more likely one was it would just be Anna's parents. He was worried that either one of them might be suffering from some illness or infirmity. Arthur was ten years older than Linda and she was forty when she had Anna.

'My elderly parents,' was how Anna had introduced them to him twelve years ago. And later on, Linda had told him how they had tried for a child for a long time before they were blessed with the arrival of lovely little Anna, the sweetest child you could ever wish to meet. You mean she was spoilt rotten, thought Ben at the time.

But then he remembered his own childhood, how good his parents had been to him, the sacrifices they'd made and the love and care he was so fortunate to have experienced. Perhaps he was spoilt, too. When Linda had explained that after Anna's birth there was no prospect of further pregnancies, he understood how Anna had become the focus of their lives and love.

He imagined how Arthur might break the bad news. 'My dear boy, there's something I must tell you; it's Linda. She's got..' Or, 'Now Ben, you should be aware that it looks as if my number is coming up pretty soon and... '

How do you reply to such news, he thought. 'I'm so terribly sorry, Arthur', or, 'Oh what bad luck! Surely, something can be done.'

It all seemed so trite. He decided he would offer to help in any way he could. He had money in the bank and, thanks to his sabbatical, time on his hands. He could help out, run errands, research cures, and generally help the family out in any way he could.

The family. The thought made him think of how he would react if Anna was there at the house when he arrived. A peck on the cheek? One on each cheek? Hands on the shoulders, or arms around her slender waist? With a, 'Hi Anna! You look great! Keeping well, then? And I understand you have some little ones? Congratulations!'.

With any luck, George should be at work, being a Monday. Ben wondered how he would handle it if, perish the thought, his ex-best-mate did happen to be there. Should he shake hands? Give him a man-hug? Punch his lights out?

He paid off the taxi, opened the little wooden gate and walked up the gravel path to the faded blue front door. His heart sank when he noticed there was no people-carrier parked in the yard with two child-seats strapped onto the back seat as he had imagined, or rather hoped. Never mind, he thought. I have twelve months.

Or she could arrive later, and join them for lunch at the pub. Then a walk across the fields back to the farmhouse for coffee, chatting away, taking the long route through the wood, holding her hand while she climbed over the style, like in the old days.

He smoothed down his light brown hair and practised his smile, then rang the doorbell and heard the distant tinkle from the kitchen. He took a deep breath and slowly let it out, relaxing as he did so. He heard a lock turn, and the door opened.

His jaw dropped. A shrunken little old lady with completely white hair stood in the doorway. She greeted him with a frightened stare from dull eyes sunk deep in their sockets.

"Er... Linda?" It was all Ben could manage. She moved forward and raised her trembling arms towards him. He took a step towards her and responded, careful not to crush her as they embraced. She held onto him, and he listened to her quiet sobs.

2

Ben looked up to see Arthur shuffling across the hall towards them.

"Ben, my dear, dear boy. So good to see you." He gently eased his wife from Ben's arms and tenderly pointed her frail frame towards the drawing room. The men shook hands then had a quick hug, long enough for Ben to feel the tremble in the old man's arms. Arthur ushered Ben outside through the front door and closed it behind him.

The two of them stood in the porch. "Sorry about that, Ben, to drag you out of the house, but I think it's best if we leave Linda for the moment." He glanced at his watch. "May I suggest we walk to the pub and have a warmer into the bank? Then when we feel like it, we can grab ourselves a sandwich or something."

Ben was glad to see Arthur. For a man of his age he was doing well despite the hair loss and the unsteadiness. Shorter than he remembered, but still a lanky six-footer.

"Good plan, Arthur. Great to be here... Is, er, is Linda okay?"

Arthur sighed. "It's a long story, I'm afraid. It'll take time. Shall we head off and talk on the way?" He went inside, reappearing ten seconds later wearing an ancient

Barbour and a tweed cap. He closed the front door behind him.

"Has it got anything to do with – Anna?" Ben remained on the porch, waiting for an answer before following Arthur who had started walking across the yard to the back gate.

Arthur stopped and turned to Ben. "It's a difficult story to tell. It won't be easy for me. You must forgive me, but I need to tell it in my own way."

"Anna's OK, isn't she? Nothing's happened to her, has it?" Ben caught up with Arthur so he could hear the reply, and the two men walked side by side. Arthur began his story.

"I'm not sure how much you know about what happened to Anna after you left. She was upset about you going – in fact, we all were – but after the long vac she went back to Cambridge and continued her studies. She was determined to get a first, bless her. And she did. Threw herself into her work. As you know, she's all we have…"

Ben's heart thumped when he detected the present tense; at least that was one possibility safely put out of the way. Somehow it brought him closer to her. He nodded, allowing her dad to continue.

"And we were concerned for her, as you can imagine. You young people these days, you have to work so hard at your studies. I mean in my day, it was mornings only – and even then, only if we felt like it!" He chuckled at the memory; then the sombre mood returned as they followed the footpath through the field.

It was a fresh and sunny morning, the sort which sometimes happens in early March, a sign that spring is on the way. Fortunately, there was no March wind to carry away Arthur's words.

"One of her friends, George Marshall, kept an eye on her. Do you know George? In her year, he was... Yes, of course you do. You played rugby together, didn't you?"

Ben smiled.

"Anyway, in their last year, they saw quite a bit of each other." Ben was reminded of the 'Dear John' letter which Anna had sent him, along with the plane ticket he'd bought her.

Arthur continued. "Then after they graduated, they both got jobs in London, and I suppose it was natural that they got to know each other better. Don't get me wrong, we liked George, but he wasn't – how can I put it – he wasn't 'you'. We had such high hopes for you and Anna. But perhaps it wasn't meant to be..."

It bloody well was meant to be, Ben wanted to say but didn't. They walked in silence for a few paces. Ben was itching to tell him to get on with it but thought it impolite.

"The two of them got engaged, and we had the wedding down here in June 2012, the year after she graduated. Lovely wedding. Beautiful weather. And Anna looked a million dollars.

"They went to Greece for their honeymoon and had a wonderful time; then it was back to work for both of them, each determined to follow their chosen career. Then Mother Nature played her part, and the twins were conceived. Anna's hopes of George becoming one of those 'house husbands' or whatever they're called nowadays went straight out of the window. She became a full-time mum.

"Of course, her mother and I were absolutely over the moon when we heard she was expecting. But poor Anna, she had a bad time of it, both before and after the birth. And there was no question of her going back to work after two weeks.

"It was wonderful for us, as Anna relied on us a lot – at least on Linda. I was not much of a modern grandad – not a nappy-daddy, I'm afraid. But I did play with them and help out where I could, collecting them from Fulham and taking them back again. I think I probably saw more of them than their father did, except when he was on holiday which wasn't much of the time. George was such a hard worker, leaving the house every morning before six and not getting back until after nine. But with a family to support..."

Serves you right, George, for poaching her.

They continued walking side by side along the footpath between two fields until they reached the road and the Jolly Farmer opposite. Arthur was telling Ben how wonderful the twin girls were – absolute darlings – as they crossed over to the pub.

"They sound delightful. You must be very proud of them. How old are they now?"

"Ben. Let's sit down there, in the garden on one of those picnic bench things. Do you fancy a coffee perhaps?"

Ben nodded.

"I'll pop in and order them. Do take a seat. Shan't be long."

Ben sat at the picnic table, enjoying the spring sunshine. The sums came automatically to him. Married in 2012. They probably waited a year or two, so the twins could have been born around 2014 or 15.

Arthur came to join him. "Two coffees coming up.

Americanos, I think they now call them, with milk on the side. She'll bring them out to us. Now, where were we?"

"I asked you how old the twins are – but let me guess... Five? Six? They must be at full-time school now, which should have eased the pressure on Anna-. What is it?... Arthur?"

Arthur was leaning on his elbows, his forehead resting on his hands, his palms pressing his eyes. He took a deep breath, lowered his hands, raised his head and looked Ben in the eye. "They're... not with us anymore. Our two little angels have gone. Just four years old. Four years! Four wonderful years for us, then gone..."

Ben was stunned. "Good God!... I'm so sorry... What was the... What happened, Arthur?"

The barmaid arrived carrying a brown plastic tray. "Here you are, then, gents, two americanos, and I brought you a couple of biscuits, those with chocolate on one side." Her smile was not returned, but Arthur managed to thank her, and the two men watched her return to the building.

When the coast was clear, Arthur leant towards Ben so he could lower his voice. "A car crash. So sad. Anna was driving. No other vehicle involved. Not Anna's fault, mind. Not at all. Ice on the road. Unsalted. No grit. Black ice. And the canal, running alongside the road. No kerb. Just a grass verge. Dear little things... Snowing... Dark..."

"What about Anna? Was she hurt?"

A long sigh from Arthur. "No. Not seriously. A few bumps and scratches. And the hypothermia, of course. She tried, Ben, so hard. Still waist deep in water when the police arrived. She was trying to open the rear door..."

Ben reached for his coffee cup, with both hands, then poured in the milk as he tried to hold the little jug steady.

Arthur nodded when Ben offered to put some milk in his cup, but he made no attempt to stir it, let alone pick it up.

They sat there in silence, except occasionally Ben would mumble something like 'Oh my God', or 'Good Lord' or some other expression of shock and sympathy.

"Mr Black!" the voice came from the pub back doorway, and a rotund middle-aged figure in country tweeds approached the bench with a big smile on his weathered face. "Just the man. I've a brace of pheasants for you, Mr Black, in the pickup, going cheap. Your missus will love 'em. Hang 'em for two weeks, and they will be gorgeous for Easter."

Arthur looked up and smiled. "Bill, my dear chap, that's awfully kind of you. How cheap is cheap?"

"Nothing for you. A gift. To cheer you up, a little early Easter prezzy for you both."

"Thanks, Bill, much appreciated. Oh, sorry Bill, this is Ben, my... er, friend – a friend of Anna's actually, down here for the day. Ben, this is Bill who works at the Manor."

"Game's my game, Ben. Pleased to meet you. But I'd better be getting on. Otherwise I'll be late for dinner. And the missus won't be too pleased, I can tell you!"

Arthur stood up and uncoiled himself from the picnic bench. He shook hands with Bill and thanked him again for the pheasants, and fished his wallet out of the back pocket of his trousers. He extracted a ten-pound note and gave it to Bill, explaining it was an early Easter present. Bill's eyes lit up and said he'd drop the pheasants round to the farmhouse on his way home. He wished them well and departed.

Arthur sat down again and turned to Ben. "Now, I want to hear all about what you've been up to for the past ten years. I cannot believe you've escaped the clutches of some oriental beauty for that long."

Between sips of coffee, Ben started from the day he came down to the farmhouse to say goodbye. He explained about his year-long post-graduate training course as an intern at Standard Chartered, then how he managed to work his way up the ladder and become a deputy fund manager. Arthur asked the right questions, and the lighter mood brought on by Bill's brief appearance continued.

It wasn't until the walk back to the farmhouse after their ploughman's lunch that Ben dared ask the question which had been on his mind since hearing the shocking news.

"Arthur, the accident. The twins. That was so tragic. How did Anna and George cope with that? Must have affected them profoundly. I mean, how do you ever get over such a tragedy?"

"I can only speak for Anna. She didn't. Hasn't. As far as we know, she hasn't got over it yet. But we hope time will heal. About six months after it happened, George and Anna split up. I don't know the ins and outs of it all, but apparently it often happens after a thing like that. There were arguments, about who should have done what, I suspect. A lot of 'if only so-and-so had done such-and-such'.

"Anna had her faith to support her, but I think even that faltered. She came to stay with us after the break-up. Linda was marvellous with her, so patient. Naturally, Linda herself was as upset as anyone, but she was a rock. Held us all together, in the weeks that followed, in the hospital, then the funeral... Difficult times, Ben."

They walked on in silence, then Ben asked, "Linda. Is she OK? She doesn't seem much of a rock at the moment.

I don't mean to pry, but she's not her old self. Is something else the matter with her?"

Arthur let out a big sigh. "I'm afraid her strength eventually ran out. It was a double bereavement. She was so close to Anna. In some ways, they were like sisters. Her only daughter. Her only child, for that matter."

"But you said Anna wasn't seriously hurt. Presumably, she recovered from the hypothermia. And she stayed with you after the split."

"That's true. It wasn't a physical thing. She had a breakdown of sorts, but she more or less got over it before she... Ah, there's Linda, in the garden with her trowel as usual... Linda! Why don't you show Ben the garden? I'm sure he'd love to see what you've been doing." He winked at Ben, and Ben played his part.

He was in no hurry to leave, but when the taxi arrived at two-thirty, he felt it was time to go. Arthur saw him to the front gate. They had a quick hug. As Arthur turned around to head back to the front door, Ben stopped him.

"Arthur, what happened? You said Anna had almost got over the breakdown, then she did something. What was that?"

"She left."

"What? She went back to George?"

"No. It was about eighteen months ago now. She just... left. Didn't say where she was going. She disappeared. Went missing. Nobody has heard from her, none of her friends. We've no idea where she is. It was too much for Linda. She cracked. She'd lost her lovely little granddaughters; then her own daughter disappears off the face of the earth."

"Jesus! That really is terrible." Ben felt a stabbing pain

in his heart and an ache behind the eyes, yet he realised it was nothing compared to how her parents must have felt. "Arthur, if I can help in any way... Is there anything I can do?"

Arthur turned and looked towards the house. Linda had gone inside and was standing in the drawing room window looking out at the two men by the gate. "Yes, Ben. There is."

"Sure. Honestly, I'd love to help if I can. What d'you have in mind?"

"Find Anna. And bring her back to us."

3

Ben was lost in thought when the train trundled into Victoria Station, but his struggling against the tide of home-bound commuters brought him back to reality as he made his way to the taxi rank outside. He joined the queue, and the enforced wait allowed his mind to drift back to his mission.

Mission impossible, more like, he thought. What the hell have I let myself in for? But he had offered to help, and remembering Linda's gaunt face at the window, he knew he must at least have a go at finding her daughter. And the last thing he wanted to do was to waste his sabbatical doing nothing. He wanted to achieve something worthwhile. And he wanted to make it up with Anna – if she'd have him.

He relaxed back in the roomy London cab, stretching his legs out enjoying the private space it gave him as it slowly made its way through the rush-hour traffic and around the endless road-works. Not that he was in a rush. He had nothing to rush back to, except a bland hotel room which could have been in any big city in any corner of the world. Nothing to look forward to that evening, except perhaps a quick one in the bar, then a room-service snack before hitting the sack. It had been a long day, and handling jet-lag was not one of his major talents.

As he expected, Tuesday arrived early on his doorstep; at 4.22 am according to the glowing green figures of the hotel clock on the bedside table. According to Hong Kong time, he'd had a good lie-in, and he felt top-notch after a deep sleep undisturbed by air turbulence or crew announcements. He was ready for whatever the day held for him. He remembered the mission and a thought struck him: if he did find Anna, and if she hadn't got hitched up to another interloper, and if she would forgive him for being so selfish in taking the Hong Kong job in the first place, then he might just get his life with her back on track.

Like it was 'always meant to be', as his old nan used to say. His head warned him to be prepared that something bad might have happened to Anna following her disappearing act. But his heart told him she was alive and well. Logic then kicked in. If she is dead, I'll arrange whatever needs to be arranged so her parents can have a funeral and grieve properly. And I can treasure my fond memory of her and find myself a soul-mate who will help me get over the loss.

If she's alive, back to Plan A. Ten years behind schedule, but few of his mates had tied the knot by his age, and when you're thirty-four, you think you've got loads of time.

"Yes sir!" He saluted his reflection in the wide mirror above the twin basins. "I accept the mission!" Then he fished out his gym kit from his cabin bag, put it on and made his way down to the basement following the signs to the Wellness Suite.

It was a cavernous space, deep below the streets of

Hounslow, its cream-painted concrete walls lit by industrial fluorescent fittings bolted to the off-white ceiling.

When he found he wasn't the only one working out on the machines, he wished he'd showered and cleaned his teeth. She reminded him of Yang Mi, the lusciously beautiful Chinese film star. He clocked the sky-blue Lycra gym suit – and the sparkly trainers. As for his unshaven state, he hoped she'd find his stubble acceptable and not think he was some layabout off the streets or was staying in the hotel as a guest of the Department of Health and Social Security.

Not that he cared that much about what she thought of him. He wasn't on the prowl. But a fellow guest, a female, to share a table with at meal times would be an acceptable distraction.

A phobia of his to which he happily admitted was that he couldn't bear to walk into a restaurant and sit at a table on his own. It was so sad, but there was also the danger that some unsavoury character would ask if they might join him. There was only one thing worse than dining alone, he reckoned, and that was sitting at a table with a strange man. If he was alone, his solution was to arm himself with a good book. It helped avoid eye contact if a fellow male guest happened to drift by, in find-a-friend mode or simply looking to expand his network of business acquaintances.

By the time he walked into the Breakfast Hall, it was beginning to get light. He chose the smallest table in the far corner of the room hoping no-one would disturb him. He placed his copy of *Shōgun* on one of the white faux-china side plates, grabbed a cup and saucer and made his way to the drinks bar. For him, the day didn't really begin until he'd had his first coffee. And there she was, the black-haired girl who'd been working on the cross-trainer, helping herself to a green tea.

"Zǎoshang hǎo. Nǐ jīntiān hǎo ma?" he said in his best Chinese. The standard morning greeting came easily enough to him.

She turned around and smiled at him. "Fēicháng hǎo, xièxiè nǐ, xiānshēng. Nǐ hǎo ma? And how did you know I speak Chinese?"

"Saw you on the plane. And, you look the part. I mean, you don't look Chinese, but having been in Hong Kong for ten years, I recognise Hongkongers at fifty paces." Not a good start, he thought, as he watched her smile fade.

"Are you saying I look Eurasian?" The question flustered Ben, but before he had a chance to mumble a reply, she said, "Because I am." She looked him up and down and smiled. Ben wondered if she found his embarrassment amusing. The meeting had suddenly got personal.

He tried again. "Are you staying here, at the hotel?"

She laughed. "Would I be having breakfast here if I wasn't?" She turned around and walked back to her table on the opposite side of the hall to where Ben had reserved his place.

He saw her again at the main reception desk on his way back to his room. She was waiting for the young blonde girl with a nose stud to come off the phone.

"Hello again!" he said. He thought about saying 'we can't go on meeting like this', but he'd used the line a couple of times and knew that the probability of it working was low. He thought he'd hedge his bets with the truth. "Look, we're both on our own here, and I hate sitting in a restaurant by myself, and I wondered if we could share a table this evening?"

"I might," she replied, "if I don't get a better offer."

The desk clerk with the nose stud was off the phone, and a couple of guests were standing close behind the Chinese girl anxiously waiting their turn, almost pushing her towards the desk.

"Yes, madam," said the nose stud, "and what can I do for you today?" It was Ben's cue to slink off. Just as well, he thought. I must make a start.

The first thing he did when he got back in his room was to phone the farmhouse again. He heard Linda's quiet greeting and was pleased she didn't put the phone down.

"Hello, Ben. I'm sorry about yesterday. I wasn't very brave, I'm afraid. But I'm glad you liked the garden. It's what keeps me going. And looking after Arthur. Or rather he looks after me. Perhaps a bit of both. We've only got each other, now."

"Linda, it was lovely to see you, after all this time, but I was devastated to hear the sad news. My condolences, of course, to you both..."

"Well, we were so pleased – relieved – to hear you're going to find Anna for us. It's been such a worry. The police, well... I suppose they are very busy. And it's not as if Anna is a little girl any more. It's so good of you to offer. And to bring her back! That would be wonderful. I know you'll succeed."

No pressure, then, thought Ben. "I'll do my best, Linda. Can I just ask if you have George's mobile number? I thought I'd start there."

"I think we do, dear. It's been some time. Let me pass you over to Arthur."

"Morning Ben. Thanks for coming to see us yesterday. You've given us hope. We're so grateful. You're after George's number. Yes, I think we have it here somewhere..."

The phone call had brought back dreadful images of the awful tragedy faced so bravely by Linda and Arthur, and all thoughts of the Yang Mi look-alike were knocked out of Ben's mind. He steeled himself for his next call. He knew it would be difficult.

"Hi, George. It's me, Ben."

"I know a few Bens. Ben who?"

"Ben Bellamy, your old mate."

"You! Ex-mate, you mean. Not even an emailed Christmas card. All these years. What the fuck do you want? You're not after money, are you? Because if you-"

"No George. I'm certainly not. And don't blame me for the loss of contact. You know why that was."

"So why phone now? And how the fuck did you get my number?"

"Arthur gave it to me. I went down to see them yesterday. They told me all about it. The twins and Anna. I'm so sorry, George. Really sorry."

There was a deep sigh on the other end of the phone. "Yeah, alright. Er, thanks. Thanks for calling... See you around..."

"Hang on, George. Can we meet?"

"Meet? What the fuck for? Old times sake? You must be joking."

"George. I need your help. I need to find Anna. It's not

for me. Not just me. It's her mum. She's desperate. Please, George?"

Another deep sigh. "Where are you?"

"Thanks, George. London. Just started a sabbatical."

"Tonight then. After seven. At my local in Fulham. Whore's Bed, if you know where that is. If you don't, ask someone."

Boar's Head, thought Ben. One of George's little habits. Then he remembered the Chinese girl, and that he had half-asked her to dine with him that evening. "Sorry, George. I'm busy then. What about lunch today?"

"Er, yeah. Alright. Let's get the fucking thing over with. I work in Holborn. D'you know The Ship? Near Holborn tube station. In a back alley. Make it 12.30. I can spare you an hour. And it's on you, mate."

"Sure, George. It'll be my pleasure. And I'm looking forw-"

George had rung off.

The taxi made good speed along the dual carriageway, but when it hit the A4 into central London, the traffic slowed it right down to a walking pace. And that's what Ben decided to do, walk. He'd left in good time but didn't relish spending it in the back of a slow-moving taxi, so he got the cabbie to drop him off in the Strand, and he walked up Kingsway to Holborn.

Outside the tube station, there was a man sitting in a doorway of an empty shop. From his tattered clothes, scuffed shoes and unwashed state, Ben cleverly deduced he was homeless. Three things about the guy surprised him. For a start, his hat was on his head and not upturned at his feet in the begging position. Secondly, he had a dog beside him, a collie who looked in better nick than he did. And he was reading a book.

"Excuse me, mate?" Ben asked him. "D'you know a pub around here called The Ship?"

"Yes, sir." A croaky voice, the result of sleeping rough during a British winter. "Go up to the traffic lights, turn right, then take first right down a passage and it's on your right. All right. Ha! Alright, then!" He chuckled at his own joke.

Ben smiled, thanked the man for his help and gave him a twenty-pound note. The tramp's laugh broke into a cough. "Blimey, mate! You're in a good mood this merry morning, aren't you?"

Ben walked on, but turned and smiled when he heard the man say, "Thank you, sir, thank you. And good luck to you, sir."

That's what Ben needed right now. Some luck. Lots of it.

He found The Ship – alright – and he smiled. Twenty pounds is a lot if you're homeless, but nothing for me, he thought. I'll just leave twenty pounds less to those who inherit all my worldly goods – if they haven't been promised in a pre-nuptial to some siren of womanhood in the meantime.

4

He was halfway through his first pint when George arrived ten minutes late. He stood up and offered George his hand. "George, great to see you! Good of you to meet me so soon. What can I get you?"

George just stood there with his hands in his pockets. "Hi. I suggest we go upstairs. There's a restaurant where we can sit and talk quietly without being disturbed. And the food's good."

"Sure, George. You lead the way." Ben left his beer on the bar and followed his ex-mate to the restaurant. It was empty, and George chose a table in the corner. The waitress brought them menu cards and a wine list. They scanned them in silence, then George announced he would be having the steak. Ben chose likewise and caught the waitress's eye.

The two men circled each other cautiously, talking about their jobs and their prospects, and the merits or otherwise of London as a financial centre compared with Hong Kong. After ten minutes, the waitress appeared.

"Two rares for you, gents, with home-made chips and veggies of the day. And your carafe of water. The wine waiter will bring your Shiraz in a jiffy. Enjoy your meal!"

After the wine waiter had left them to it, George opened the batting. "Let's get one thing straight. You fucked off to the Far East and left your so-called girl-friend in Cambridge. She had no choice. Did you really expect her to give up her course and follow you out there?"

"No, but I didn't expect my best friend to marry her." Ben remained calm. "I thought she'd wait for me. We were unofficially engaged. Sort-of. Not committed to each other in the sense of making vows, but I did expect we'd marry when I returned after my first year. By then, I think we would have both been ready."

"Well I can tell you," said George, jabbing his fork at Ben, "that if I hadn't watched out for her – on your behalf, I might add – some other bugger would have moved in."

"Watching out for my fiancée does not include marrying her. And take that fork out of my face."

The two men continued to eat in silence. ThenBen sighed and put down his knife and fork. "George. I made a mistake. I know that now. It wasn't your fault."

"Ben. Look. We fell in love. It wasn't meant to happen but it did. That's all there is to it. I'm sorry."

"Well, I'm sorry it didn't work out better for you. For both of you. I really am sorry about what happened. It must have been terrible."

"It was worse than terrible... You don't know the half of it... I guess her parents told you about the crash. Their version, I should imagine."

"OK, give me yours."

George let out a sigh, had a slug of wine and begun, stopping now and then to chew on a lump of Aberdeen Angus.

"She'd been to some charity lunch. I'd agreed to pick

the girls up from a birthday party, but I got caught up at work. I texted her to let her know, but she didn't look at her phone. The party hosts – the parents – phoned her to ask what was up and she got in the car and rushed around there to collect them. She should have called a taxi. The weather was terrible, and I guess she would have had a glass or three at the lunch do."

"But you can't blame her if you were meant to be picking up the girls?"

George put down his knife and fork. "Ben. Shut up and listen." He took another glug at his wine glass. "On the way back she skidded. That's the trouble with fourbies. People think they're fireproof on ice, and don't appreciate they have no more braking power than any other car.

"Anyway, the car left the road and slid down a bank into a canal. Not a deep one. About five foot, I suppose, covered in a thin layer of ice. That broke, of course, and the car rolled into the middle. Ended up on its side. God knows how Anna got out, but the twins didn't.

"She was still trying to open the rear door when the police arrived, but the doors were child-locked. The police tried but had to wait for a fire engine. In the end, they got a crane and winched the thing out – girls still in their child seats. Rushed to hospital, along with Anna and one of the policemen who'd been up to their necks in water trying to get at the girls.

"DOA, apparently. Not Anna and the policeman, just my two lovely treasures. The hospital must have got my number from Anna – not that she was making much sense. I arrived about half an hour after it happened, thanks to the police car that drove me down from the office, blue light doing its thing. Sirens the lot. Anna was conscious but in a bad way. I don't think she knew the girls hadn't made it.

"When the organ donor people came, they thought Anna knew, so it was a terrible shock for her. She refused. She said they'd be OK. She kept saying 'please God, please God' over and over again. It was our first serious disagreement, ever. About donating their organs. And I don't think we really recovered.

"I took time off until after the funeral, and we supported each other. Crying ourselves to sleep each night. Anna recovered from her hypothermia, but mentally she was broken. I went back to work which took my mind off it, but she had nothing to distract her.

"I dreaded coming home each evening, and so I started working later and later. That upset her even more. And she blamed me for the accident. 'If only you'd come home when you said you would' — that kind of thing.

"Actually, I think we both felt guilty, which didn't help matters. She got counselling which was good for her, but I think the bloke took her side. I became the outlet for her inner rage. Six months it lasted, then we split. She went back to her parents. I stayed in Fulham."

Ben swallowed and stared into his glass. Finally he looked up. "So, where is she now, George?"

"Blowed if I know. Frankly, I don't really care. We were finished when she left. Our girls had gone, so had our love. Nothing to hold us together. I had to start a new life, and I assumed she had done the same. Her parents phoned me up a couple of times, asking if she'd come back, but there was no way she would have done that. It was over."

"Where do you think she might have gone? Any ideas?"

"God knows. Actually, he probably does." George smiled. "After all, she talked to him enough."

"Funny, that," said Ben. "She was a bit religious. Had a thing about it. Searching for something... You don't think she might have done anything stupid?"

"Like top herself? Nope. Not Anna. That's something she was sure about. Her body belonged to God. She would never have self-harmed, let alone killed herself. I think that's why she was so anti organ donation. She reckoned it wasn't up to us to give bits away, whether we were alive or dead... Such a pity..."

"What was such a pity?"

"Her refusing to give her permission for the girls'-. You know, to donate their organs. They could have saved a few children's lives, and given sight to the blind and God knows what else. The hospital were upset. Two lovely girls, undamaged, apart from having lungs full of water. But Anna wouldn't have it..."

"Could she have gone to friends? Was there someone she was really close to, who would have taken her in?"

"No. When Linda first rang me, to ask if she'd returned, I did a ring round. None of them had seen her or had had any contact. They all assumed she was lying low, recovering from the trauma. Some felt guilty they hadn't kept in contact after the crash, but having written their letters of condolence, they probably felt they didn't want to intrude. Very awkward for them, of course. I've been there done that, but on the receiving end..."

"What about the police? Were they called? Was she reported as a missing person?"

"Dunno. Wasn't up to me. I think her parents did. I did my bit for Linda and Arthur, going through our phone book. We'd formally separated, for good. Parted. Went our separate ways. I wasn't going to walk into the nearest police station and say my estranged wife had disappeared."

"What about money? Assuming she is OK, how would she be coping financially?"

"We had a joint account for everyday things, and she hasn't touched that since we separated. She also has her own savings account, so I guess she would have survived on that. 'What's yours is ours and what's mine is mine'. Same old."

"Was she on Facebook? Twitter?"

"Never touched them – at least as far as I know."

"Emails?"

"She took her iPad with her when she moved back to her parents' place near Cranbrook. So, I've no idea. She was a keen googler, and followed blogs – especially those dealing with religion."

"Has any post arrived for her since she left?"

"Not really. Catalogues and things. Free magazines, of course. 'On Religion' was one. Monthly, I think. She read bits out to me. Put me 'off religion', it did. Charity mailouts. Some Christmas cards from people I've never met. Oh, and statements from one of her credit card companies. No expenditure, though. Zero to pay. But they keep coming... Madness. I forwarded all but the junk onto her, at her parents' place, until she did a runner. Then there was no point, and it all went in the bin."

"Anything else, George?"

"Yep. A coffee, then I must get back to the office. Otherwise, they might think I've been enjoying myself."

When Ben got back to his hotel room, he inspected the inside of his eyelids for a few hours, setting his alarm for six. He watched the news, showered and changed and made his way down to the dining room clutching his book.

He hoped he wouldn't be reading it. At least not for long, until the Yang Mi look-alike arrived.

As he entered the hotel restaurant, he scanned the tables, but there was no sign of her among the few early diners scattered randomly around the room. He chose a table – laid up for two – near the entrance to be sure he didn't miss her. He started to read, keeping one eye on the double doors. A waiter came up and asked him if he would like an aperitif. He ordered a prosecco and returned to his book. He was half-way into his second glass and totally absorbed by the sad account of how the heroine became a geisha girl when he heard her voice.

"Wǒ hěn gāoxìng nǐ zài zhèlǐ!" she said with a broad smile on her face.

Ben leapt to his feet and beamed at the apparition in front of him. "And I'm pleased to see you, too. Please. Come and join me," he said, as he went around the table to pull out her chair. "Would you care for a glass of prosecco, or something else?"

"That would be great, thank you. Thank God you're here! There's an American who keeps trying to chat me up, and I know if I sit on my own he'll want to join me. You know what they're like, and I'm not at all interested in that sort of thing. Like you, I hate sitting alone, as it's an open invitation for any male who happens to be passing. At least I know you won't try anything."

Ben felt like saying, 'thanks a lot', but at that moment the wine waiter arrived, and he ordered a prosecco for the lady.

"The name's Ben, by the way, and I'm a hedge-row manager earning $235,000 a year with bonuses." Fortunately, she recognised his poor attempt at an American accent and giggled.

"And I'm Ling, " she announced stretching out her hand across the table towards him. He reciprocated, being very careful not to knock over his tall wineglass.

"I work in IT... And I'm happily married," she added with a twinkle in her eye, "so you'll be perfectly safe, too."

His line about not wanting to eat alone was good, not only because it was true, but it avoided any doubt about the commitment: it was not a date. It did not convey any interest of a sexual nature, leaving each party free at the end of the meal to get up from the table and go on their way. On this occasion, he wondered if that wasn't such a desirable arrangement after all. But a married woman? That was not his style.

The usual small-talk followed. When their 'waitress-for-the-evening' brought the oversize menu cards, the subject turned to the food on offer, and they discussed the merits of hotel help-yourself buffets over the *a la carte*. They agreed that being able to see what you're getting and control the portion size overcame the seductive, mouth-watering descriptions on the menu.

He followed her towards the table laden with starters, watching her slender hips sway from side to side beneath her tight black dress. He noticed the black high heels, and the sheer stockings emphasising the gentle curves of her legs. And the long, black shiny hair which danced around her shoulders as she walked, revealing the occasional brief glimpse of the fair skin on her slender neck.

On the way back to their table, Ben summoned the wine waiter and asked for a bottle of red. When it came, the man asked which room number it should go on. "402," Ben said without thinking, realising a moment later that he had been too quick. But then getting a married woman's room number wasn't going to lead anywhere. Not in Ben's case.

"So, Ling, why are you here in London?"

"My brother's getting married on Saturday, and I'm here to represent the family at the wedding. And you? Do you live here?"

"No, not really. I'm with Standard Chartered in Hong Kong, but they've granted me a twelve-month sabbatical."

"How wonderful? What are you planning to do?"

"Oh, this and that." Ben was embarrassed that he hadn't planned anything in detail, although he had his bucket list. "Look up some old buddies, spend time with my parents in Cape Town. I'm hoping to get my skipper's licence. Not that I have a yacht, but I love sailing, and with a skipper's ticket I can charter one. And I'm going to do a PADI course. That stands for the Professional and, er, Amateur Diving Institute. It's a..."

"Similar to the Professional Association of Diving Instructors course?" Ling smiled.

"Just testing," Ben said. "And I've got some errands to run, and a couple of reunions. Should be fun. I had lunch today with an old friend. Hadn't seen him for ten years. Great fun. Talked about old times. We were at uni together." He looked down at his food as the haunting images came flooding back.

"Ben, you look sad. Had he changed since you last saw him?"

Damn it, thought Ben. It was the last subject he wanted to get onto, but her raised eyebrows and those big eyes looking directly into his demanded an answer.

"No. Not at all! Same old George!" He could see it wasn't working. He bit his lip and looked away. "I suppose we all change a bit. I mean, ten years. It's a long time..."

He made the mistake of returning her gaze, and seeing the sympathy in her eyes and the gentle smile on this beautiful creature sitting opposite him was enough to make him crack.

"We were good mates, but when I left uni and went to Hong Kong, we sort-of lost touch. There was a girl..."

Ben remembered an army friend telling him about resistance to interrogation techniques. How once you start spilling the beans, there's no stopping. And that's what happened to Ben that evening. It all came out. Everything. How he and Anna had planned to get married and have a big family, to make up for neither of them having any brothers or sisters. And how he wanted to earn some money and make some headway in his career beforehand.

Ling listened patiently as Ben explained about his best friend George, and then about the tragedy and Anna's subsequent disappearance. And how he promised her parents he would find her. When the tears welled up, Ling extended a hand across the table and laid it gently on his.

The dessert trolley came and went, and over coffee Ben finally reached the end of his story.

"I'm so sorry, Ben. Is there anything I can do to help?"

"That's kind, but I've just got to work my way through it. Go through the possibilities. Get some advice from Siri. Hang on a sec..."

Ben took out his wallet from the inside pocket of his jacket and pulled out a photograph. "This is Anna. In 2010." He passed it across the table to Ling.

"She's beautiful! I love her hair!" Ling paused. "And she has a kind face. She's strong. You must love her very much." She passed the photo back and smiled at Ben.

"It's a few years' old now, but at least it's something to go on," said Ben. "but first, I've got to find myself an Airbnb and get out of this place."

He saw the look on Ling's face, the deliberate turning down of the corners of her perfectly formed mouth in an exaggerated way as if to say I'm only pretending to be sad and I don't really mind if I never see you again.

"But I'm booked in here for a few more days, so why don't we do the same again tomorrow? I'll let you know if I make any progress in finding Anna."

Ling smiled. "That would be nice. You can fight off that American for me."

5

Wednesday for Ben began at 6.30 am, a slight improvement in the jet-lag situation. He'd enjoyed Ling's company and had appreciated her offer of help, even though he knew there wasn't much she could do. And he convinced himself it was a good thing – bearing in mind his mission – that any friendship which might or might not be developing with this electrically attractive beauty would be entirely platonic.

He thought he'd give the rowing machine a go and he made his way down to the basement. He was not fussed at all that there was no sign of Ling, although it did occur to him that it was a bit of a waste of hotel water having a shower before and after his workout. And when he met her leaving the Breakfast Hall as he was going in, he did a mental shrug of the shoulders, as if to say to himself 'see if I care'.

"Zǎoshang hǎo xiānshēng. Zhù nǐ shuì gè hǎo jué?"

"Yes, thanks, Ling. And you?"

"Really well, thank you. And Ben, thanks for last night. I enjoyed it, but I was sorry to hear about Anna."

"That's OK. I hope I didn't bore you."

"Not at all. Are you dining in the hotel tonight? I just wondered if we might..."

"Yes, definitely," said Ben, failing to hide his enthusiasm. "I'll be coming down to eat at about eight-ish after the Channel Four News. See you then?"

"Most certainly, kind sir." Ling smiled and did an almost imperceptible curtsey, then added, "if I don't get a better offer in the meantime."

Ben smiled, and they wished each other a good day. Cleaning his teeth before breakfast hadn't been such a bad idea.

He needed to return to Uplands and make some inquiries. Arthur answered the phone and seemed pleased to hear Ben's voice. "Come whenever you can, dear boy. You know you're always welcome here. And stay for a spot of lunch – if you can spare us the time."

It was just before eleven when Ben rang the doorbell of the farmhouse. When Arthur opened it and welcomed him in, the smell of fresh coffee wafted out from the kitchen.

"Coffee, tea, Ben? What can I get you?"

"Coffee, please. Normal milk and no sugar, if I may."

Arthur reached up for two mugs hanging on the oak beam above the Aga, then picked up the jug from the hot plate and brought it over to the table. As he went back to the fridge for the milk, he explained the situation. "Now, Linda's gone shopping with a friend from the village, so now's a good time for us to talk turkey if you see what I mean. It's better if she, er..."

"Sure, Arthur, I get the picture. Can I start by asking a few questions? I'll try not to sound like a policeman, but

I need to get a few facts straight, about how Anna... How she disappeared."

"You go right ahead, Ben. I'll try and help. And I'll try not to be silly..."

They were sitting at the kitchen table, on opposite sides. Arthur's elbows were resting on the ancient scrubbed pine. Ben noticed he was blinking, and he realised how hard it must be for anyone to re-live such a tragedy. But he knew he would have to ask the awkward questions and to do this he would be scratching at a sore – or rather a deep wound which was only just beginning to heal — one which would inevitably leave a permanent scar.

"Timings, Arthur. Can we start by going over a few dates, please? When was the -, when did it happen, the accident?"

"That's an easy one. 5th January 2018. A Friday. George was meant to be coming home early, but..." Arthur's words trailed off, and he lowered his head.

"And the funeral?"

"God, it must have been a couple of weeks. They had to do an... establish exactly why they... And the coroner had to give his permission."

"Sure, Arthur, I understand." Ben needed to go carefully, knowing his next question might be even harder for Arthur to cope with. Ben had to ask it. "Were the girls buried, or were they..."

"Cremated? Burnt?" Ben saw the frown, the clenched fists. He guessed it was Arthur's way of keeping it together. "The latter..."

It was Ben's turn to sigh. It meant there was no graveyard to visit. No graves for a grieving mother to tend. Her babies were gone, leaving only a few pounds of ash scattered over some rose bushes, along with everybody else's. Nothing left to keep Anna in south-west London, or indeed in south-east England, he thought. Or in England, for that matter.

"Arthur, can you tell me when Anna and George split up?"

"Yes. It was shortly after their sixth wedding anniversary, 16th June 2018. A couple of weeks later."

"And when did she come here?"

"Straight away. She came straight here. She came home. Obviously, we welcomed her into our arms, and in a way, we were so pleased she came to us... But it was so sad that those two young adults couldn't make it work. Couldn't hold it together and support each other through it. Tragic. She arrived by taxi with just two suitcases..."

Ben said nothing. He waited for Arthur to carry on, in his own time. A big sigh from Arthur, then he continued. "We didn't know she was coming. I was in the garden, and this black London cab stopped outside the gate. She didn't say much. When I saw it was her, I ran down the path and took her into my arms, my little girl. I heard the sobs – we'd had lots of those – but on that occasion my tears were silent. I could feel them rolling down my cheeks and into her blonde hair. But I knew I had to be strong.

"I realised what had happened, that they'd split up. The two cases confirmed it. I took them up to her room – her old room – and she followed me. Didn't say a word... I left her there. Linda was out playing bridge, but when she came back, she sensed something was different. It must have been the expression on my face. To be honest, I didn't know whether to laugh or cry. In some ways, it was like the returning of the prodigal son – daughter, in this case – but it wasn't something to be celebrated.

"We hadn't interfered between the two of them –

George and Anna. Of course, we knew things weren't going well from after the funeral. I mean how could they? But we hoped they'd get over it; settle down into their new life without their lovely girls." Arthur lifted his hands to cover his eyes. He took two deep breaths, raised his proud head and continued.

"About a week later, a van arrived with her things. George had got a removal company to pack them up and send them over. Good of him. Four boxes, in the barn. She never opened them all. God knows what's in them."

Ben sensed it was a good time to move on. "Arthur, can you tell me about what happened on the day she... went?"

"It was a Tuesday, 13th October. In the morning; fine day. She'd been with us about four months. We had good days and bad days. She never mentioned the twins or George for that matter. Linda and I hoped she was moving on, looking forwards, preparing herself for her future. Poor girl, just twenty-nine! A lifetime ahead of her, though. But she'd aged. Not surprising, really."

"Arthur, did she say anything before she left? How did she leave?"

"That's the mystery. We were both out at the time, at the garden centre choosing some shrubs. She didn't want to come, and we thought she'd be safe on her own. A grown woman, for God's sake!

"No note. No sign of her. We thought she'd just gone for a walk. Across the fields. She often did that but was never longer than about two hours. So when she wasn't back by lunchtime, we got a bit worried. We wondered if she'd sprained an ankle or something, but then we realised she'd phone us. She had a mobile, you know."

"Sorry, Arthur, can I just ask how she left? Was there a car she could have taken?"

"There was Linda's car in the garage. When she came back, we got it taxed and insured for Anna to use, but she never did. She said she was never going to drive again. The bus stop's miles away, so someone must have picked her up, a taxi perhaps. She'd done that before. Did I say she'd taken a suitcase? Well, she had. We went up to her room to check. That's when we realised she hadn't gone for a walk."

Ben had to ask the next question. He hoped Arthur would see it coming and would not be too shocked. He phrased it carefully. "Do you think she left of her own free will?"

"Yes. I do. You see, she packed her case; a few clothes, according to Linda. Her mum was good at that kind of thing, of knowing what was in Anna's wardrobe and tucked away in her chest of drawers. Always the mother hen! And Anna took her phone. You don't do that if you're kidnapped!"

Unless the kidnapper wants to cover their tracks, thought Ben. Another difficult question which Ben wanted to ask, more of a request: "Arthur, would you mind if I were to have a look in her room? Seems a good place to start."

"Not at all. You're welcome. Linda keeps it nice, for when Anna comes back. When you find her. If she *wants* to come back."

It made Ben realise the hurt those parents must feel when they think of that particular possibility, of their beloved daughter wanting to break off all contact. A runaway. How you must blame yourself – or your spouse. Something said or not said, done or not done. Some irritating habit or manner. Or simply that your child finds your company tiresome. Not that it was likely in Anna's case. She got on well with both of them, and they allowed her free rein to do whatever she liked.

Her bedroom was as he remembered it, all those years ago, when he would creep along the corridor from the guest room and snuggle up with her under the duvet until an hour before dawn, when he would creep back again, carefully avoiding the floorboard which squeaked.

The room was neat and tidy, clean linen and puffed up pillows on the divan bed, a little glass vase of fresh meadow flowers on the chest of drawers. A pile of magazines neatly stacked beside her bed. And her iPad on her bedside table.

He opened it and tapped the screen. Nothing. It was dead. Silly me, he thought. Nearly two years, what do you expect? And he doubted either Arthur or Linda had even thought of looking at it, let alone putting it on charge.

He heard the sound of the front door opening. He guessed it was Linda.

Arthur heard it too and looked at his watch. "Goodness, it's half-past twelve! And I forgot to put the quiche in the oven."

"My fault, Arthur. I've been asking too many questions."

"Not at all, dear boy. But now Linda's back it might be better to let it be for now... Let's go and join her."

The quiche was followed by his favourite: Linda's apple crumble, accompanied by lashings of double cream from the farm up the lane. Talk was of the lovely springtime weather and the possibilities of another good summer. Linda wanted to hear all about Hong Kong, and whether Ben had had any experience of typhoons.

As usual, he talked it up. He felt it his duty to dwell on the many good points about the country he now called home, rather than depress people with the bad bits, the almost unbearable heat and stifling humidity during the summer, the incessant insects, the overcrowding and the traffic, the noise. It was not everyone's idea of paradise, but Ben liked it, the excitement of the place, the work ethic and the exotic food.

After coffee, he looked at his watch and declared it was time to go. Arthur offered to take him to the station, and he accepted. As they walked across the yard to the car, Ben remembered the iPad in Anna's room and asked Arthur if he could borrow it.

"My dear boy. Have it — yours to keep. I'm sure Anna wouldn't mind. I'll get it for you while you say goodbye to Linda."

A few minutes later, Arthur returned, puffing. "Here we are. Now, let me just show you those boxes of hers. They're in the barn."

Ben had two more questions he had to ask, as the men walked across the farmyard. "Arthur, did you report the absence to the police?"

"Yes. Two days later. They asked lots of questions and added her to the list of missing persons. But they weren't hopeful, Anna being a mature adult who was technically still married. Unless we had some sort of proof of a crime, which of course we hadn't."

"Did you ever hear from her, after she left?" Ben thought it unlike Anna to cause her parents any unnecessary worry.

"Not a dickie-bird. Nothing. Some sick joker left a message on our phone, about a week after she left, telling us not to worry and saying she was fine. But it wasn't Anna. Linda said it sounded more like a Dalek!"

A text-to-speech message thought Ben. From a mobile to a land-line phone. His heart thumped.

There were four boxes in the barn: what used to be called tea-chests made out of thin plywood. Three of them had been opened, but the lids had been replaced. Ben read the letters scrawled on them with a black marker pen. 'BKS & MISC', 'CLOTHES & SHOES', 'KITCH & BATH'. George had done a good job, under the circumstances.

Ben looked at the fourth chest and noticed the lid was screwed down. It looked as if it had never been opened since its arrival two years ago. On it were just the two initials, 'L & J'. Clothes, he guessed. Shoes, dolls, cuddly toys, melamine mugs and plates covered in colourful cartoon characters, favourite games, picture books...

On the train back to Charing Cross Ben wondered how long Linda and Arthur would remain in that house. It was far too big for just the pair of them, with Anna gone and little prospect of them filling it with guests. And with them not being in the best of health, he imagined it was quite a struggle maintaining and running the place.

They should move to somewhere more manageable, he thought. Within walking distance of shops; perhaps a little village house. Not that it was any of his business, but he thought he might mention it to Arthur the next time he saw him.

6

When Ben got back to his hotel room, he extracted his phone charger from his cabin bag and put Anna's iPad on charge. Brilliant, he thought, as the screen burst into life – probably for the first time in ages. He thought he'd leave it while he showered and changed, then do a bit of delving before it was time to go down to dinner and meet Ling, if she hadn't had a better offer.

Great, he thought, when he came out of the shower and noticed the little battery icon showed it was taking a charge. While he still had one of the hotel's thick and fluffy bath towels around his waist, he sat down at the writing desk with Anna's iPad and pressed the central button which brought all the icons up onto the screen. Luckily, she hadn't locked it.

He began by swiping it sideways so he could look at all the apps. The usual ones were there, but no social media. No Facebook, Twitter, Snapchat or Instagram. No Words-with-Friends, Whatsapp? or any blogs.

Why have an iPad if you don't use it, he thought. His shoulders dropped, and he decided to get dressed and watch the news on the large wall TV at the end of his king-size double bed.

There was nothing exciting or interesting going on in the world, apart from a few proxy wars and government lies. After the adverts, his mind drifted back to Anna's unhelpful iPad. Perhaps she'd become a very private person and wasn't into all that social stuff. Perhaps she just used it to look things up, and for email.

E-mail. Of course! He jumped up and went back to the writing desk. His finger hovered over the Thunderbird icon. Was it right to read someone else's email, without their permission? But this was Anna's iPad, his ex-girlfriend's, a person with whom he'd had intimate relations. And someone he'd abandoned, who had become someone else's girlfriend, then fiancée then wife. What a fool...

"And that's Channel Four news. It's goodnight from Kathy and me." The weather forecast followed, predicting a mixture of sunshine and showers for the South East, light winds and a touch of early morning fog in low lying areas which would clear later in the day... It was time to go. But he couldn't resist it. He justified it on the grounds that it was in Anna's best interests for him to find her, and looking through her electronic correspondence might help his mission.

He started with her inbox, because it was less private. At least it wouldn't be mail she had written. The damn thing was empty. He had no choice, so he selected her outbox. Nothing. Browsing history? Blank. He yanked out the charging cable, grabbed his book – in case Ling had had a better offer – and made his way to the lift. He pressed the ground-floor button and hoped no-one from the three floors below him would interrupt his vertical journey down to street level; he was in no mood to make polite conversation with strangers.

Ling was sitting at a table for two, near the entrance, when Ben arrived in the dining room. It was rapidly filling up with diners.

"Thank goodness you're here," she said, "judging by the inquiries I've had in the last ten minutes, you'd think this was the only spare seat in the room. What kept you?"

"Sorry, I was, er... looking into something."

"Hey, Ben, where's the smile? Aren't you pleased to see me?"

"Of course I am," he beamed. "And I'm pleased you didn't get a better offer."

"Ah! But I did! But both were just too good-looking for me. Too tempting," she said, giving him her wicked smile. "Jīntiānguò de yúkuài ma?"

"Yes, thanks. Great... Actually, not so great. What about you?"

"I have sore feet, walking around London, seeing all the sights I didn't see last time. Nice weather, too. But why was your day not so good?"

"Well. I went back to Anna's parents' house, in Kent, to try and find out some more information about how she disappeared. She hadn't taken much, just the one suitcase. Left a lot of her clothes behind, and hadn't unpacked the boxes her husband had sent — not all of them. But she did leave her iPad in her bedroom, and her father said I could take it. I thought it might give me some clues."

"And did it?"

"No. Disappointing. I charged it up, but when I switched it on there was zilch. No social media – and her email boxes were empty. Either she never used the damn thing, or she must have deleted everything before she went. All her addresses. So, frankly, I'm a bit unhappy about that."

"What a shame!" Ling seemed genuinely disappointed. "I assume the deletion was before she went, so that was well over a year ago. That makes it difficult. Had she wiped the memory, do you know?"

"Haven't a clue. Shall we go and get some starters, and I'll catch the wine waiter's eye. Red or white?"

During the meal, he asked her to tell him about her day, and he found her animated enthusiasm attractive. He told her of his experiences last time he was in London and the sights he enjoyed the most, which included St. Paul's Cathedral. He was surprised she hadn't visited it and that it wasn't on her list.

"Really? It's a wonderful building, built by Christopher Wren, and it's where Prince Charles and Princess Diana got spliced. It's awe-inspiring!"

"Ben, I know it's a famous place, but I'm not a religious person in that way. I find God in nature, not buildings. Not that I'm looking for him – or rather it. Or she. Or they. If there is an intelligent power who created the world, the universe, I don't want to pretend it's a person."

Ben nodded in approval. Makes a change to hear that, he thought.

Ling must have sensed he was relaxed about her thoughts on the matter, and she continued. "It's like gravity. We know it's there, and we don't fully understand it. It's essential to our lives, yet it can cause all sorts of disasters. You cannot doubt its existence, but we don't think of it as a person. We don't worship gravity. We don't talk to it."

Ben smiled. His sentiments entirely. "Neither do we blame it if we fall off a balcony or a bridge collapses. And we don't praise it if it stops us drifting high into the sky like Mary Poppins."

Ling giggled.

"Anna was looking for God, in the traditional sense, a person she could talk to and listen to. At least she was when we were at uni. Perhaps she's found him. Although it must have been difficult for her when... I mean, how can you forgive your god if he lets something like that happen."

"The poor girl." Ling frowned as she said it, and her eyes stopped twinkling. They sat in silence for a few moments.

Ben appreciated that. He enjoyed conversation – banter and discussion – but he never felt the need to fill every moment with chatter, and it was a great relief to him that his companion thought the same.

The wine waiter broke their private reverie as he topped up their glasses. Ben remembered Ling's earlier question about the iPad.

"Just going back to Anna's computer, you asked about the memory wiping. I assume if there was stuff there in her email folders, it would have all been wiped off when she deleted it."

"Ah," said Ling, smiling again, "deleting and wiping are not the same thing. When you wipe a drive, it overwrites all the deleted data, but when you delete something on a computer – which is what most people do – you merely delete its heading: its signpost, if you like, which helps the computer locate the data. So, if the data hasn't been overwritten, it's still there."

"And if it has been overwritten?" Ben paused with a

spoonful of tiramisu between his overladen bowl and his mouth.

"Gone. Forever. Fragments might remain, but there might not be much left of the original document. But if Anna deleted those files and created no new ones, only the sign-posts would be lost."

Ben put his spoon down. "So, is there a way of finding the data without the sign-posts?"

"Oh yes. It takes time, but with a bit of patience it's possible."

"How, Ling? You must tell me how."

"Not so fast, Ben. First thing is you'll need a keyboard. Did Anna's iPad come with one?"

"No. Just the touchscreen."

"In that case, you'll need to get hold of a compatible keyboard. You can't get into the command mode with just a touch screen because it won't allow you to use the correct key combinations – holding down one key when you press another."

"Where can I get one from?"

"I expect most computer shops would sell you one, or you can get one on line, but it's not that simple. You need to know the right routines, and those aren't so easy to get hold of, because they could be used for illegal purposes, like hacking into state secrets."

Ben put his spoon back in the empty bowl and let out a big sigh as he slumped back in his chair. He was not an IT man. He used computers every day of his life, but he treated them like one would treat a mobile phone: you use them all the time, but you don't have to know what the wiggly amps are doing.

Ling leaned forward on her seat and looked at Ben with raised eyebrows. "Or you could get someone else to do it. Someone who knows how and has the right keyboard. They could restore the sign-posts, then you – with a bit of luck – might be able to see the files in her inbox and sent box."

"Where am I going to find a shady character like that to hack into the damn thing?"

"Am I shady enough for you?" Ling smiled and put her head slightly on one side. Her eyes were twinkling again. "Of course, I won't read the files, just make them visible again – assuming they've not been overwritten or wiped."

For Ben, the penny slowly dropped. "You mean you could... get them back? How cool! That would be so kind, Ling!"

"It would be a pleasure. You offered to help Anna's parents, and last night I offered to help you. It's the least I can do. But remember, she might have wiped them."

Ling made it sound so logical and sensible, and Ben felt invigourated at the prospect of making some progress in his mission.

"Wow! When would you be able to have a crack at it?" he said, remembering she was flying home in five days.

Ling looked at her watch. "Give me fifteen minutes. Then bring the iPad to my room. Five-three-six. On the fifth floor."

The two friends got up from the table and ascended together to the fourth floor. Ling remained in the lift while Ben walked to his room. His heart was racing as if he'd run up the stairs. He grabbed Anna's iPad and made his way up to Room 536.

Ling placed the iPad on the antique writing desk – identical to the one in Ben's room – and sat down in front of it. She connected the iPad to the keyboard of her laptop and settled down to work. Ben stood behind her so he could look over her shoulder at the screen, although he found it difficult to stop his eyes being drawn to her shiny black hair, her square shoulders, and, if he leaned slightly forward, the smooth pale skin above the neckline of her dark blue dress.

She rattled away at the keys and Ben watched the screen, leaning forward slightly so he could get a better view. The screen went blank; then small white characters began to form on the black background. She tapped away, a seemingly meaningless string of characters and punctuation marks. The screen scrolled up, went blank for a few moments, then a list of dates appeared. Ling looked up at Ben and smiled. "Anna's inbox!" She scrolled down the long list.

"My God!" said Ben. There are loads of them!" Without really thinking he put his right hand on her shoulder, a sort of pat on the back for work done well. But it lingered there, for just a moment longer than it needed to.

She looked up at him and giggled. "We've done it. Now let's try and get her sent box." Yes, thought Ben, all right then.

Ling warned Ben that there could be gaps in the documents if Anna had deleted them at different times and then created further files. It was just a matter of luck. But Ben was not discouraged. He was after names and email addresses which he could follow up, rather than the detail in the correspondence.

Ben was torn between returning to his room straight away to read through the restored documents, or somehow prolonging the evening in Room 536. Since leaving Anna ten years previously, he had experienced a few affairs, some shorter than others. But having lost

Anna to George, he knew how much misery infidelity could do to a relationship – for him it was a kind of bereavement. While he was as much driven by his instincts as any other healthy thirty-four-year-old male, he was overruled by his conscience. That's the trouble with adultery, he thought. If it doesn't go well you regret it. And if it does go well you regret it even more.

7

The lingering effects of jet-lag were creeping up on Ben as he arrived back at his hotel room, tired but happy that somewhere within the iPad he was clutching there was perhaps the vital clue. He managed to scan through the list of incoming emails, but nothing exciting caught his eye, and much of it seemed to be the usual junk. He reckoned a fresh start in the morning might be the way to tackle the task ahead of him.

Predictably, he woke up before the dawn but decided to try and get back to sleep until a sensible hour. But half his brain was still on Hong Kong time, so he found himself lying on his back staring at the artex ceiling, just visible in the faint glow of the bedside clock. He thought about Anna's emails and the secrets they might hold, and how he would go about tracing her contacts, the ones Ling had found.

He recalled his time the pre4vious evening in Ling's company. Her smile, her giggle and those twinkly eyes. Her husband's a lucky bloke, he thought, when he reminded himself of her status. Anyway, you have a mission. Think of Linda and Arthur and the promise you made to them. He imagined them rattling around in their six-bedroom farmhouse, alone, waiting for their beloved daughter to return, wondering if they would ever see her again.

With those thoughts of Anna in mind, he eventually drifted off, back into the land of nod until the sun, streaming through the undrawn curtains, prised open his eyelids. He looked at his watch and reckoned he could just about make breakfast.

He was pleased he'd got down in time, just before ten, but disappointed there was no sign of Ling. No doubt off doing some early sight-seeing, on such a lovely spring morning. But he had work to do. No lingering in the breakfast room for him, hoping she might walk in. After a boiled egg, toast and a cup of stewed hotel coffee, he returned to his room to read through the emails, hoping to spot some vital clue.

He began with the latest one.

"Dear Anna Marshall,
It gives me great pleasure to inform you that your application to join our community on Gorith Island has been accepted. Attached are some guidance notes for what to bring with you and your travel itinerary and documents. We suggest you transfer these to your mobile phone so you have them with you at all times. We wish you a pleasant journey and look forward very much to welcoming you.
Bless you and bon voyage,
Gorith"

Gorith Island, he thought. Sounds Welsh, perhaps like Caldey Island – or Ramsey. A 'community', eh? Commune, more like. Knowing Anna, it was something religious. Some sort of course, or gathering, a retreat, or whatever.

He read the email again. Sounds like a bloke's name, he thought, and he's got his own island. Must be wealthy. A guru? A cult leader, perhaps? Ben had heard about the moonies. And the siege at Waco. He was only six when that happened, but it was in the news on its twenty-fifth anniversary. He recalled that lots of people died. But the name Gorith didn't ring any bells for him, so he did what everyone does when they want to find out about something.

First, he typed in 'Gorith Island' into Google's search box and selected maps:

> Maps can't find *Gorith Island*. Make sure your search is spelled correctly. Try adding a city, state, or zip code.

Next, he tried just 'Gorith' on its own:

> *Gorith*, ». m. (rhith) A faint appearance; a phantom, or illusion, a. That partly appears; illusive Et — CortttTgyfarehawr. He i« an Utuiire gretler. TaHeiiit; Gorithiad ...

Straight from William Owen's 'Dictionary of the Welsh Language', published in 1832. He was right on one score, thought Ben. Gorith and his island were indeed illusive. Perhaps also a phantom. But the good news was that Gorith had never made the news. Which meant he couldn't have done anything really bad. But how the hell do you find him or his island if Google has never heard of him? Unfortunately, there were no attachments to the email telling him how to get there.

Obviously, the name had been changed to Gorith, so his

next attempt was to look at all the islands around Great Britain and make a list of those that could have recently become a base for some kind of closed community. That ruled out all those which had substantial populations, or were well-established tourist destinations, but that still left about thirty. Then he discarded any that were simply too small to sustain any population, let alone a self-contained commune. He was ended up with nineteen. But having looked them all up on Wikipedia, he was no nearer in establishing which one had been renamed after its rich new owner.

The bright sunshine streaming through his window persuaded him that a brisk walk would clear his mind, now cluttered up with useless information about Britain's many islands. As he entered the large revolving door leading out from Reception into the big wide world of the west London suburbs, he spotted Ling on her way in and waved through the glass. She did the same, and both of them decided to keep going round and meet the other. Fortunately, Ling had the sense to step outside, and she watched Ben slowly go around again, trapped by the glazed doors.

She was tapping her foot on the pavement, making a big thing of looking at her watch, then rolling her eyes. Ben got the joke and laughed, and the two embraced in that oh so English way when the English are trying to be like the French.

"Hey, thanks for last night!. You were wonderful!" said Ben, as a hotel guest, a middle-aged male was alighting from a taxi. He looked back and smiled at the couple.

"A pleasure," said Ling. "I love tinkering around with

those things. They are so easy compared to others. Anyway, I was glad to help. Have you had any success?"

"Not really. But I did find an email from a person called Gorith. He said her application had been accepted to attend a course or seminar, I guess, on his island. I've no idea where it is. And, believe it not, neither has Google. The email said there were two attachments, some instructions and travel docs, but they weren't there."

"Ah," said Ling, "that can happen, I'm afraid. The link gets lost."

"Not to worry. If she synced them with her mobile, she might have deleted them straight afterwards. The email didn't say much else. Just 'Bless you' at the end." Ben pursed his lips in disapproval and shrugged his shoulders. He didn't want Ling to see his frustration, so he smiled and decided to change the subject. "What are you planning to do this morning? Fancy going into civilisation for a bite of lunch?"

Half an hour and a taxi-ride later they were in a small Italian restaurant in Hammersmith decorated with plastic grape-vines and fake fishing nets, no doubt designed to conjure up the products of both vineyards and the sea which could be found chalked up on the menu board. They ordered spaghetti bolognese and a bottle of house red; rough stuff, but it went well with the rich sauce and the home-made focaccia.

"So, young lady, how do I find an island that nobody's heard of?"

"Hmm. Difficult. I would imagine some of these religious communities can be quite secretive; they don't want to be discovered. We don't know for sure that Anna took Gorith up on his offer. Or, she might have gone there for the seminar and come back. Was there a date on the email?"

"Can't remember, Ling, but it was the last one on the list, the most recent. And from the dates I did see, none of them was more recent than October 2018. She received no emails after she disappeared. At least none arrived on her iPad. It was probably switched off."

"Ben, here's a thought. We know someone who has heard of it!" Ben couldn't understand why Ling was so enthusiastic.

"Okay, so who might that be?"

"Who do you think?"

Ben frowned as he tried to follow Ling's train of thought. "Dunno. I give up."

"Anna. She must have heard of it. Otherwise, how would she have applied to attend whatever it was?"

"Er, but she's disappeared. She might still be there. How can we ask her if we don't know where she is?"

"Silly boy! We don't *ask* her. We find out *how* she discovered it!"

"How can we do that?"

"Perhaps she read about it, or saw an advert... in a magazine, or newspaper-"

"That's a thought. There's a pile of magazines in her room at her parents' place. And I think her ex mentioned one called 'On Religion'. He made a joke about it. Said it put him off religion."

"Worth a try?"

"Sure. I'll go there this afternoon and bring them back. I'll let you know how I get on this evening. I take it you'll be dining in the hotel?"

"Not so, Ben. Tonight we are having the rehearsal for my brother's wedding, and I need to be there. We are then going out for a meal, and Sasha's parents have offered me a bed for the night. She's the bride, and her parents have a flat in Pimlico. In fact, they suggested I also stay there tomorrow and over the weekend. I fly back to Hong Kong on Sunday evening, so it makes sense for me to check out of the hotel this afternoon."

Ben frowned. "So when am I going to see you again – to let you know how I get on?"

"Well, time's short, but how about you showing me St. Paul's Cathedral tomorrow morning – and then lunch?"

Ben relaxed his furrowed brow and he smiled. "Sure thing. Eleven, say? Happy to do that – if I don't get a better offer!" Ling giggled, leaned forward across the table and ruffled his hair.

By 3.00 pm he was in the Dover-bound train from Charing Cross for the third time that week, on his way to Uplands Farmhouse. He'd phoned ahead to make sure Arthur was going to be around, and he explained the reason for his visit. Arthur seemed pleased he was going to see Ben again and promised he'd put the kettle on.

He arrived in good time for tea, and as the two men sat at the kitchen table with their mugs in front of them, Ben brought up the subject of moving house.

"Arthur, I know it's none of my business, but have you and Linda thought about moving? Perhaps somewhere more convenient, easier to manage? I mean, now Anna has gone…"

It was a foolish thing to say, and Arthur took it badly. "Oh, Ben! You don't sound very hopeful! For Heaven's sake don't tell Linda!"

"No, Arthur, I am hopeful. Really I am. I was just thinking of you, and coping with a place this size."

"Well, we would like to move. We love this place, and it does have happy memories, but for oldies like us it's not very practical. But we couldn't sell it without Anna's blessing. It's her home – and her inheritance."

"Arthur. I'm sure she'd understand. And if – er, rather when – she comes back she may want to work and live in London, to have her own home."

"It's not that simple. Uplands is her home, her house. She actually owns it. Shortly after she married, we made it over to her. Our financial adviser persuaded us to sign the papers, to save inheritance tax. We didn't make a big thing of it, because we thought it wise not to let George know. We wanted it to be an asset just in her name..."

Ben, for once, was lost for words. Anna's parents were trapped in this big house, and he could see no way out of this mess for them. He wished he hadn't brought the subject up.

"You said you were hopeful, Ben. About finding her? May I ask what progress you've had?"

"Sure, Arthur. I don't want to raise your hopes, but I think she went on a course of some description, to an island, perhaps a Christian community of some sort, a retreat. At least I know the name of the place. It's Gorith Island. Does it mean anything to you?"

"I don't think so. Is it off the coast of Wales perhaps?"

"I don't know, but I'm hoping to find some reference to it in those magazines of hers, the ones George forwarded to her when she stayed here. I think she may have read about the place."

"Ah yes! The magazines. Can I be of any help? Could we go through them together?"

There were ten of them in all. Each man took five and

they worked their way through them, scanning each article for the name Gorith – or any reference to islands, or retreats, or indeed anything that might have caught Anna's eye and persuaded her to up-sticks and disappear for nearly two years.

Ben sighed when he put his last one back on the table. A few minutes later Arthur finished, and the two men looked at each other. Neither had found anything.

"Well, what a shame!" said Arthur. "Nothing of any relevance as far as I could see."

"Sorry Arthur, but many thanks for helping."

"That's okay. Happy to help. Interesting magazines. Never looked at any of them before. Nice pictures, but not my cup of tea. All that stuff, full of hope and optimism. I'm surprised they allowed that advert."

"What was that?"

"Oh, a classified one, inside the back page," said Arthur. "I noticed it because it seemed out of place."

"Why was that?"

"Strange typeface. Old English. Just said 'PARADISE IS NOWHERE' and gave a phone number. Can you imagine anyone calling them?"

Ben picked a magazine off his pile. He hadn't noticed the classifieds in the back. He glanced down them. One caught his eye. It too had a strange typeface and an equally depressing message. 'FREEDOM IS NOWHERE'. He reached for another issue and looked down the back page. 'PEACE IS NOWHERE'. The telephone numbers were the same, starting with 07, a UK mobile. Right now, he thought, we're the ones getting nowhere, and he slumped back in his chair.

He looked up at Arthur who was trying to read the advert he had just spotted.

"Ben?"

"Yes, Arthur?"

Arthur was squinting at the upside down advert. "Doesn't that say 'PEACE IS NOW HERE'?"

Ben grabbed another magazine and found what he was looking for: 'FREEDOM IS NOW HERE'. He recalled the ad Arthur had first spotted. He wondered if Anna had found paradise.

8

He tapped the number into his phone but stopped short of making the call in front of Arthur. The last thing he wanted to do was raise his hopes, only to have them dashed should the adverts have been a false trail. After all, they were two years old. But once he was safely on the train heading back to London, he woke up his mobile and made the call.

Two rings and a click later, a woman's voice came onto the line. Plummy, very English, but computer generated. It reminded Ben of Alexa, Amazon's avatar which obeys your every command. Or those talking satnavs which tell you ever so politely to take the next turning on the left.

You've reached the London offices of the Gorith Foundation.

He wanted to leap up off his seat and run up and down the carriage.

Please select one of the following: One for donations, Two to hear about our exciting residential programmes or Three for general information.

Ben pressed Three.

> Welcome to our general information department.

Same voice, Ben noted.

> You will need to register before we can send you our information pack. To do this, please respond to the text message we will send you in a few moments. We have your mobile number.

The line went dead. Ben held his phone out in front of him, staring at the screen. Twenty seconds later, there was a ping and a message to say he had a new SMS. He tapped the bubble and read it.

> Thank you for your interest in the Gorith Foundation. Please reply to this text stating your full name, age, physical address and email address. Your personal details will not be revealed outside the Gorith Foundation. Our privacy policy will be forwarded with the general information which will be sent to your email address within twenty-four hours.

Ben replied, as per the instructions, even though he was always reluctant to give personal information to strange people – or strange computers. At least they didn't ask me for my bank details, he thought.

He wanted to tell Ling about the progress, as she was the one who had suggested looking in those magazines. Then he realised he didn't have her phone number, or her email address, or where she was now staying – or indeed any details about her, not even her surname. It would have to wait until he met her tomorrow, at St Paul's Cathedral at 11.00 am. The thought that she might not turn up made his mouth go dry.

He spotted her from about fifty paces standing outside the tourists' entrance. He couldn't help but smile as he quickened his pace towards her.

"Wǒ hěn gāoxìng jiàn dào nǐ!" he said, beaming.

"Wǒ yě hěn gāoxìng jiàn dào nǐ," she replied, doing her little curtsy with her head to one side. "I dreaded the thought of wandering around here on my own. So, how are you?"

"Fine, thanks, and I've got some news! But how are you, and how did the rehearsal and everything go last night?"

"I'm well, and all went okay last night – and I've got some news for you!"

"Ladies first, then!"

"Well, I told my brother – Donnie – and Sasha that I had met this gorgeous Englishman at my hotel, and they suggested I brought him along to the Wedding tomorrow, as my guest."

Ben smiled down sweetly at Ling, at the thought of her being on his arm at such an important family event. Then she added, "but he couldn't come, so would you like to accompany me there instead?"

As soon as the smug smile left his face, Ling did her giggle which confirmed to Ben it was a tease but left him wondering if he had been officially invited. "Yes, I would like to join you – if that's okay?"

"Of course it is. I'd like you to meet Donnie. I think you'd get on well with him. Now, what's your news?"

"We found it! The link!"

"Who's we and what's the link?"

"Arthur and me. Anna's dad. We went through her

magazines. The religious ones, and we found an ad. It said 'PARADISE IS NOW HERE' in funny writing, but the squiggle at the end of the 'w' made it look as if it was joined up to the word 'HERE', so we thought it said 'paradise is nowhere'. And there were others, in the classified ads section, about peace and freedom – all with a phone number which I phoned and, guess what?"

"Gorith Island?"

"How did you know that?"

"You told me about Gorith yesterday."

"Anyway, it was the Gorith Foundation, and I've asked them to send me details."

"Ben, that's fantastic news. You must be pleased."

"Well, it was you who suggested looking in those mags. Brilliant!"

"So have you got the brochure yet?"

"Nah. But they said twenty-four hours. So it might arrive today, or in the morning. Not much we can do in the meantime – so shall we have a look over this old church?"

Ling took Ben's arm, and he led her through the gate up to the ticket booth. He paid the entrance fee, and they began their tour clutching their electronic guides.

By one-thirty, they were cathedralled out and decided to go and grab a bite. Ling thought it would be fun to have a traditional English pub lunch, so Ben extracted his phone and used an app to find traditional pubs in the neighbourhood. They settled on the Punch Tavern, at the eastern end of Fleet Street just a few minutes walk from St Pauls.

Ling loved the oak panelling in the main saloon and the ornate Victorian decor throughout. After a quick tour around the place they settled at a table near the window.

Ben went to the bar and ordered two pints of bitter and two pork pies, and asked for some proper English mustard. He felt a bit mean subjecting Ling to such a meal, but it was exactly what she wanted. He warned her to go steady on the mustard, though after a couple of mouthfuls of pie her eyes were streaming.

"You must drink some beer with it. It will cool things down," said Ben.

Ling spluttered a cough and managed to tell him, in a husky voice, that she was absolutely fine.

Coffee followed, and when Ben lifted his cup to take the first sip his phone bleeped. An email had arrived. The do-not-reply address was a garble of letters and numbers, but the subject line told him who it was from: Paradise Now.

"It's from them," he said in a whisper, "the Gorith people." He started reading.

"Hey, wise guy, read it out. And there's no need to whisper!"

"Okay Okay... Here we go... Dear Mr Bellamy. Thank you for your kind inquiry and for providing details about your goodself. These will remain confidential, on the understanding that this e-mail is confidential to you as the intended recipient. If you have received it in error, please delete it from your system now. Any unauthorised use, disclosure to a third party, or copying is not permitted."

Ben put his phone back in his jacket pocket, gave a big sigh and said, "Sorry, Ling. Can't read it out to you. You're not authorised, I'm afraid."

The kick on his left shin under the table changed his mind about authorisation, and he fished out his mobile and continued reading.

"The Gorith Foundation was set up some years ago to

establish a closed community able to live and prosper outside the mainstream of international interaction; to exist independently in a world of ever-closer interdependence and competition, in an environment in tune with nature, yet unconstrained by any particular belief, faith, philosophy or political doctrine. A paradise where freedom, tolerance, choice and peace prevail; a community where love triumphs over hate, good over evil and-"

"Sounds good to me," said Ling. "When can I go there?"

"No, Ling. I've come across this sort of scam before. It's a cult. They lure vulnerable people there with all kinds of promises, then brainwash them to believe in some ridiculous concept, and milk them of their money. Like that lot in Oregon, back in the eighties, which took over a small town and made life hell for the inhabitants.

"No doubt this 'Gorith Foundation' is similar. Probably squatting illegally on some island off Wales having set up a commune under a quack Guru named Gorith. That guy in Oregon, Bhagwan Shree, I think he was called. He had nine Rolls-Royces. Nine!"

"Yes, Ben. I saw the film. *Wild Wild Country*, wasn't it? On Netflix."

"That's right. I saw a few episodes. Evil lot. God, I hope Anna hasn't got involved in that kind of rubbish."

"But they can't all be as bad as that," said Ling. "Remember the Pilgrim Fathers, or the monks at Holy Island, or in dozens of other places. Humankind has always striven to find an alternative to mainstream society, a better way of getting along together."

"Yeah, and what about Jonestown? Remember? The mass suicide by cyaninde poisoning? More like the mass murder of hundreds of people, including children. That's hardly a better way of getting along together. For all we know Anna might already be dead."

"Yes, Ben. That was terrible. But for every evil cult they're probably hundreds that are not evil. You can't dismiss them all simply because you don't understand them."

"What I do understand is that I'm going to have to get Anna off that island ASAP. Before they fry her brain completely, or do something even worse. They've probably already drained her of her savings."

Ben stopped, as he remembered what Arthur said about putting Uplands in her name. He felt his neck going red. *Oh my God! Perhaps Gorith has got the house in his clutches as well.* He imagined Linda opening her front door to find a couple of bailiffs on her doorstep handing her an eviction order.

"Read on, Ben."

"Do you really want to hear any more of this nonsense?"

"Er, yes. It might say where the island is, or give you some more clues," said Ling.

"Good point. Where did I get to? Here we are... A community isolated both from the depravity of so-called modern civilisation and from the deprivations of primitive society. A metaphorical island in a sea of geo-political turmoil, and a real island set in a sea of tranquillity: Gorith Island... Then it lists some physical details – area 12.46 sq km-"

"Ben. I can't picture that. How far across would that be?"

"Depends on its shape. If it were circular, its diameter would be about, er, four kays. If it's square, about three-and-a-half by three-and-a-half. Or it could be 12 kays long by one kay wide. Take your pick... Coastline 21.36 kays...

Vegetation 'mixed' whatever that means... Population 479 'Gorithians', so it looks as if they've taken over the place... Nearest international airport – God!"

"What is it, Ben?... Ben!... Speak to me!"

"Er, sorry Ling. Christmas Island. Its nearest airport is on Christmas Island, in the Indian Ocean."

"Indian Ocean? I thought Christmas Island was in the Pacific."

"No, Ling. You're thinking of Easter Island-"

Ling frowned. "Hmm, so you know what I'm thinking?"

Ben noticed the twinkle had gone and it dawned on him that the English idiom he had used could be taken the wrong way. Before he had a chance to explain, Ling continued. "So, Uri Geller, tell me what I'm thinking now!"

"Er... that I'm a bit of a plonker?"

"Half right. So which bit am I thinking of right now?" she asked.

Ben was mortified by the thought that he had upset her. How stupid, after all the help she had given him and asking him to the wedding the following day. Her question flustered him, and without thinking, he replied, "Dickhead, I suppose."

Ling giggled, her hand shot up in front of her mouth and her twinkly eyes scanned the room. When Ben realised what he had said he felt his neck going red again – and clearly his companion found his discomfort highly amusing. "Wrong!" she said, and then added, "at that particular moment."

He busied himself with his phone, googling Christmas Island. He smiled when he read the first few lines of the Wikipedia entry and passed his phone over to Ling. "Just take a look at that, girl!"

Ling read it out. "The Territory of Christmas Island is an Australian external territory comprising the island of the same name. Christmas Island is located in the Indian Ocean."

"One-all, I believe?"

After lunch in the Punch Tavern, they decided to go their separate ways. Ling got the pub to order her a taxi to her brother's parents-in-law-to-be, and Ben decided to take the Tube back to his dreary hotel.

They said their goodbyes outside the pub as they waited for Ling's taxi to arrive. "Ben, thanks so much for today. It was fun. I'm so pleased about the progress you're making with Anna. At least you now have a good idea of where she might be, and I'm sure you will be her knight in shining armour, riding to her rescue on a white horse..." Ling looked away.

He noticed she wasn't smiling and suspected she was missing her husband. Ben was used to being alone – or rather being lonely which was quite a different matter. He remembered how he missed Anna when he first went out to Hong Kong, and he thought how much harder it must be to be separated from a loving spouse after a few years of marriage, even if it was only for a week. At least Ling would be reunited with her husband in a couple of days and be back to marital bliss.

For Ben, though, his Anna seemed a long way away. How on earth was he going to get to some God-forsaken Island in the Indian Ocean, and when would he be able to set off? What would he do once he got there, and how would he spring his beloved from Gorith's grasp? He'd need more than a white horse.

The arrival of the taxi brought Ben back to reality. "Hey,

what about tomorrow?" he asked. "The wedding? Where shall I meet you? What time? And what should I wear?"

"Oh my God! Let's meet there, at the In and Out Club. Three o'clock. A suit, I think. I'm so glad you're coming. Should be fun. See you!"

9

He watched the taxi drive away, not sure why he felt low. He thought it was probably a combination of things: his worries about Anna being on that cult island on the other side of the world, his commitment to her parents, and wrestling with the problem of how he could save her.

It reminded him of the World War Two film *Saving Private Ryan*, which starred Tom Hanks as Captain Miller, the ranger tasked with finding Ryan, the only surviving son of four, his brothers having all been killed in action. But Ben was no ranger captain. His military experience was zilch, and the only conflict he had ever been involved in was a minor punch-up on the rugby field.

Captain Miller of the US Marine Corps had a hand-picked team of six soldiers to help him. Ben's 'team' comprised Arthur, who was unlikely to set foot outside of Kent, and Ling, who would be catching a plane back to Hong Kong the following day. How ironic, he thought. *Here am I, on a year's sabbatical in England, and my best – only – side-kick for my mission is going back to where I have just come from. Why the hell has she got to do that?*

He had to remind himself Ling had a husband and home there – and he consoled himself that at least he'd see her at the wedding the next day. His spirits rose, but then evaporated into thin air when he realised that afterwards, she'd be walking out of his life for ever.

To cap it all, he had yet to unpack his two suitcases, inside one of which was his best suit, the one he had brought with him in case he had to attend any formal functions, like funerals, where his more casual wear would not be acceptable. By now, the lightweight suit would be well and truly crumpled.

His plan had been to wait until he got settled in his Airbnb before unpacking properly. Not that he had brought much with him, on the basis that he could afford to buy whatever extra clothes he might need once he got to London. But not a new suit, for God's sake. Not if you live in Hong Kong where suits are made to measure overnight at a fraction of the Saville Row cost and are twice the quality.

Fortunately, the hotel came up trumps. After breakfast the following morning, he returned to his room and found his freshly pressed suit hanging in the wardrobe and his black oxfords highly polished on the shoe rack. His favourite white silk shirt – still in its clear plastic wrapper straight from the hotel laundry – was lying on the bed. He knew it had been a sensible decision to extend his stay in the hotel for those extra three days, although he felt the time had now come to make the break and find more suitable accommodation.

The 'Business Centre', on the first floor, was a suite of rooms, one of which was a windowless, airless room with five computer stations for the use of guests. Ben settled himself down at one of them and logged in, giving his name and room number. He was the only guest there.

Luckily, the ancient desktop machine was a Microsoft, his preference when it came to simple searching, and his fingers flew over the keys without him having to think too hard about what they were doing. It made a pleasant change from using the touchscreen on his phone which was not designed to handle the heavy touch of his thumbs.

He found it fascinating looking through the three-hundred-plus London homes on the Airbnb website. But he wasn't sure what he wanted, or how long he would be staying there.

His original idea had been to take a small flat for a year, to use as a base for him and his clobber, enabling him to come and go as he pleased. However, his plans for completing a master's certificate sailing course, a diving course, looking up old friends and visiting his parents in Cape Town were shattered by his self-inflicted mission to rescue his Anna. Now that he knew – or thought he knew – that she had been tricked into joining some cult and had probably been brainwashed and fleeced by some pseudo-guru on a faraway island, his priorities had changed.

He needed to talk to Ling. She would know what to do. It had been Ling's idea to look through Anna's magazines, and she really did seem anxious to help. At least he would see her at the wedding. But he appreciated that the opportunity of discussing the matter with her in private would be limited. As for the two of them sitting down together in front of a computer, searching possible locations for Gorith Island – forget it.

He wondered what Ling would say if he asked her the simple question: where do I start? Her answer, he guessed, would be 'with what you know'. Not much, but the little he did know was a starting point. The nearest international airport to Gorith Island was the one on

Christmas Island; in other words, there was no international airport nearer than that one. Be grateful for what you've got, he told himself.

Somewhere deep in his brain, an LED lit up. He closed down the Airbnb website and googled Christmas Island and selected maps. He zoomed out and was staggered to see the dot of Christmas Island shrink to nothing amid the vastness of the Indian Ocean.

On further zooming out he brought into view the land mass of Australia and the islands of the Indonesian Archipelago to the east, and the Maldives, Sri Lanka and the Cocos Islands to the west. He selected the print icon, and after a couple of seconds the hotel printer burst into life and with a quiet chunter produced his hard copy.

Next, he looked up international airports in the area and marked them on his 'chart' with one of the hotel's cheap ballpoint pens: Perth, Jakarta, Kuala Lumpur, Cocos, Colombo and Gan. He drew a straight line from each airport to Christmas Island, then, by eye, he marked their midpoints with a cross.

From each cross, he drew in both directions a perpendicular line which indicated to him all the places which were equidistant from that airport to Christmas Island. This would tell him that Gorith Island had to be on the Christmas Island side of the line. By doing this for each airport, he ended up with an irregular six-sided polygon around Christmas Island in which Gorith Island must lie.

He was proud of his achievement, but the smug smile was wiped off his face when he realised the box he had drawn covered several thousand square miles of ocean. He exchanged the pen for the mouse and zoomed into the area on the screen.

He began searching it for any signs of land, but after about half an hour he gave up, realising that even if he managed to find out where Gorith Island was, he had no way of getting there. If only he had his masters' certificate, he would be able to buy or charter a yacht and sail around the Indian Ocean looking for Anna. Shouldn't take more than a couple of decades.

Time for a coffee, he thought. Then an early bite of lunch followed by a brisk walk before changing into his glad rags. He was pleased he'd packed his Royal Hong Kong Yacht Club tie, as he reckoned that some of the guests might recognise it and take the trouble to talk to him.

The black cab dropped him outside the In and Out Club in the north-east corner of St James's Square, with twenty minutes to spare. Luckily, it was a fine afternoon, and he was happy to enjoy the tranquillity of the gardens in the centre of the square before stationing himself at the entrance to the club so he wouldn't miss Ling.

At about ten to three, the guests started to arrive, so he took up his position by the door. It was not a wise thing to do, as some of the arrivals seemed to think he was an usher and asked him lots of questions to which he did not know the answer, like where the Ladies' was. He got around that problem by holding his mobile to his ear and pretending to engage in some important conversation, turning his back on the stream of guests arriving, but every now and then scanning the queue for Ling.

Three o'clock was approaching fast, and he wondered if he had the right place. Then someone behind him tapped him on the shoulder.

"So who are you phoning? Is she a secret girl-friend you haven't told me about?"

Ben spun around. "Ling! How lovely to see you!" And without any awkwardness, they both leaned forward and exchanged kisses on both cheeks." Ben stood back and admired the apparition in front of him.

She was wearing a coral dress which shimmered in the sunshine and a hat in white lace with a cluster of rosebuds of matching pink. Her white high heels and purse of white leather completed the picture of elegance, but what caught his eye was the necklace worn high around her slim neck. The diamonds, all the size of garden peas, dazzled in the sunlight."

She must have noticed his eyes taking in every detail and his mouth gaping at the sight. She smiled and said, "It's not mine. My grandmother lent it to me for the occasion."

"Well, it certainly suits you. Are they... surely they can't be real?"

"Shh, Ben," she giggled and looked around her. "Of course they are, silly boy!"

"Wow!" was all Ben could say in reply.

"Hey, but you're a bit of a wow yourself, you know. That suit! And those shoes! I didn't know the young men of today ever polished their shoes!" Ben just smiled.

"Let's go inside and take our seats," said Ling, slipping her arm in his and guiding him through the double doors into the ornate reception hall and up the wide staircase to the first floor. "Have you been here before?" she asked.

"Never," said Ben as they made their way to the room where the ceremony was to take place. "It's amazing. Just look at those chandeliers!"

"I know. They're beautiful. They gave us a guided tour

on Thursday. The building dates back to the seventeenth century, but the club has only been here since 1996."

After they had taken their seats, two rows from the front on the groom's side, Ling confided in Ben that the bride wasn't due to arrive until three fifteen, which gave her a chance to ask Ben if he'd made any plans for his mission.

"Mission impossible," he replied. "I mean, how the hell am I going to find this island. And if I manage to do that, how on earth can I get there? And if I manage to get there, will I be able to find Anna and escape with her back to civilisation?"

"Steady, Ben. One step at a time. It can't be too difficult to get to the island. After all, if Anna managed it, so can you."

"What do you mean? She was probably taken there, by Gorith or his merry men. Kidnapped! Dragged there in chains, under protest-"

"Ben, you know that is hardly likely," said Ling, smiling at the handsome young man sitting beside her. "Why don't you do what she did?"

"What? Fall for their lies? Get seduced by their promises? You must be joking."

"No, Ben. Not that. Just apply to go on one of their residential programmes – retreats, or whatever they call them. Like Anna did. If your application is successful, they'll then send you a plane ticket and joining instructions, and voila! Before you know it, you'll be indoctrinated!"

"Ling, please don't joke about it. I might succumb, and then we'd both be trapped."

"Nonsense, Ben. Cults like that prey on the weak.

You're strong! And you have a mission to complete. You'd be fine."

"Okay. I get there. I find Anna. How do we get back? Will they just give us a plane ticket each and wish us well on our way? I think not. These cults are highly secretive because if people found out about them, the authorities would take action. Like at Waco. They'd send in the National Guard. Or the SAS!... Or rather the SAAS if it's an Australian territory..."

"Shush, Ben. She's coming."

The faraway sound of a lone Scottish piper rose up the stairs, getting louder as he led the bride's party up the grand staircase into the ceremony room. Everyone rose to their feet and turned around to watch them, including a beaming bridegroom and his best man. A beautiful girl in a stunning cream wedding dress, gliding slowly arm-in-arm with her proud father and followed by two endearing little bridesmaids diligently holding up the end of Sasha's long train.

"The bride's nieces," whispered Ling as the two little ones passed them. "Aren't they absolutely gorgeous?"

Ben thought they would be about the age Anna's twins would now be if it hadn't have been for the accident. Ling must have seen the mood change in him, as she surreptitiously dug an elbow into his side. He got the message and smiled like everyone else in the room.

The skirl of the pipes turned into a whimper then came to an untuneful stop as the bride and her father reached the ornate gilt table behind which the Mistress of Ceremonies was standing, smiling generously at the young couple whom she was about to join in civil matrimony.

10

The marriage ceremony reached its inevitable conclusion with the happy couple enjoying a lingering kiss. As they made their way slowly towards the double doors leading out onto the landing, the piper began a delightful rendition of that cheery Scottish tune which always reminded Ben of porridge.

The couple certainly looked happy, but Ben wondered how he would feel if he were in Donnie's shoes, getting spliced for life 'unto death us do part'. The thought opened the old wound, the itch of guilt that he had let Anna down, the dread that he'd made an awful mistake by running away to Hong Kong.

No eligible woman he had met since then had come close to being like his Anna, and this realisation toughened his resolve to find her and put matters right. As they were meant to be. He could do it, and he would, whatever it took.

He was relieved that there was no 'greeting line', as Ling would have been taken away from him to be part of it. But she explained she had to get around the reception room and meet as many guests as possible and pass on her mother's good wishes.

She insisted that Ben accompanied her, explaining that this was his role for the afternoon. The last thing she wanted was to get stuck with someone. A wedding reception was not an occasion where one could just walk off.

Of course, he was proud to be at her side. Seeing the many glances of approval which she inspired among the male and female guests made him appreciate her enchanting presence. No wonder they kept dragging her off for photographs, he thought.

They made their rounds, each with a glass of vintage champagne in hand, and Ling made a special effort to introduce Ben to everyone they met. Some of the guests raised their eyebrows quizzically at Ben when they shook hands with him, briefly pointing their eyes at Ling when they did so.

Ling was quick to notice when this happened, and she laughed it off saying they were 'just good friends'. To the people she knew really well, she explained that Ben was engaged to a lovely girl called Anna who was away on a course and that he was hoping they'd get married when she returned.

Ben's tie went down well with the Hong Kong contingent who immediately recognised the emblem and were anxious to talk about boaty things. Ben was happy to do so, but no sooner would a discussion begin about the merits of steel hulls versus fibreglass ones, when Ling would drag him away to meet the next group of guests.

Finally, they managed to reach the bride and groom, and Ling took great delight in introducing her brother Donnie to Ben. The two men shook hands, and when Donnie noticed the tie, he immediately started to talk about sailing.

Meanwhile, Ling admired Sasha's ring, and the two girls shared a couple of private jokes, sniggering behind cupped hands to make sure the men couldn't hear them. Donnie explained to Ben that a wedding present from his father's firm, Jason Mardine, was the loan of their yacht, berthed in St Katharine Docks in East London.

"My goodness!" said Ben, "that's some wedding present!"

"Ah, but there's a catch to it," said Donnie. "It's brand new. And the firm want it delivered to Hong Kong. So that's the deal. Sash and I are going to sail her back."

"Bloody hell!" said Ben. "Just the two of you? When are you off?"

"Just us, at the moment, but we may get crew for some of the legs. Not that it's vital. She's been fitted out for single-handed blue-water cruising, so the two of us should be able to manage it. We've got a couple of shakedown weeks here first, getting up to speed with it. Getting to know the ropes – literally! And getting any snagging done, then we're off."

"Sounds like a busy honeymoon ahead?"

Donnie laughed. "Actually we've been together for two years, here in London, so we've kind of done that bit. The voyage should be fun, though. We're really looking forward to it. The yacht herself is a-"

"LORDS, LADIES and GENTLEMEN!" It was the master of ceremonies, dressed in his finery of a scarlet tailcoat, white gloves and black trousers with gold stripes down the sides. "Will you kindly make your way downstairs to the banqueting hall and take your PLACES for the WEDDING BREAKFAST!"

The crowd bunched up as guests slowly made their way towards the stairs. Ling hung on to Ben's arm, explaining that she didn't want to lose him. "Why do they call it a breakfast? It's teatime."

"Hang on, Ling. Wait one," he said, as he extracted his phone and turned it back on. "Here we are…'It's referred to as 'breakfast' as the couple are starting a new day together from the moment of their marriage, whatever time of day that happens to be. The wedding feast is their first meal as newlyweds. Traditionally, couples used to fast from the night before their wedding, only breaking the fast after their vows.' So there you have it."

"Ah so!" said Ling, imitating the Chinese stereotyped way of indicating one has understood something. It made Ben smile. Ling was so English in her character that he had almost forgotten she was from Hong Kong. But now the place had been handed over, she was technically Chinese.

Ben summoned up the courage to whisper the question. "Ling, is Donnie really your brother?"

"Yes, Ben. Same parents, if that's what you mean. Baby brother, actually. Three years younger than me. Why do you ask?"

"The red hair. The pale skin?"

"Simple. He's a throwback. The Scottish gene, rearing its ugly head. Not that Donnie's ugly. But he says I'm the throwback. And who's to say?"

Ling had warned Ben that all couples would be split up for the meal, but she made sure Ben found his place and introduced him to the two girls on either side of him before she made her way to the top table. Just before she reached her place, he noticed her turn towards him and frown. At the same time, she discreetly lifted one finger, as a nursery teacher might: a warning to be good. His look in return made her smile; it was as if to say 'Who me? Would I ever not be good?'

Ben enjoyed the meal. The food was stunning; and despite his best efforts, his wine glass never got below half full, thanks to the diligence of the liveried waiters. The music provided by the string quartet was delightful, and at just the right volume to enable him to converse comfortably with the two young ladies on either side of him, neither of whom were sporting any kind of hardware on the ring finger of their left hand. Their enthusiastic laughter at his jokes had the harmful effect of encouraging him, and he soon found that the rest of the guests around the round table were eagerly listening in.

After coffee had been served, the staff hurriedly distributed the generously filled champagne flutes in preparation for the speeches, and Ben turned his chair around so he would be facing the top table. He caught Ling's eye and gave her a little wave of his fingers as if to say hi, I'm still here and I'm thinking of you. She smiled and reciprocated.

A gavel banged on its sound block. "LORDS, LADIES and GENTLEMEN. PRAY SILENCE for the FATHER of the BRIDE!"

Sasha's dad said all the right things, embarrassing his daughter with tales of her potty training and saying what a wonderful son he had gained in Donnie. Eventually, the toast to the newlywed couple was proposed, and the assembled company rose to their feet and drank to their good health and happiness. Loud applause followed, then further scraping of chairs as everybody regained their seats for Donnie's speech.

His was short and sweet, complimenting Sasha's mother and thanking her and her husband for the hand of her lovely daughter. He proposed the traditional toast to the two little bridesmaids which brought everyone to their feet with loud cheers, anxious to show their appreciation and have another good slurp from their champagne glasses.

The best man did his stuff, replying on behalf of the bridesmaids and having everyone in fits of laughter at his outrageous tales of Donnie in his younger days. The theme of his speech was clearly about sailing, with suitable innuendos about sheets and booms and bowsprits.

When everybody started to get up and go back upstairs to the reception room for dancing, Ben was glad of the opportunity to stretch his legs and breathe the cooler air in the hall. And to find Ling and keep her out of trouble, because that was why she'd invited him.

Despite having had a steady girlfriend for two years who was a ballet dancer, Ben was not that keen on tripping the light fantastic. But after a few drinks, he usually managed to struggle onto the dance floor and make a fool of himself – if the occasion demanded it. Sasha's and Donnie's wedding was no exception. When the happy couple were halfway through the first waltz, they encouraged all their guests to join them, and Ben found himself being dragged onto the dance floor by one of his table companions.

She was certainly a whizz on her feet, guiding Ben gracefully through the throng of dancers and clearly enjoying herself. It reminded him of Anna, and he held her even closer as their bodies twirled together as they circumnavigated the small dance floor, in perfect time to Tchaikovsky's *Waltz of the Flowers*. He smiled soppily as he recalled those happy days at Cambridge when he first met Anna at a 21st birthday party.

He was brought back to the present by a tap on the shoulder. It was Ling. She suggested that, as she had been good enough to invite him along, might he be that much of a gentleman to ask her to dance?

He had never seen her cross, and he thought he'd lighten the mood by teasing her. "Oooh," he said, "you're so sexy when you're grumpy." It did not work, although he had to admit that, actually, her frown across her unblemished forehead and the pout with those gorgeous red lips did look quite attractive.

They danced to a delightful rendition of *Sweet Caroline* followed by *Dancing Queen*; then Ling said she ought to go and talk to her brother, as she wouldn't be seeing him for some time.

"You've probably forgotten that I fly back to Hong Kong tomorrow."

"Ling, I do remember. You're off tomorrow. I understand. Let me come with you."

Her eyes lit up and she smiled. "Ben, do you really mean it?"

"Sure."

"How wonderful! You might have trouble getting a ticket, though."

"Er... sorry, Ling. I meant I'll come over with you to talk to Donnie. I want to find out more about his yacht."

"Hmm. Don't feel you have to." Ling frowned. "And if you want to go and chat up that frump you were dancing with earlier, you just go right ahead."

Ben took Ling's arm and led her over to Donnie who was having a deep conversation with his new father-in-law. Ling joined in, leaving Ben standing there until he managed to catch Donnie's eye. Ling continued talking to Sasha's dad, leaving the two boys to talk sailing.

"An Oyster, eh?" asked Ben. "Wow! What model?"

"An 885. Series 2. Bluewater spec with four cabins. LOA 27m and her displacement is around 150 tons. You must come and see her. How about Monday?"

"Thanks, Donnie, I'd love to. What's her name?"

"*Juli-Emma*. Come along about eleven. We should be on board by then. St Katharine Docks. Near Tower Bridge."

"Hey, Donnie babe!" It was Sasha. "Come and meet Eddie and Nat. Over here."

Ben seized his chance to have a private word with Ling and wheeled her away to the relative quietness of the landing.

"Look, I'm sorry I wasn't a good escort. It's just that I don't normally drink before six in the evening, and I think the champagne went to my head a bit."

"That's okay." She turned away from him and looked at her watch.

"Ling. Listen. I am really grateful to you for being such a good... friend and helping me with my mission, to find Anna. You've been marvellous, and inviting me along today was really kind. And I have enjoyed it – especially when we danced. You and I, that is. It was special."

Ling sighed. "I'm sorry, too. It's just that I'm staying with Sasha's parents tonight, and the car is coming for us at ten, and I've still got some cousins to see. Her dad doesn't want to stay for the disco, and they offered me a lift. I said yes, so you and I really ought to say goodbye now, while we have a chance.

"Let me know how the mission goes – and good luck. I'm sure you'll succeed. Donnie's got my details, and he can give them to you on Monday. That's if you're interested in staying in touch."

"Of course, Ling. We're pals." He extended his arms towards her and she responded. They had a little brother-and-sisterly hug and then she pulled away and took a paper tissue from her white leather purse.

"I hate goodbyes," she said and forced out a laugh. "Take care!" She turned and walked off across the landing to the reception room.

"Have a good flight!" he called after her, as she disappeared out of sight.

Well, that's it, he said to himself. Job done. Escorting over. Might as well go back to the hotel and do some serious planning. No point in staying here.

11

Sunday morning, early. Ben had been in London for just one week. In some ways the time had rushed by, but when you're staying in an airport hotel, the days can drag. He kicked himself that he hadn't yet made the move into more suitable accommodation, but then he had achieved other things.

He'd made contact with Anna's parents, met her slimeball of an ex-husband, and had taken on what he still reckoned was an impossible mission to rescue his damsel in distress. He had yet to book himself onto a yachtmaster's course but he thought he'd sound out Donnie on where to go for the best training when he met him the following day.

The other thing he had promised himself was to take exercise every morning, but on this particular morning he did not feel up to descending into the basement. He had a real napper-zapper of a headache and felt slightly nauseous. He wondered if he had flu.

He made it down to breakfast and managed a bowl of muesli and two cups of coffee. Following a return to his room, he made his way back to the hotel's Business

Centre. Not surprisingly, he was the only person there. He grabbed some paper from the stack above the shared printer and sat down at one of the workstations. But before logging into the desktop, he decided to use his mobile to phone the number in the adverts he and Arthur had spotted.

As before, a couple of rings later, he heard the woman's computer-generated voice.

> You've reached the London office of the Gorith Foundation. Please select one of the following: One for donations, Two to hear about our exciting residential programmes or Three for general information.

This time he selected One.

> Welcome to our donations department, Ben. We have your mobile number. Please listen carefully to the following announcement.
>
> The Gorith Foundation welcomes donations of any kind, at any time, but a central tenet of our philosophy is that any contribution is donated by the donor without any expectation of anything in return. Likewise, we offer our members various facilities and educational training without expecting any donation from them.
>
> In other words, we do not charge our members anything, but they are welcome to make any donation they choose, at any time. This could be monetary, or a contribution of labour, time or other effort or item which they may care to donate for the good of our community.
>
> We hope you have found this announcement useful and interesting. Further details will be sent to you, should you apply to join one of our residential courses. Thank you for listening.

The line went dead. At least they're not trying to screw money out of me straight away, he thought. Softly softly catchee monkey, perhaps. Well, they're not going to make a monkey out of me.

He wondered about the other effort 'or item'. A six-bedroom Kentish farmhouse perhaps? But – and it was a big but – if what they are saying is true, they might not have forced Anna to hand over Uplands. Yet. Time was clearly a factor.

His next task was to find out about their 'exciting residential programmes'. That should be a laugh, he thought. The kind of thing Anna would love, a long weekend sitting cross-legged in some dusty hall chanting ommm or whatever until you start rising slowly off the floor. Or rather you think you are because they've hypnotised you. Or, he conceded, you have hypnotised yourself.

He dialled the number and waited for Miss Artificial Intelligence to do her thing. Then he chose Two. Same voice:

> Welcome to our residential department, Ben.

This time he noticed the quiet click before his name was mentioned.

> We have your mobile number. Please listen carefully to the following announcement. The Gorith foundation is pleased to announce that it is presently able to offer limited places on our graduate course. Its duration is three years. During this time selected applicants will be provided at no charge with board and accommodation. Students will be invited to contribute to the satisfactory running of the island, which in some respects works similarly to a kibbutz.

The curriculum is open, in that each student, after their initial induction, is free to study any subject of their choice. All learning aids are provided, and examinations are optional. Transport costs to Gorith Island will be met by the foundation. It is not necessary to bring money or credit cards except for incidental expenses on your journey.

Having successfully completed the graduate course, students are then welcome to join our post-graduate community and remain on the island until they choose to leave it. The option to leave the island is not encouraged during the graduate course, as students may not have qualified as suitable ambassadors to return to the wider world until they have completed their full training.

We hope you have found this announcement useful and interesting. If you wish to apply for the graduate course, please select the hash key, and we will send you an application form. Thank you for listening.

Ben pressed the hash key. Three flaming years, he thought, and he wondered if it was some kind of hoax. But then, Anna had actually disappeared, having had her application accepted, and they had, apparently, sent her travel documents.

He didn't like the idea that leaving Gorith Island 'is not encouraged'. Perhaps it's a prison, he thought. Like Devil's Island, in the book *Papillon*, by Henri Charriere. A brilliant true story which he had read as a boy, describing how the author escaped from the penal colony in French Guiana by improvising a raft using sacks of coconuts.

He reckoned if Henri Charriere could escape a proper high-security prison, he would be able to walk away from a bunch of loonies without any trouble. He recalled one of the adverts: 'Freedom is now here'. Can't be too many restraints, then. Perhaps not *walk* away, as it's an island, in an ocean. But he could surely make a boat of some sort – or steal one – and he would drift back to civilisation on the trade winds having improvised a sail.

He remembered how Captain Bligh had been cast adrift in an open boat following the mutiny aboard HMS Bounty and sailed 4,000 miles to the Dutch East Indies. He would do the same. Or rather they would, he and Anna, together. He had to remind himself that was the whole purpose of him going there. If he decided to go. At least that wasn't a decision he had to make there and then, as he would have to wait for the application form.

His next task was to google St Katharine Docks and work out how to get there. Not only did he find out it was Central London's only marina, but that it was:

> Steeped in heritage and truly unique... a home to a collection of high-quality offices, restaurants and bars... St. Katharine Docks offers great facilities in an iconic setting... visitors can enjoy the unique experience of sailing up the Thames and mooring right next to the Tower of London and Tower Bridge... We welcome vessels from all over the world.

Sounds my sort of place, he thought, as he flipped through the stunning photos, not only of the historic buildings but also of the fascinating collection of ships, boats and barges moored there. When I get my yacht, that's where I'm going to keep it, he decided.

He checked the mooring fees, as he guessed they would be expensive in Central London, and so close to the City and Canary Wharf. But they turned out to be very reasonable. For a modest craft of, say, 20m it was a mere £9.10 per night, and that VAT was included. Then he re-read the column headings on the price list. Slight change of plan, he thought, when he found that the £9.10 figure per night was also *per metre* of overall length. The bowsprit would have to go.

But how wonderful it would be to live there, he mused. A thought occurred to him and he retrieved the Airbnb site. He chose London as his location and ticked the box for boats. Among the sixty-one on offer, up popped a picture of St Katharine Docks with a rather nice looking oldy-worldy yacht in the foreground. He made a note of the name: *Samara*. He wrote down all the details and made up his mind he would have a look at the vessel after his meeting with Donnie.

It was back to the St Katharine Docks website for details of how to get there.

> Opposite the Tower of London and a short stroll from Tower Hill underground, St. Katharine Docks has some of the best transport links in London. You can reach us by boat, tube, bus, train or car.

Easy peasy, he thought. A tube to Tower Hill and I'll walk from there if it's fine; one change, from the Picadilly to the Circle line. Quicker than a taxi. Sorted.

He left the hotel early, arriving in plenty of time to have a nose around the place before his meeting on board *Juli-Emma* with Donnie and Sasha. He loved the docks and was quite excited about the prospect of living there. At least until he set off for Gorith Island.

He recognised *Samara* from the Airbnb photo and went over to her to get a better view. Just as he got there, a man emerged from her, saw Ben staring at her and asked, "Can I help you?" in the way English people do when they really mean 'what the hell do you want?'.

"Lovely boat," Ben said. "I gather it's on Airbnb?"

"Sorry. Booked up fully until the end of September," the man said as he walked away.

Ben gasped when he saw *Juli-Emma*. She was stunning. Truly in the super-yacht class. And Donnie was rightly very proud of her. He welcomed Ben on board with a warm handshake and gave him a conducted tour of the deck, explaining how things worked and what they were made of.

"Look at this, Ben. It's a captive reel mainsheet system... And over here we have an anchor-rocker on the bow prodder – makes handling of large anchors much easier !... Now, that mast is carbon fibre... Note we've gone for the raised deck option. It gives an extra foot of headroom down below and better views. Come on. Let's go down and I'll show you!"

They stepped down into the spacious cockpit and made their way between the two helming stations to the companionway ladder. Ben was blown away by both the space and the superb quality of it all. Donnie led the way into the main saloon. "See what I mean about the views?"

"Sure do!" Ben said, "and the space! It's vast!"

"Well, she's over six metres in the beam, so there's lots of room. And dad wants to use her for entertaining clients and influencers – you know what I mean?"

"Sure!" said Ben, guessing as to the sort of people Donnie's father had in mind.

"The fact it's a sailing yacht and not just another Tupperware gin palace sends the right eco-messages – although, between you and me, I reckon she'll do more sea miles under power. The engine's a Cummings Turbo-charged QSL9-330 which churns out 246 kilowatts..."

The tour ended with them back at the main saloon, with Donnie patiently answering Ben's questions. The interrogation finally came to an end when Sasha popped her head around the door, and Ben jumped to his feet.

"Sasha! How wonderful! And what a change from Saturday," he said, looking at her jeans and tee-shirt. "I must say the wedding was absolutely super, one of the best. Really – and thanks again, both of you, for inviting me."

"Glad to have you aboard," said Donnie, "although it was my big sister who pleaded your case."

"On bended knee," Sasha added with a smirk. "Only joking. But you two seemed to be getting on all right. Is this, er, quite a new thing, you two together?"

"No, not at all," Ben said, smoothing down his right eyebrow. "I mean, yes, it's new – in that we haven't known each other for long. And, no." He forced out a chuckle at the ridiculous suggestion, "there's no 'thing' going on. Not at all."

Donnie and Sasha sat there, across the saloon table from Ben, looking at him with eyebrows raised in expectation of an explanation. He squirmed on the cream leather chair. "We're just pals, really. Met in the hotel. Ling's been amazingly kind in giving me some advice. About a friend of mine from uni days who's disappeared – ex-fiancee, actually, who's got mixed up in one of those modern church things. There really is nothing in it, between me and Ling... And with Ling being happily married..."

Sasha cast a glance at her husband. She leant forward towards Ben. "Er, Ben. What did she tell -"

"Honeybun, my love, you couldn't fix us a coffee, could you? Or would you prefer tea, Ben? We've got both, green and black. Now, tell me. How much ocean sailing have you done?"

"To be honest, not a great deal. I took it up ten years ago when I first arrived in Hong Kong. And it was glorious for me, getting out on the water. I'm not qualified at all, but I was hoping that during my sabbatical I'd do a course which would give me my yacht-masters' certificate. In fact, I was going to ask for your advice on that one. You know, the best way to tackle it?"

"Yeah. You can do a crash course, but their objective will be to coach you for the oral and written exams. You'll pass them, but will you make a good skipper? My recommendation is to get some serious ocean sailing under your belt first. Some bluewater experience – then you'll sail through the exams – no pun intended – and you won't need a crash course. And you'll be a real skipper!"

Sasha returned from below with three mugs of coffee and a plate of plain chocolate suggestives, all on a small tray which she had carefully balanced on one hand. One hand for the ship, Ben thought. A rule he'd learnt the hard way in his early sailing days.

"There we are, boys. Dig in. Has he managed to recruit you yet?" Sasha smiled at Ben.

"I'm not sure what you mean."

"Just coming on to that, Ben. Here's the thing. As you know, we're sailing *Juli-Emma* back to Hong Kong, leaving in a couple of weeks. Should be fun, and Sash and I should be able to cope. With all the gear on board and the control systems, you could actually sail this tub single-handed.

"But we don't want it to be an endurance test. I think I mentioned at the wedding that if the right person came along we'd take them on as crew. Not for the whole thing, but for some of the legs. They could fly out and join us for a week or so, then we could drop them off at the nearest airport. What d'you think?"

"Wow!" Ben was lost for words.

"Think about it. No rush. I know you've got things planned, finding that girl of yours, but maybe when you come back we could arrange something. For you both, perhaps. Does she sail?"

"No." He wanted to add 'not yet' as a plan started to hatch in his mind.

"I'll tell you what, Ben, if you fancied a taster, why don't you join us tomorrow? We're taking *Juli-Emma* back to the yard in Southampton to get a few things sorted. Leaving about tennish, on the high tide. Should be there by midnight.

"You could spend the night on board and leave the following morning. Or stay a few days, in the crew cabin. Our plan is to set off for Hongkers the following week, so you'd have to leave by then. Unless you wanted to stay for that first leg?"

"I don't know about that. But the sail to Southampton would be great. Are you sure? That would be fantastic."

"Of course! Bring your things – in case you decide to stay."

12

As Ben retraced his steps to Tower Hill Tube Station, his mind buzzed with possibilities. He went through all the what-ifs, wondering what would work and what wouldn't. He had visions of *Juli-Emma* sailing into a little harbour on Gorith Island, him jumping on to the jetty and demanding to see Gorith in person. 'Take me to your leader!' He smiled at the thought.

He would insist on seeing Anna Marshall. She would run into his arms and they would sail away together. A honeymoon in Hong Kong, then a first-class flight back to Heathrow and a chauffeur-driven limousine down to Uplands.

Mission accomplished.

Then he remembered the six-sided box he'd drawn on his improvised A-4 sea chart, around Christmas Island Airport, and that he hadn't a clue where Gorith Island was among those hundreds of thousands of square miles. Ling was right. The only way of finding it was to go there on a course, with the Gorith Foundation meeting the costs of his trip; that aspect of the venture appealed to him, being an economist.

It had to be the three-year graduate course as it was

the only one on offer. Not that he had the time or the inclination to stay for three years. He would drop out once he found Anna. He hoped the application form would soon arrive and he could make a start.

He continued to day-dream on the Tube, as it lurched its way under London, trundling westwards towards Heathrow. A thought struck him: if Donnie can't take me there, could he at least provide my means of escape? Once I'm there, I phone him the lat and long of the island and arrange the pick-up. I get the girl, we run to the secret rendezvous on the beach, at the dead of night, where Donnie is waiting with the dinghy. We plane across the ocean swell to the mothership and set sail.

Hardly a dinghy, he thought, as he remembered the brand new, state-of-the-art rigid inflatable boat strapped down on the fore-deck of *Juli-Emma*. More like the kind of thing commandos use. He saw himself with a blackened face wearing a green beret.

Yes, he thought. The plan's got legs. If Donnie just happened to be in the area with nothing better to do. He assumed that ocean sailing for fun must include stop-offs at islands if only to break the monotony of making passage across seemingly endless expanses of sea-water.

The reception desk was free when he arrived at the hotel sometime after two, so he took the opportunity of informing them of his departure the following morning early and asked them to book him a cab. While the girl with the nose stud made notes, his phone pinged telling him an email had arrived, and a glance of the screen confirmed it was from the Gorith Foundation.

Once in his room, he opened it and read it. Attached was an application form for the graduate course on Gorith island. Phew, he thought. Phase One complete. It was a typical form, requiring the usual personal details including passport number, office and date of issue, the number and type of driving licence if held, details of any county court judgments and a summary of assets and liabilities. Then more personal details including school record, educational and professional qualifications, religion and hobbies, and date of availability.

He reckoned it was a cross between a mortgage request and a job application – or perhaps a combination of both. But there was a final question which concerned him: 'why do you wish to undertake this course?'. He reckoned he'd have to give that some thought. No rush, though. I'll do it on board *Juli-Emma*, once I've sounded out Donnie.

A warm welcome was waiting for him when he arrived at the quay-side. Donnie grabbed one of his suitcases and Sasha took his cabin bag. Ben could hardly believe he had the crew quarters all to himself, a vast cabin with two double bunks, its own bathroom and a kitchenette. After settling in, he joined Sasha and Donnie in the saloon where a steamy hot cup of coffee and biscuits were waiting for him.

Donnie looked at his watch. "Let's see. Another ten minutes, I guess." When he saw the puzzled look on Ben's face, he explained. "We're all set to sail, but we're waiting for the lock. It's not like a canal lock as it's only got one gate, so they can only open it two hours either side of high tide. Otherwise, the dock would empty. We're booked to go first, so I don't expect much of a delay. Now, the safety briefing."

Ben was impressed by Donnie's clear and confident address, which reminded him of the safety announcements on the cross-channel ferries of his childhood. Donnie did use the phrase 'donning your life-jacket', but there was no mention of 'muster stations'. Ben noted the locker with the flares and how to select the emergency radio channel.

"A question, if I may?" said Ben.

"Fire away!"

"Why *Juli-Emma*?" Ben had been wondering who the woman – or rather lady – was, or whether there were two of them.

Donnie laughed. "Have you ever tried to name a boat?"

"No Donnie, I've never had that privilege, but I guess it must be difficult."

"You're right. Nigh-well impossible. It was a major board item for six months, would you believe it?"

"Why? What were the issues?"

"Well, Dad was determined it should be identified with the firm. He said it was important that corporate guests on board should realise it wasn't just any old tub chartered for the day. Not a plaything which remained in the harbour for most of the time, hired out for parties, but a proper ocean cruiser that evoked the history of the company. He wants our guests to be reminded of where we'd come from."

"Sounds sensible to me."

"But but but! Our security people said it would be too risky to sail the seven seas with the company name emblazoned on the bow for all to see, including nice people like Somali pirates. Not that we've got a valuable cargo to steal. But the people on board could be at risk. Ransom targets. Anyway, we all agreed he had a point – especially those of us who would be sailing her."

"So, the girls' names. Where did they spring from?"

"Someone suggested Juliet Mike – the firm's initials according to the phonetic alphabet. Anyway, we all thought it was a bit obvious. Even pirates might guess they were initials. And Juliet Mike didn't sound like a yacht. So it became Juliet M, then Juliet Emma – a bit of a mouthful, that one. Finally, some bright spark came up with *Juli-Emma*."

"Donnie, Babe! Don't be so modest! Your dad said it was you!"

"Was it? I'd forgotten. Anyway, you, Ben – as our first VIP aboard – have just proved that it works. It made you curious enough to ask, and we've proved it's our own boat!"

"Ship, darling! You keep saying she's a ship!"

"Sorry, Honeybun. You're right. Sort of."

"Forgive me," said Ben, "but where does the distinction lie? And isn't *Juli-Emma* a yacht?"

"A very good question."

The message came over the vessel's radio. The swing bridge across the lock had been swung clear and they were to proceed. Ten minutes later they were in the tidal waters of the Thames, motoring slowly towards the open estuary and the North Sea.

Both the boys were in the cockpit, with Donnie was at the port helm. He smiled at Ben as he carefully manoeuvred *Juli-Emma* along the busy waterway. "For your information, Ben, she is now a ship!" He laughed at Ben's screwed up face. "I'll explain later!"

As they passed Canvey Island, the estuary widened to over five kilometres. It was Ben's turn to take the wheel. He'd been at Donnie's side since leaving the docks and had been watching him closely, following his course on the repeater screen. Donnie had answered his questions patiently, and obviously thought Ben capable of helming the ship.

He told Ben to keep her on the course through the various waypoints which the computer had selected in order to avoid running aground. With a draught of over three metres, it was kind of important.

It would also keep him clear the wreck of the SS Montgomery. Not something you would want to run into, bearing in mind there was 1,400 tons of wartime explosive still on board capable of throwing a 300 metre wide column of water and debris nearly 3,000 metres into the air and generate a wave 5 metres high – and blow out almost every window in Sheerness.

"Christ!" said Ben. "That wouldn't be a good start to a maiden voyage." He wasn't sure if he wanted the responsibility of helming, but Donnie insisted.

"Ben, I'm going below. Give me a shout when you get bored and I'll put it into auto."

"Thanks. I'm fine!" Ben realised that his helming efforts were not required, but once clear of the munitions ship he loved the feeling of being at the controls. They were running before the steady westerly, helped along by the out-going tide and achieving a peak speed of some 12 knots SOG, sizzling through the water in the bright sunshine. This is what it's all about, he thought. How wonderful!

It reminded him of his last trip to Cape Town when he'd spent a day sailing with his father on a friend's yacht. It crossed his mind that Donnie might be going via the Cape, rather than Suez; he wondered, if that were so, he might join him there for his next leg – if the mission permitted it, of course. It would give him the chance of seeing his parents.

When Margate slipped by them on the starboard side, Donnie popped his head up and told Ben to keep her on one-eighty after passing well clear of the headland. Once safely out of the estuary, Donnie broke out the genoa and Ben felt the power surge as the yacht heeled over and took the force-five westerly on its starboard beam.

A glance at the cockpit display told him they were making a steady 15 knots. Not for long, though, because after twenty minutes – which only seemed like ten to Ben – Donnie announced it was time to switch back to motor power.

"Sorry, Ben. But if we stick to sail we'll never make it by midnight. I've set an in-shore course well clear of the TSS-"

"TSS, Donnie?"

"Traffic Separation Scheme. Basically a one-way system for big ships. We'll stick to the inshore traffic zone between those main traffic-lanes and the coast. It's reserved for local traffic, fishing and small craft like us. We'll be passing close in to Dungeness and then Beachy Head, then a straight run to Selsey and up the Solent. Into wind, but the engine will keep us at a respectable ten knots. Sea state's good. Come and join us for a spot of lunch."

Donnie let Sasha and Ben enjoy the sandwiches she'd prepared, while he kept watch. "It's almost like a self-drive car," he explained. "The alarms and control systems are so sophisticated that we humans aren't really necessary any more. To be honest, I can't get used to it. I have to see what's around me with my own eyes, especially in the Channel. It's so busy."

Sasha quickly finished eating and said, "Babe, why don't you eat and let me keep an eye out, and you can show Ben the chart-screen."

"Being very much old school, Dad wanted a flat horizontal display which mimicked a chart table. Something he could lean on! This one uses a full res four-kay monitor, and using the blue-toothed ruler and pen, you can treat it almost like a real chart. But of course, you can do so much more."

The display showed their course and the way-points, with the little icon of a boat creeping along past Dungeness. Ben looked out of the window and saw the two nuclear power stations, giants rising out of an almost featureless flat headland.

Donnie put his thumb and forefinger on a small black pad in the corner of the display and zoomed out, like on a smartphone, and the entire coastline of southern England appeared. "Here. Have a go," he said.

Ben found it fascinating. He could zoom out and see the whole world on the display. "Hey! it's like Google Earth!", he said.

"Sure. You can select Google Earth if you want. Like on any computer. Have a play."

Ben panned the display down and zoomed in on Cape Town. On the Google Earth option, he was able to look at his parents' house. Then he moved out and across to the Indian Ocean and reverted to the sea chart. A big place, he thought.

After lunch and coffee, the two men sat outside on the deck enjoying the sunshine. Visibility was good, so Donnie was smiling and relaxed. He told Ben that the radar would warn of any vessel within thirty nautical miles which could pose a danger, and then it would automatically change and alter speed as necessary – assuming they were not under sail, although automatic reefing of the main and jib was possible.

Ben thought it was an apt moment to sound Donnie out about that big sister of his. "So Donnie, has Ling caught the sailing bug as well?"

"No," said Donnie, "not this sort of thing. Not Ocean sailing, but she's brilliant in dinghies. Single-handed stuff. Much better than I am."

"Single-handed? Does her husband sail?"

"Husband? I wish!" Donnie smiled at Ben.

"You wish he sailed, you mean?" said Ben.

Donnie laughed. "Nah... "

Ben looked at Donnie and raised his eyebrows. "Well?"

Donnie laughed again, an awkward laugh and turned away.

"Your sister does have a husband, doesn't she?"

"I think I've let the cat out of the bag. Look, I'll be straight with you. She's not married – but you mustn't blame her if she said otherwise. There is a reason for that, and it's a bit sad, really. Nothing to do with you, though. It's her way of, of handling things."

Ben was confused. "What things, Donnie?"

"Oh, personal stuff." Donnie sighed and looked at Ben. "Ling's lovely, and I love her dearly. Throughout my childhood she was like a mother to me. I suppose she's one of those natural mums – loves babies, thinks they're all beautiful, yearns for a family of her own, but..."

"But what?" Ben asked.

"She, er, can't have any."

"Why on earth not? She looks pretty healthy to me."

"Don't ask me to explain the technicalities. About eggs and stuff. Anyway, she can't conceive."

"That's terrible! Surely there is something that can be done. What about IVF?"

"Ah. That's the point. You need an egg and a male seed. If you don't have either..."

"But surely it's possible to get them from somewhere. There are sperm banks, and I would have thought in this day and age one could have an egg or embryo transplanted from another woman..."

"Yeah, but even then I gather it's a bit of a hit-and-miss affair. But that's only half the story."

"So what's the other half?"

"Well, you know what she's like. Stubborn is her middle name. She wants her offspring to have at least one real parent."

"What's stopping her? Once she's found the right partner..."

"Therein lies the rub, my friend! You see, she was let down badly, some years ago. She was in a relationship with a super guy, from the island – one of the houses – but when she explained to him about her, er, predicament, he dumped her. You can't blame him. His family expected her to produce at least one son-and-heir, so he felt duty-bound.

"And having had that awful experience, she feels she cannot conceal the fact from the men she meets who show an interest – and there are plenty of them, I can tell you!"

Ben felt his neck going red.

Donnie continued. "Yet, if she tells them she can't have children, the responsible good-husband-material does a bunk, but the others – the philanderers and those cheating on their wives, older guys after a mistress, those who like the idea of sex without responsibility of any kind – those are the ones who hang around. Just the sort she cannot abide. Can you imagine Ling as a trophy wife? A bit of fluff on the side?"

"Certainly not! What a dilemma! A sort-of Catch-22 situation."

"A sort-of Catch-nothing situation, if you ask me," said Donnie. "But there is a glimmer of hope on the horizon. Dad's paying a fortune for her to undergo an experimental procedure which might cure the problem. That's why she flew back home straight after the wedding. He's determined to do what he can, for her sake – and for the family. He sees her as the matriarch-in-waiting. The power behind the throne, if you like. Which in our case passes down the female line; or has done so far."

Ben didn't get what Donnie was saying about his family, and he was reluctant to ask. And he wanted to hear more about Ling. "So, is that why she told me she was happily married?"

Donnie laughed. "Is that her latest line? Good one! Keeps them all at bay, I guess... Ben, I'm just going to test the heads, so could you take the ship for a while? Knock her out of auto and play around a bit. I'll warn Sash and you can try out a few tight turns – and an emergency stop if you like. And take the revs up. Have some fun!"

13

Ben was enjoying his time in command, putting the yacht through its paces. He guessed Donnie had got his head down, which was a compliment as it showed Donnie trusted him. And it made sense for the captain to get some rest, as *Juli-Emma* was unlikely to reach Southampton much before midnight. Someone needed to be on the ball when they arrived.

They were well past Hastings when Sasha joined Ben at the helming station. "Hi, Ben. Having fun, then?"

"Sure thing! She's amazing! I think I'm getting the feel of her, but I'm not as good as the autopilot."

"Perhaps none of us are, but there are times when you need your wits about you. The control systems are good, but Donnie says that if you rely on them too much you can find yourself in trouble."

The craft was creaming along at a steady twelve knots towards the next major landmark, Beachy Head. It was some five hundred metres away when Donnie appeared in the companionway. "Ben, take her ten degrees to port, could you?"

"Aye aye, Captain," said Ben as he spun the shiny stainless-steel wheel.

"Just to be on the safe side," Donnie explained as he joined Ben in the cockpit. "That cliff ahead is getting on for 150 metres high, so neither we nor our radar can see around the headland. Being further out will give us and the scanner a better view."

"Got it. Why have a lighthouse at the bottom of it? Surely it makes more sense to build it on top of the cliff."

"Good point, Ben. Actually, the original lighthouse was built right on the top, but they found that rising sea mist and low cloud often obscured it. Also, at one stage in its life they had to move it back because of coastal erosion, then you couldn't see it if your vessel was too close.

"Beachy Head is famous for two reasons. It's the highest coastal cliff in Britain, and, after the Golden Gate Bridge in San Fransisco, it's the world's favourite spot for suicides."

Charming, thought Ben, as he looked up the almost vertical chalk face, now frighteningly near. What a tragic way to end a life. What a waste.

His thoughts were interrupted by Donnie resuming his commentary. "The port of Newhaven is just around the corner, and you can have all manner of craft sailing in that area, from windsurfers to the Dieppe ro-ro, so we have to take care. Dad doesn't want this thing creased."

Ben liked Donnie's style. It was relaxed yet sensibly cautious. He was a safe skipper with a steady head and was an excellent example for Ben to follow.

"It's very good of you to allow me to come along," he said. "Great experience. Wonderful."

"Glad you could make it. And I'm pleased you're enjoying it. But ocean sailing is not always like this. Think what it's like in a Force Ten, at night in the middle of the North Atlantic!"

"You mean it can be even more fun?"

Donnie laughed. "So, how about joining us on a leg?"

"What d'you think of it, Ben?" piped up Sasha. "Do you like our boat – I mean ship?"

"Bring it on! Love to. But tell me about this ship/boat thing."

"Okay," said Donnie, "let's get one thing out of the way. The Royal Navy call all their submarines boats, wherever they are and whatever they're doing. Their next rule is that you can put boats on a ship, but you can't put ships on a boat. So, as we are carrying a rib – and the 'b' stands for boat, of course – we are a ship.

"Oh, that it was so simple! But there are other definitions. Some people say size matters – and you with the gorgeous long hair can stop smirking – and that anything big is a ship and anything small is a boat. But how do measure size? Tonnage or length? According to some definitions, anything under 500 tons is a boat. So you're on a boat. But another definition says anything over sixty-five feet is a ship, so *Juli-Emma* is a ship."

"So where does a yacht fit into the scheme of things?" said Ben.

"Now, that comes from a Dutch word for a fast sailing vessel designed to hunt down pirates. But unfortunately, it can now refer to motor vessels. Okay, they have their own classification 'motor yacht' but remember the 'Royal Yacht Britannia'? I think we'd all agree she's a ship. Which brings us on to usage."

Donnie instinctively scanned the horizon. "Someone once said that it's a boat when you have to do work on it, and a yacht when you take your girlfriend out on it. Others claim a yacht – motor or sail powered – is for recreational purposes, whereas a ship is generally for commercial use."

"Got it!" said Ben, "and thanks for the explanation."

"Not over yet!"

Sasha laughed and looked at Ben. "Donnie does tend to go on a bit. He's been trying to teach me the difference for two years, but I always get it wrong!"

"Just three more factors to bear in mind. I think the OED says a sailing vessel must have three masts to be a ship. Otherwise, it's a sailing *boat*. Other dictionaries say that boats tend to be those craft you find on lakes and inland waterways, whereas ships sail on oceans."

"And the last factor?" asked Ben.

"Very important, this one. If in doubt and you're talking to the owner, call it a ship."

They all laughed, and Ben sensed it was a good time to tackle Donnie about doing a leg with him.

"Donnie, I've made up my mind. I would love to join you on part of your voyage. I can't think of a better way to spend a few weeks. And it would be such a help in getting my yacht-master's."

"You're right about that. I'll train you up. What part of the voyage do you fancy?"

"It does depend on a few things. I need to fetch Anna, the girl I mentioned, but at the moment I'm not sure about dates. When do you expect to be crossing the Indian Ocean? That might just fit in-"

"Indian Ocean, Ben? No, we're stopping at Hongkers."

Ben's jaw dropped. He felt such a fool. He suddenly twigged that Donnie and Sasha were going back the other way, across the Atlantic, through the Panama Canal and across the Pacific. You stupid boy, he said to himself. *You stupid, stupid idiot.*

He realised that fitting in a leg on board *Juli-Emma* and going to Gorith Island was going to be impossible. He would have to choose one or the other. As for using Donnie's ship/yacht/boat to rescue Anna, that was just cloud cuckoo land. For now, though, he decided to put on a brave face and not say anything. He would sleep on it, then work out a new plan – and a way of telling Donnie if he decided his mission took priority. Meanwhile, he would enjoy his time on board.

They navigated their way through the sea lanes from Newhaven and threaded their way around the unpredictable manoeuvres of the sailing boats from the marina, zig-zagging across their bows. Being under power meant they had to give way to them, but Ben was delighted to steer the ship around them under the supervision of Donnie.

Sasha was sitting on the bow deck as they made their way past Brighton. Suddenly, she shouted, "man overboard! Er, not overboard, I mean in the water! Ahead! Off the starboard bow!"

Donnie grabbed his binoculars and raced up for'rd to join her. Half a minute later he was back with Ben in the cockpit. "She's right. A person in the water, about four hundred metres away. Drop revs to 500. Steer five degrees to starboard! We're going to pick him up."

He lifted his glasses. "Orange lifejacket... he's waving! He's alive! I'll take over, Ben. Call Sasha back."

Ben was impressed with the way Donnie was handling the situation, and he watched with interest as he opened the throttle and the vessel surged forward. Then Donnie cut the revs and manoeuvred Juli-Emma about and took her very slowly astern towards the man. Sasha lowered the transom swim-deck and unfolded the steps.

When the man was just a few metres away, Donnie cut the engine and carefully steered the ship towards him, then with a burst ahead, he brought *Juli-Emma* to a stop, two metres from the casualty. He was clearly weak but able to grab the pole Sasha was holding out to him.

"Thanks. That's so kind." It was a woman's voice. She was able to hold the handrail of the steps and, with Sasha's help, she dragged herself on to the swimmers' deck, trailing behind her the remains of her kite, and, on the end of a coiled plastic line, her board. "I couldn't free it. My hands were so cold. They're numb."

"Sasha. Take her down and give her a hot cup of tea, and a bowl of warm water for her hands. Make sure it's not hot. Otherwise it will hurt. Ben. You take the helm while I lower the rib. Low revs, just enough to keep some way on her."

"Thanks so much," the girl said. "I'm okay. It's just my hands. The rest of my wetsuit's fine." Sasha helped her remove the black neoprene hood, and flicked the safety catches on the harness freeing her from the kite lines which dropped to the deck of the cockpit.

Ben saw the rib swing out on its gantry which then lowered the craft gently to the water. Donnie brought it around to the stern. "She's good to go. Just keep the bows down. Don the lifejacket aboard. Use the electric engine lift when you get near the shore. And for Heaven's sake don't let her go broadside to the surf!" He laughed when Ben's jaw dropped and his eyebrows went shooting up.

Fortunately, the boys had enough time for a quick circle around the yacht together, enabling Donnie to demonstrate the basics. Ben had piloted ribs before, but not one this size, not with twin Evinrude one-fifties on the transom plate.

When the girl appeared from below carrying a tote bag, Ben realised it was now his turn to take charge of the rib. Gulp, he thought. He helped her aboard, and when both were seated Donnie freed the bow line and tossed it to Ben.

"I'm Ben, by the way." He had to shout over the roar of the engines and the rush of the headwind as they made their way toward the shore, about two kilometres away.

"And I'm Cathy." She smiled at him, and he grinned back. He guessed her hood was in the bag with the remains of the kite kit, as he took a glance at her long blonde hair streaming out behind her. She reminded him of Anna. He wondered if Cathy also had blue eyes and a slim but shapely figure hidden beneath the black wetsuit. But there was no time to day-dream as the surf, breaking on the shoreline, was suddenly getting alarmingly close.

"Where to, madam?" he asked.

Cathy laughed. "Can you see the light-blue beach hut? Just to the left of that tall building behind it? That's where my stuff is. If you can drop me there – but don't go through the surf. I'm happy to swim ashore. My hands are fine, now."

Ben was relieved about not having to risk manoeuvring in the surf, and more than happy to drop her off exactly in line with the blue beach hut. This is what I need, he thought as he spun the rib around, if I'm going to escape with Anna from Gorith Island.

Having delivered his passenger, he eased the throttle forward, and the craft seemed to skim across the tops of the waves as he made his way back. I could outrun anything in this, he thought.

Once back on board, it was a straight run westwards for Selsey Bill. Saving Cathy had taken his mind off his problems, but then he recalled Donnie's comments about Ling. He realised that not having a sister to quiz about such things, he knew absolutely nothing about a woman's workings.

It was not something a growing lad would ask his mum, certainly not in the late Twentieth Century when it was bad enough learning about his own body. And although he did hang out with girls in his mid-teens, how women worked biologically wasn't a topic of conversation. So when Donnie went down to check the engine temperatures, he decided to get Sasha's take on Ling.

"He told you, did he?" said Sasha. "After ticking me off for asking if you two were an item?"

"Well, he didn't exactly tell me. It just came out in conversation. But I'm pleased he did, as it explained some things. But I'm afraid my knowledge of human biology is not good. I know they're having a lot of break-throughs with genetic engineering and transplants. I just hope they can do something for Ling. It must be so hard to come to terms with the fact you can't have children."

"Yes and no, Ben. And not everybody wants children. If you've an understanding husband, you can have a good life together achieving fulfilment in other ways. Or you can adopt."

"But you can't do either," said Ben, "if you don't have a partner – and if Ling goes around telling people she's happily married, she's hardly likely to find one. Not that it mattered in my case, as I have Anna, or I hope I will have when I find her, and the plan is to have a big family." *If I* find her, he thought. And if she still wants to be with me. At least I know she can have kids.

"Ben, I'm really pleased for you," said Sasha, "and I'm sure it will all go well... As for Ling, I can understand her reticence where meeting men. Being infertile is not something you blurt out when you're introduced to some handsome, eligible young hulk. We're all concerned about her, and you can imagine how anxious her parents are. But let's hope the treatment goes well."

"What's the problem?"

"Anovulation, I gather."

"A what?"

"All one word, Ben. It's when the ovaries fail to release an egg when they're meant to. I don't know what the problem is in Ling's case – Donnie's hopeless at communicating such things. But I understand that most of the time the condition can be treated with medication. It's rare, but sometimes a woman doesn't have any eggs to release, even though her ovaries work perfectly well in other respects."

"Other respects? I thought that was their job, to release eggs."

"Part of their job, Ben. They do lots of other things, too. They're endocrine glands which secrete estrogens and progesterones." She must have noticed Ben's eyeballs glazing over. "Anyway, that's the gist of it. Any questions?"

"Thanks, Sasha. That's most helpful. I do have one question: can a woman with that problem have an ovary transplant."

"Very difficult, apparently, because of the gland function – they're part of a whole-body system – and also tissue matching. What they are trying to do now is graft the skin of a healthy ovary onto a defective one."

"The skin? How does that help?"

"All the eggs are in the skin. So, if the graft takes, the patient retains the original ovary which continues to play its part in the endocrine system, but with a fresh skin around it containing hundreds of eggs. Problem solved! If they can get it to work.

"It's very much at the pioneering stage. There's a clinic in Beijing working on it. Tissue match is still a hurdle, but I expect they'll eventually crack it. Better than IVF, as it's more natural. And if the op is successful, you can go on popping out lots of children, at least until the menopause."

"Interesting. Let's hope they can do something for Ling. You certainly know a great deal about it. And you explain it so well."

"Steady on, Ben! Don't quote me! I'm not a medical person, so I might have got it wrong. I'm just telling you what I've been told, or read in a magazine at the hairdressers'. Or in the Daily Mail."

Ben found the conversation with Sasha fascinating. It made him realise what a sheltered life he'd led when it came to such matters. He recalled his biology lessons at school, only up to GSCE level, when the embarrassed master had very quickly skimmed over the delicate subject of human reproduction. How things have changed, he thought. Now everyone talks about everything.

Juli-Emma arrived at the Ocean Village Marina just after midnight, and by half-past, all three crew members were ready for bed. Ben crashed out on one of his four bunks in the crew cabin, having been awake for over eighteen hours.

14

"Fuck!" said Ben. He rarely swore, at least not out loud. But when he woke up and worked out where he was, the disappointment of his predicament hit him like a sledgehammer. In fact, there were four hits.

1. Having clocked out of that miserable hotel, he'd failed to find any accommodation and had nowhere to go.

2. His hopes of living in St Katharine Docks and enjoying the many delights and convenience of Central London had evaporated into thin air.

3. His plan for rescuing Anna had flown out of the porthole.

4. If he were to continue his mission and sign up for that flaming course on Gorith Island, he would have to break the news to his new-found ship-mates that he had changed his mind: he would not be joining them for a leg of their journey back to Hong Kong.

He tried to work out how he would do it. Then he gave up. *Get up, you daft bugger. Stop feeling sorry for yourself.*

After a stingingly hot shower followed by a wet shave, he donned a clean tee-shirt and shorts and made his way through to the saloon. The smell of fried eggs and bacon wafted through from the galley, and Sasha appeared with a mug of coffee and a ready smile.

"Hi, Ben. Sleep okay?"

"Yes, thanks. Like a log. A ship's log." He chuckled at his pathetic attempt at humour, and Sasha was kind enough to laugh.

"How do you like your eggs? Easy over or sunny side?"

"As they come, please."

Eggs. He recalled the discussion he'd had with Sasha the day before and realised it was another depressing thought to add to his misery. That his dear friend Ling had a medical problem which would effect the rest of her life – if they couldn't find a cure. Shame, he thought. She'd make a good mum – and a good wife.

"Hey, Bosun, why the frown?" It was Donnie, striding into the saloon as if he owned the place. Which, in a way, he did.

"Me?" said Ben, putting on a false smile. "Was I frowning? Nothing to frown about, not after yesterday."

"You did pretty well, I must say. You're a natural. And Sash and I are delighted you're going to join us for a leg, aren't we, Honeybun?"

"Sure, Babe. Absolutely!"

"Ben. After breakfast, I'd like to show you our route back home so you can decide which part appeals to you. We've got some real treats in store!"

The two men leaned over the horizontal screen, and Donnie brought up on the display the route he had planned back to Hong Kong. He talked Ben through the first leg, out of the Solent and down the English Channel to Ushant.

"To where?" asked Ben.

"Ushant, a French island thirty kays off the coast of Brittany. It's France's most westerly point. Then it's 'head south 'til the butter melts', across the Bay of Biscay – that should be fun – and south to the warmer climes of Gran Canaria. There, we turn right and follow the trade winds to St Lucia in the sunny Caribbean."

"When do you reckon you'll be there?"

"Good question. We've got a few things to sort out here over the next few days, but all being well we'll leave before the Easter weekend. For planning purposes, let's say Wednesday 3rd April. Ten days to the Canaries and then fifteen to St Lucia, so we should arrive before the end of the month.

"That part of our voyage is not the most interesting. It's a long haul running before the wind from Gran with no landfall until St Lucia. But if you joined us there, you could experience the delights of island hopping through the Caribbean, then the Panama Canal. Now that would be fun!"

"Sounds great!" said Ben. He tried to sound enthusiastic. As much as he loved the idea, he reckoned it was out of the question. He had to get to Anna as quickly as possible, and he knew he wouldn't enjoy the sailing if he abandoned or postponed his rescue attempt. How could he ever face Arthur and Linda again?

On the other hand, there was no point in going to Gorith Island until he'd worked out his escape route. He remembered the warning: 'leaving the island is not encouraged'. Gorith is not going to make it easy for me, especially if I am springing one of his captives. He had his own Catch-22 situation, and he wasn't sure how to get out of it.

"Once through the canal, we head off for the

Galapagos," said Donnie, "then head due west to the Line Islands." He pointed them out to Ben on the chart table. Ben knew about the famous Galapagos but had never heard of the Line Islands.

"We aren't going south to Tahiti for two reasons. A, it's become very touristy, and at this time of year finding a good mooring will be difficult. And B, our route will be shorter. We don't have much time to play with, and anyway, we don't want to be in the Pacific when the season ends."

"Season?" said Ben, wondering if there was such a thing in the equatorial Pacific.

"Yep, the sailing season. You see, the weather can turn nasty towards the end of the year, and while *Juli-Emma* is built to handle the odd typhoon or two, they are best avoided."

Ben was pleased to hear that. While he had every confidence in Donnie, he was relieved to hear he wasn't a storm-chaser.

"Then we're going to island-hop through Kiribas, taking in the Phoenix Islands and the Gilbert Islands, then run for home! Should be back in time for the party."

"What's that? A welcoming party?"

"I suppose it could be, but for Sash and me it's our second wedding celebration. Her parents were keen to have the wedding in London, in the spring, but my parents – along with a lot of our rellies – couldn't make it, so Dad's laying on a second wedding celebration at home for all the Hongkongers. And any of Sash's lot who want to come over. You would be most welcome to come. I'd like you to meet Dad. He's the boss, the tai pan of Jason Mardine. No doubt there would be other people you'd know, and my sister would be there."

Ben lost concentration for a moment, as Donnie continued with his presentation.

"The Republic of Kiribas comprises what used to be the Gilbert and Ellice Islands, plus the Phoenix and Line ones, here." He pointed to the chart. "Kiribas is a sovereign state with a population of 110,000. Used to be a British Colony, then got independence in 1979. It actually consists of thirty-two atolls and reef islands with a total land mass of 800 square kilometres, but it's spread over three and a half million square kilometres. That's a lot of sea!"

"Wowsers!" said Ben, trying to sound enthusiastic. He guessed Donnie had read up about it and let him continue.

"Kiribas straddles both the equator and the 180th meridian, although the International Date Line goes around Kiribas and swings far to the east. It's a great place for getting off the tourist trail and going to places where few have been before, and people who want to understand a country – not just see it. And the bird-life is amazing. There's world-class fishing, too. They say that Kiribas will challenge your view of how life should be and show you a less complicated way of living where family and community come first."

Ben nodded wisely as if everyone's view of life should be challenged and they should all be seeking a less complicated way of living. If it were less complicated, he thought, I'd be out of a job. Bird-watching and fishing had not been on his hobby list for many years, but then he wondered if they might be a good counterbalance to studying arbitrage and asset mixes, delta hedges and hurdle rates, leverage and lock-up periods.

Stop it, he said to himself. You're on a sabbatical, for Heaven's sake. He let Donnie carry on with his oral travelogue.

"The capital of Kiribas is Tarawa, here. It's the site of one of the bloodiest battles of World War II."

"Really?"

"Yep... " Donnie looked at his watch. "Oh shit! Sorry, Ben, I've got to go. I need to be at the shipyard at ten. Look, why don't you have a good look at our route, then over lunch we can discuss possibilities.

Ben liked the prospect of visiting uninhabited islands where few had ventured before. Of trying his hand at deep-sea fishing and swimming in tropical lagoons.

He zoomed in on the chart and noted that the first landfall for *Juli-Emma* after the Galapagos was an island called Kiritimati, one of the Line Islands as Donnie had said. On the chart it was a tiny light brown speck surround by almost endless blue. Ben switched to Google Earth and zoomed in. He saw that in the north-west corner there was an airport.

That would work well, he thought. Fly to Kiritimati, explore the islands, some fishing and bird-watching and sail back to Hong Kong and attend the wedding celebration. Perhaps his dream of being Anna's knight in armour was just that, a dream. A stupid idea which he had no chance of pulling off.

He smiled when he remembered the homeless guy in London who had wished him good luck. Was it only a week ago? He didn't begrudge him the twenty pounds, but in terms of a return on investment, he had to admit that so far the yield had been disappointing.

"Sorry, guys!" It was Donnie, returning late for lunch. "Got caught up at the yard. They tried to flog me a towed turbine!"

Sasha did not look too pleased that 'Babe' was late for

her carefully prepared salade Niçoise. "And did they succeed?" she said, raising her eyebrows.

"Yes," replied Donnie. "Or rather no, they didn't succeed, because *I* decided myself we needed more generator capacity to cope with the extra demand from all the electrical kit we've had installed."

"You mean from all the extra electrical gadgets which *they* decided we would need?"

Donnie frowned and glared at Honeybun. "Sasha, are you saying that if you cross the Atlantic and then the Pacific you don't need the right kit?"

Ben thought it was a good moment to change the subject. "Talking of crossing the Pacific, I very much like the idea of joining you for that final leg, from the Line Islands back to Hong Kong-"

"Splendid!" said Donnie. He turned to Sasha. "Isn't that great news, Honeybun?"

"Sure is, Babe! I think it's wonderful. We'll be a great crew, and we'll have a lot of fun. And Ben will be able to come to the party! You will, won't you?" said Sasha, smiling at Ben.

"Sorry. I can't. Join you, I mean. For that last leg."

"What are you saying?" said Donnie.

"I said I liked the idea. But I can't. I've got to find Anna. I've promised."

Sasha was the first to speak. "Oh, Ben. That's such a shame, but I'm sure you're doing the right thing. She must be a lovely girl and you deserve her. I understand how you owe it to her and her parents, but I think you also owe it to yourself as well. It's always best, in the long run, to do what's right, to let your conscience be your guide."

Donnie was next. "What a pity! That last leg, it's the best, the most interesting and the sailing will be the most varied. The experience would be invaluable when it comes to taking your yacht-masters. Honestly, Ben, you wouldn't regret it. It's the chance of a lifetime!"

"I know, Donnie, but-"

"Ben. Think about it. Over lunch. This afternoon. Let's discuss it this evening, over a jug or two."

"Okay," replied Ben, but he knew there was no way he was going to change his mind. Anna came first.

It was a short walk from the quayside to the steakhouse Donnie had chosen, an attractive restaurant with some interesting artwork and a nice atmosphere. He insisted dinner was on him, and that it was to celebrate Ben passing the *Juli-Emma* crewman's test. Not having to drive anywhere was a relief, and as the following day would be spent quayside, the three friends were able to celebrate in true style.

The food was excellent, and when the time came for coffee, Donnie discreetly asked the waitress for three malt whiskeys.

"Oh, Donnie-Babe," said Sasha, "I don't think I could manage one, not after all that wine."

"Nonsense. Of course you can! Ben, you're up for it, aren't you?"

"Sure thing, boss," said Ben, then wished he'd had the courage to follow Sasha's line.

"Good-good-good! It's my Scottish heritage, laddie. A wee dram once in a while – but I have to warrrn ye. *Juli-Emma* is a dry ship. Y'know wha' I mean?"

"Certainly," said Ben, "a very sensible rule."

"So it doesn't put you off?" Donnie had dropped the exaggerated Scottish accent, much to Ben's relief.

"Not at all," replied Ben.

"So, come and join us in Kiribas, and we'll sail into Hongkers together!"

"A question, if I may, Donnie. A minor point, but I noticed the chart table called it Kiribati. Is it a misprint, or is Kiribas another place entirely?"

"No, and no! Not a misprint, and it's the same place." Donnie smiled at the confusion written all over Ben's face. "It's a long story..."

Ben saw Sasha looking at the ceiling, and he suggested to Donnie it could wait for another time.

"No, laddie, ye need to ken these things!"

"In that case," blurted out Sasha, "speak PROPER ENGLISH for Heaven's sake!" Her tone was good-natured, but it was enough to put Donnie well and truly in his place. It made Ben smile.

Donnie made a point of clearing his throat and began. "The Gilbert Islands, which – as you know – form the main part of the Republic of Kiribas, were named after the British Mariner, Thomas Gilbert, who came across them in 1788 when he was pioneering a passage from Sydney to Canton."

Sasha did a mock yawn, and her husband of less than a week pretended to be offended but carried on regardless.

"The locals referred to the islands as the Gilberts, but the language of the day couldn't cope with double consonants – or 'L's – so it sounded more like Giribas. This morphed into Kiribas and that's what the locals call their nation to this day."

"So where did the 't' and the 'i' come from?" asked Sasha, suddenly interested.

"Ah! In the Gilbertese language, when it became a written language in eighteen-whatever-it-was, a 't' and an 'i' together signified the sound of an 's'. So, that's why 'Kiribas' is actually spelt K-I-R-I-B-A-T-I-"

"Thank you, Donald. I think we've got it," said Sasha.

"By George she's got it!" declared Ben. "So, a name written down, like Kiritimati, is not pronounced like that at all. It would be 'Kiri' then an 's', then 'ma' followed by another 's', which makes-"

Ben leapt to his feet. The blood had drained from his face. He said it very softly: "Christmas. Christmas Island."

"Smack on, laddie," said Donnie, "discovered by Father Christmas in 1777."

Sasha gave him a look which had the desired effect.

"Actually, it was named by Captain James Cook of the Royal Navy who first went there on Christmas Eve. Now interestingly, the other Christmas Island, the one in the Indian Ocean, was named by Captain Mynors of the East India Company, when he sailed past it on Christmas Day, in 1643, so-"

Ben was not listening. "I'm sorry," he said. "I need to check something on my phone. It's in my cabin. Please excuse me..."

15

Ben was almost in a trance as he stumbled along the quay back to the boat. It wasn't the wine and the whiskey which was befuddling his brain, but the realisation that his life might be about to change for ever. He tapped in *Juli-Emma*'s entry code and went to his cabin. His mobile was lying on his bunk being charged. He knew that this small, rather irritating electronic bit of wizardry held the answer. He hardly dared to pick it up.

He scrolled through his emails and opened the one from the Gorith Foundation which described its island. He opened it and found what he was looking for: *Nearest International Airport – Christmas Island CXI*. A moment or two later, Google told him CXI was the IATA code for Cassidy International Airport, 'located north of Banana, a settlement on Kiritimati in Kiribati'. He had the right one.

Sasha and Donnie were strolling along the quay, arm in arm, when Ben met them. He was out of breath but managed to say it: "I'm up for it. Definitely. That last leg. From Kiribas to Hong Kong!"

"Wonderful news, Ben!" said Donnie, "I had a feeling you'd change your mind. Good for you, mate!"

"Ben, what about Anna?" said Sasha.

"Can she come too?"

"What?" said Sasha and Donnie, almost in unison.

"I think I've found her! I think she's in Kiribas. On an island. She disappeared after her children, er, died. We think she's joined a religious sect – a cult – on a place called Gorith Island- "

"Steady, Ben. Take it slowly," said Donnie. "Who's 'we' for a start?"

"Your sister, Ling. She helped. Came up with some really good ideas – and hacked Anna's iPad so we found her emails. Some of them."

"Trust her," said Donnie, "she's a whizz at that sort of thing."

"There was an email from some shady organisation called the Gorith Foundation. Anyway, I was able to get in touch with them, and they sent me some details which said that the nearest international airport to Gorith Island was on Christmas Island. I thought it was in the Indian Ocean- "

"Hang on, Ben. How do you know it's not that one?"

"I checked the details they sent. Just now. On my phone. The airport code, CXI. It's the one in Kiribas."

Donnie made a silent whistle, while Sasha beamed first at Donnie then at Ben. "How wonderful! So you can both join us for that final leg. We'll be a foursome! And when we get to Hong Kong, you can both come to the party!"

Her eyes were shining in the twinkling light from the quayside lamp posts being reflected off the water. "It could be a joint celebration! Donnie and me, and you and Anna! We could announce your engagement!"

"Not so fast, Honeybun. We need to think this through. Let's get on board so we can do some proper planning."

The three of them were leaning over the chart table. Donnie had zoomed the display on Kiritimati. "Tell me, Ben. How do you plan to find this island she's on?"

"That's easy! I'm applying to do a course there, and they'll send me the travel documents – air tickets and instructions."

"What next?"

"I arrive on the island and find Anna, and then you pick us up from there – if you wouldn't mind, that is."

"I'm certainly up for it! What a maiden voyage for *Juli-Emma*! Rescuing an English woman and her partner from the clutches of an evil cult. Imagine the reception we'd get when we sail into Hongkers Harbour! Dad would love it! He'd revel in it, at the club. The papers would be full of it. And it was always part of our plan to explore some of these islands!"

"Donnie, Babe. How will we know which island to go to? There're hundreds."

Donnie zoomed out until Kiritimati was just a dot. "Ben, over to you. Ideas, please?"

"Once I'm there, I'll phone you with the lat and long, and we can arrange the pick-up."

"How will you know the co-ords?"

"My phone should tell me. It's got GPS."

"Good point," acknowledged Donnie.

It was Sasha's turn. "Does Kiribas have mobile phone coverage?"

"Ah. The main islands, almost certainly," said Donnie.

"But by the sound it, Gorith Island isn't one of the main ones," said Sasha. "And look, Donnie. Look how far apart they are! That's just the Line Islands! They couldn't have mobile coverage over the whole area."

"Well, Honeybun, we know Gorith Island is near the airport on Christmas Island-"

"No, Babe. We don't know that. The nearest airport is the one on Christmas Island. It's not the same thing. It could be thousands of miles away!"

Ben listened patiently to the exchange, and his earlier elation at finding the right Christmas Island began to evaporate when he realised the problem. He'd thought of smuggling into Gorith Island a radio or satellite phone, but then he guessed he might be searched on arrival. Gorith and his acolytes wouldn't want people making contact with the outside world.

It was getting late, and his head was throbbing. "Hey, guys. Would you mind if I...?"

"Sure, Ben. Go ahead. We won't be far behind. Let's all sleep on it and share our thoughts in the morning. Sleep well."

"You, too."

The two paracetamol helped Ben get some sleep, but at four o'clock in the morning he was wide awake, lying on his back trying to come up with a solution. Again, he asked himself: what would Ling do? 'Go back to what you know' she'd say. Had he done that in the first place, he might have noticed the airport code and saved himself a lot of heartache.

She's right, he thought. What do we know? Then it came to him, his discussion with Ling about the size of the island. And it's coastline. Perhaps that clever chart table can do some clever things, he thought. At least he had something to throw into the discussion at the breakfast table. And with that comforting thought, he fell asleep.

Rain was beating down on the cabin roof when he woke up with the dawn. He took it as a bad sign. At breakfast, Donnie said it was just what was needed. Now he knew Ben was going to join them, he could fit him out with all the wet weather gear and take out the rib again, perhaps down the Solent and across to Cowes for lunch.

"First things first," said Donnie, as the three of them tucked into beans on toast with a fried egg on top. "Any further thoughts on the escape plan?"

Ben explained his idea about using the measurements of the island to help identify it.

"Brilliant! You're a genius," said Donnie.

"But I don't see how we can arrange the pick-up," said Sasha, "if we can't make contact beforehand."

"Good point. We'll need a fail-safe plan. Something we can arrange before Ben leaves. A date, time and place. Ben, when will you get there?"

"Don't know. I'm sending my application off today-"

"But how do you know it will be accepted?" asked Sasha.

"I don't. Just hoping." Ben looked at the pair of them and shrugged his shoulders. "I could hear back from them straight away, or it could take weeks. The form asked for an availability date, and I'm going to say as soon as possible because the sooner I get there the better. I hate to think of what they are doing to her. And I've no idea how long it will take me to find her once I'm there. They might have her locked up somewhere – although they do say they believe in freedom and choice."

"So," said Donnie, stroking his chin, "a few unknowns to cope with... It's going to take a while for us to get there – four months at least – so you'll probably be there first.

Why don't you get that application off now, and maybe you'll hear back before we set off?"

"Good thinking. I'll do that right away."

Filling in the application form took much longer than Ben had thought. And he had to include a signed statement giving the Gorith Foundation the authority to access his medical records. This had to be witnessed by someone who was not a relative, and they had to provide passport or driving license details. Fortunately, all this could be done electronically, and Sasha was more than happy to witness the digital document.

The remaining hurdle was answering the question, 'why do you want to do this course?'. He could hardly give the true reason, but he had been brought up to tell the truth – and some wag at uni had once told him that liars need to have good memories. He settled on 'to experience the peace, tranquillity and freedom which Gorith Island offers'. He wanted to add, 'without being brainwashed', but thought better of it.

"All done," he announced when he finally joined the happy couple in the main saloon. "It's gone. The die is cast!"

"Well done!" said Donnie. "Let's hope you get an answer soon, and we can start to do some serious planning. Who's for lunch in Cowes?"

Ben felt cosy in his brand new wet weather gear, as the three of them whizzed across the water towards the Isle of Wight. The wind had dropped, and the rain had flattened the sheltered water, so the rib gave them a relatively smooth ride. Donnie had phoned ahead to book a table for lunch at the Royal Yacht Squadron, and they arrived in good time.

"Been here before, Ben?" asked Donnie as they struggled out of their waterproofs in the men's changing room.

"Who me? You must be joking!" Ben remembered hearing about the RYS, perhaps the most prestigious yacht club in the world. Certainly one of the oldest, dating back to the early nineteenth Century. He wondered how the hell Donnie had managed to become a member and join such personages as the Prince of Monaco and King Constantine of Greece.

"We're early for lunch, so let me show you around," said Donnie, and the three of them went on a tour of the club premises, Cowes Castle. Donnie explained it had originally been built by Henry VIII to protect England against the threat of invasion from France, but continued in use as a fortification until the middle of the 19th century, very briefly seeing action during the Civil War. The Squadron took it on as their new clubhouse in 1854.

"Now, Ben. This is important. The club became the Royal Yacht Squadron in 1833, but its association with the Royal Navy began shortly after Trafalgar when Sir Thomas Hardy – of kiss-me-quick fame – became a senior member.

"And, in 1829, the Admiralty issued a warrant allowing members of the Squadron to sail under the Navy's White Ensign, rather than the merchant Red Ensign flown by all the other buggers. So technically, when you're on board *Juli-Emma*, you're in the Navy and I can keel-haul you if I feel like it."

As Ben expected, lunch was first class. While they were

relaxing in the club lounge with their coffee, he felt his phone vibrating. It was an email.

"Guys! It's from them."

"That was quick," said Sasha. "Are they acknowledging your application?"

"Probably just telling me I've forgotten to answer one of their stupid questions. Damn difficult filling in one of those forms on a mobile. I should have done it on my iPad... Bloody hell!"

"What's up, Bosun? Thrown it back at you? They do that sometimes. You get through the whole damn thing then they tell you you've missed out a digit in your passport number or whatever."

"Oh, Ben!" It was Sasha. "Don't be upset. When we get back to the boat you can use our lap-top. You can forward their email to us, then reply-"

"It's not that... They've accepted me! On the course! Already!"

"Brilliant! Well done indeed. Great news."

Donnie's congratulations made Ben feel he'd achieved something really important; then he came down to earth with a thud when he realised he'd been accepted to join a load of weirdos on some secret island. He read the letter out to them:-

Dear Ben Bellamy,

It gives me great pleasure to inform you that your application to join our community on Gorith Island has been accepted. Attached are some guidance notes for what to bring with you and your travel itinerary and documents. We suggest you transfer these to your mobile phone so you have them with you at all times. We wish you a pleasant journey and look forward very much to welcoming you.

Bless you and bon voyage,
Gorith

"Travel itinerary!" said Sasha. "It might help us find the island! Read it out, Ben."

"Sure. Heathrow to Los Angeles. Los Angeles to Honolulu. Honolulu to Kiritimati. Sorry, Christmas Island! Must get used to saying it properly. Ferry to Gorith Island!"

"A ferry! Can't be that far. Twenty miles? Any other details."

"Yes, Sasha. It says ferry from Cassidy Airport. Nothing about a transfer to the harbour. Could be a helicopter?"

"Possibly," said Donnie, "which means it could be up to 200 miles away. What about timings?"

Ben looked at the tickets. "Ah! Heathrow to Los Angeles – my God! It's first class! They can't be short of a quid or two. Here we are. Take-off local time is 21.30 on the 27th."

"Which month, Ben?" asked Donnie.

"March 2020."

"You mean tomorrow?"

Ben thought Donnie was being daft. Then Ben realised it was him who was going round the twist. "Christ!"

The three of them sat bolt upright and looked at each other, waiting for one of them to say something. Eventually, Donnie broke the spell. "I think we'd better get back. Get around that chart and do some planning..."

Ben was concerned. "I'm going to have to see Anna's parents before I leave. To brief them up on what's happening."

"Can't you email them?" asked Sasha.

Ben smiled. "They don't do email. Or mobile phones.

Arthur's in his eighties, and Linda's not far behind. I'll have to go and see them and explain everything. Otherwise, they'll be worried."

"You're right," said Sasha. "You go. What about leaving early in the morning, then going straight to Heathrow after you've seen them? Take what you need and leave the rest of your stuff on board."

"Good idea," said Ben. "But what about the planning? How are we going to meet up?"

"You just worry about sorting yourself out for tomorrow. Donnie will work on all that side of things, won't you, Babe? He loves that kind of stuff, sitting at the chart table and pouring over nautical maps, guidebooks, websites and weather reports. It'll keep him out of trouble."

"Thank you, Sasha," said Donnie. "Hopefully we'll be able to keep in contact by phone, text or email until you take off from Honolulu. From there on it might be difficult."

"I feel bad about leaving you to do all the work, but what I can do when we get back to the boat is to draw an area on the chart in which the island must be so that its nearest airport is the one on Christmas Island. I worked out the method last week when I thought Gorith Island was in the Indian Ocean."

"Good thinking, Bosun. That'll be a start."

16

Ben's afternoon wasn't as productive as he'd hoped. He selected the nearest four international airports to Kiritimati and drew his lines which formed the box – but it was over 500 kilometres across: some 20,000 square kilometres which Donnie and Sasha were going to have to search. On the chart table, of course, but having tried it himself, he knew it was going to take hours. Every time he zoomed in, more islands would appear on the chart. Then they would disappear when he zoomed out to see where they were in relation to Kiritimati.

Having left his shipmates to carry on the good work, he went to his cabin and phoned Uplands. He asked Arthur if he could call in the following morning to give them a progress report and to let them know what he intended to do. Yes, Arthur said. Come for elevenses.

Next, he went carefully through the joining instructions and packed his cabin bag, the only luggage permitted. They emphasised that all he needed to take would be for the journey. Everything else could be found on the island.

No alcohol or drugs, other than prescribed medication, or weapons of any kind were to be taken. It warned him there was no mobile phone coverage; that came as no surprise. The instructions said there was no need to bring money, as all bills could be settled on departure. Students were requested to tell their loved ones as little as possible about Gorith Island, but to reassure them they would be well looked after during their course. *We'll see about that.*

Finally, he checked the itinerary and found he had a two-night stop-over in Honolulu, as the onward flight to Christmas Island wasn't until the Tuesday morning. He noted that it took nearly four hours, yet arrived on the Wednesday, the day after. He wondered how his iPhone would handle crossing the International Date-Line.

That evening, the trio had supper on board. Compared to the previous evening, the mood was sombre, as none of them knew for certain what was going to happen. Ben was worried about many aspects of his adventure, not least about the possibility of getting stranded on the island, having failed in his rescue attempt. He tried to imagine how he would feel standing in front of a firing squad.

He was also very concerned about letting down Donnie and Sasha, imagining them sailing the equatorial Pacific for the next few years trying to find him because he had failed to make the rendez-vous. Or worse still, them getting into difficulties while trying to get Anna and him off the island, and *Juli-Emma* getting smashed up on some rocky coastline and all of them perishing. He kept asking himself the same questions: am I up to this? Should I risk the lives of Sasha and Donnie? And Anna?

Sasha was more concerned about Ben's safety and asked him whether the Gorithians would be armed. Ben remembered the sect in Oregon, the Rajneesh, who had their own police force armed with semi-automatic rifles. And Waco. But neither sect had a secret island surrounded by millions of square miles of ocean. "No, Sasha," he replied. "Very unlikely."

Donnie wondered if the island would have any coastal defences or boats which could give chase. "I doubt it, Donnie," said Ben. "Few boats could outrun *Juli-Emma* in full sail, in my opinion. And certainly not the rib. That thing flies!"

"Let's talk about timings," Donnie said. "Clearly, you're going to be on the island long before we're in the area. A few months, I guess. Do you think that would give you enough time to locate Anna?"

"I would hope so. There are about five hundred Gorithians living on the island – and Anna is quite striking. As long as both of us remain free to wander, I guess I'll find her in that time. I've got a photo of her which I can show to people. It's from our days at uni." He extracted it from his wallet and showed it to Sasha.

"She's lovely, Ben. But I guess that's going back a few years. We all change, you know. Could you get a more up-to-date one from her parents tomorrow?"

"Good thought, Sash. I'll do that."

"So, back to timings," said Donnie. "I believe we should time the extraction as soon as possible once we have arrived in the area. Our aim must be to get Anna out of that hell-hole ASAP."

"But Babe, we don't know when we are going to arrive. We've got two oceans to cross."

Donnie sighed. "I was just coming to that. I think we need to give Ben a 'not before' date, so at least he and Anna won't be hanging around on some beach for days, waiting for us to come and pick them up. Once they've made the break, we've got to get them out of there."

"And you don't want to be hanging around on the

shoreline waiting to pick us up," added Ben. "I think we need a cut-off date as well. If you haven't found us by then, you two head home." The thought made Ben's stomach feel funny.

"Nonsense! that's not going to happen. But somehow we've got to coordinate this operation. To do that we've got to be able to communicate."

"But, Babe, there's no mobile phone coverage, and you can't expect Ben to run the risk of smuggling in a radio. You've no idea what might happen to him – and Anna – if they were caught with it."

"Right again, Honeybun. There must be some way of doing it. I dunno, high tech, low tech?"

"Any tech?" chipped in Ben.

"I know," said Sasha smiling, "semaphore!"

The men looked at her as if to say 'come on, woman, be serious for God's sake!'

"Or Morse code?" she added, looking at Donnie then at Ben.

Donnie rolled his eyes. Ben was lost in thought, unconsciously rubbing his stubbly chin. He'd shaved that morning, early, and as they were not hitting the nightspots that evening, he'd done nothing about his six-o'clock-shadow.

Suddenly, he jumped to his feet and rushed out of the saloon. The newly-weds exchanged glances. Less than half a minute later he returned clutching something. He held it up for them to see.

"What on earth's that?" asked Donnie.

"Looks like a make-up mirror," added Sasha.

"It's a HELIOGRAPH!" Ben could hardly contain his excitement. "Actually, it's my shaving mirror. I keep it in my sponge-bag."

"My God!" said Donnie. "That's it! You've cracked it!"

"Er, boys? Will someone explain to me what in Heaven's name is a heliograph?"

"Sure, Honeybun. Very basically, it's a mirror used for signalling. You line it up, so it reflects the sun's rays toward the person you wish to communicate with. You can tilt it, so it flashes on and off."

"Like – er- Morse code, perhaps?" said Sasha, smiling at the two men.

"Okay, Einstein," said Donnie, "one to you. It's a good idea. They have a huge range because the sun-rays – and the reflected rays – are virtually parallel. Like a laser. And near the equator, there should be plenty of sunshine. And a shaving mirror? What could be more innocuous than that? If Gorith's henchmen search Ben and find that, they are hardly likely to suspect he's planning a break-out. It's brilliant!"

"What about at night?" said Sasha.

"Oh, very funny, Sasha. Very droll," said Donnie.

"No, Babe, I'm being serious. If there is any threat, we might want to make the extraction when it's dark."

"Good point, Sasha," said Ben. "We must minimise risk." They all nodded in agreement.

"Ben. Do you have a camera?" asked Donnie.

"Yep. On my phone, but not otherwise. Why? Do you want me to record the happy event?"

"No," said Donnie, "I'm thinking of using cameras if we wanted to communicate by night, using the flash. One flash every ten seconds, for example, to guide us in. I've no idea what the range is, but if Sash and I were scanning the shoreline with binos, I reckon we'd pick up the flashes from a couple of kays out."

"Great idea, Babe. And, like the shaving mirror, a

camera is hardly likely to arouse suspicion. You'll need a good one with a powerful flash; the sort birdwatchers might have."

"Hey!" said Ben, "I listed bird-watching as one of my hobbies on my application form!"

"There you go!" said Sasha. "The perfect cover! Why don't you buy one at the airport tomorrow, and a solar charger, and spare batteries. And, you'll save the VAT!"

The brainstorming continued to well after midnight, each member of the team being spurred on by the ideas of their companions. None of them knew the Morse code, but they agreed they'd learn it. Camera flashes at night would be much more limited, and they decided to use them only to indicate position when appropriate.

Donnie agreed that he and Sasha would continue their chart search for an island which matched the area and coastline length Ben had given them. He'd explained that the difficulty was that several of the islands were atolls with lagoons, either partly or completely enclosed, so the area of such an island – and indeed its length of coastline – was a matter of subjective judgement.

The final issue which they discussed was the mechanics of picking up the two escapees. Bringing *Juli-Emma* into the harbour – if there was one – was out of the question. And sailing her too close to the shore-line would risk running aground and compromising secrecy. They all agreed the rib would have to be used for the extraction. Luckily its tanks gave it a good range, but it was not good in heavy seas. And it was noisy.

On the other hand, it had a low profile, could handle shallow water, and it was fast. With no knowledge of what to expect from the Gorithians, surprise and speed were essential: to get in there, pick up Anna and Ben and get out before 'the enemy' could react.

Donnie said they should remember the motto of the SAS: 'Who dares Wins'. Sasha chipped in with 'fools rush in where angels fear to tread', followed by Ben with 'nothing ventured nothing gained'. Then Donnie again: 'time spent in reconnaissance is seldom wasted'. But when Sasha added 'if at first you don't succeed, try, try, try again', Donnie stopped her.

"No, Honeybun. We've got to get this right first time. Once the enemy is alerted, it'll be ten times more difficult."

The following morning, there was a sad parting when the Uber arrived to take Ben to the station. Hugs and squeezes all round and a smacker on the lips for Ben from Sasha. He'd only known them for four days, but Ben reckoned that sailing together bonds you. And the planning of the mission had certainly helped. Despite the irony of splitting up and not being reunited for a couple of months, they were a team.

It was an easy journey for Ben, from Southampton Central up to Waterloo, then down to Staplehurst and a taxi from there. As usual at Uplands, a warm welcome awaited him and he was offered coffee and biscuits, and Arthur suggested that they all sat around the kitchen table. Ben was surprised but pleased that Linda was going to join them, although he knew he would have to choose his words extra carefully.

"So, Ben, you have some news for us?" Arthur smiled and looked at Linda, as if to indicate it was going to be good news.

"Yes. Sort of. I think I know where Gorith Island is."

"That's where we think Anna is, dear. Remember I told

you about those magazines? Ben and I think she's joined a community there."

Linda nodded.

"I have to say this," said Ben, clearing his throat nervously, "but there is a small chance she might be being held against her will." He noticed the open mouths. "Or simply that she is unable to get transport of any kind," added Ben.

Then Linda smiled. "That's why she hasn't come back to us! She can't! My poor baby!"

Ben continued. "But I've applied to go there, too, to do a course, so I can meet Anna and then bring her back."

"But that's wonderful, Ben," said Arthur. "Are you sure you can spare the time?"

"Absolutely!"

"So when are you off?"

"Today, actually. This evening."

"And when do you expect to return, the two of you?" Again, Arthur and Linda exchanged smiles.

"Well. It's going to take some time to get there, then I have to find Anna, and organise how we can get back."

"Will it be before the weekend?" asked Linda.

"No," said Ben, "Gorith Island is, er, far away."

"Not off Wales?" asked Arthur.

"No." Ben knew he had to be careful. He wondered if it was wise to have Linda there.

"It's a long way off... Abroad, in fact." He watched Linda's face. She was clearly waiting for him to continue.

Ben bit the bullet. "Actually, Gorith Island is in the Pacific. The Pacific Ocean. Near the Equator."

Linda gasped. "But that's so exciting! Arthur, isn't that wonderful? Ben's going all that way to find Anna. How romantic! Is it near Bali Hai?"

Arthur frowned and scratched his head.

"You know, dear. *South Pacific*. The musical! We saw it together, when I was expecting. Remember?"

"We're not absolutely sure where Gorith island is," said Ben, "but it's in a group of islands mid-way between Hawaii and Tahiti."

"I'll get the atlas," said Arthur and he struggled to his feet. A couple of minutes later he returned and opened the big book on the table. The page which Arthur turned to revealed a very familiar image to Ben: a few tiny light brown dots surrounded by lots of blue.

Linda put on her reading glasses, stood up and leant over the map. She looked to Ben and whispered, "Can I come with you?"

Arthur looked pale. Ben could understand it was a shock for him, knowing that his daughter was so far away. "How long do you think... When can we expect to see you both?"

"It's not that easy to get to. The nearest airport is on Christmas Island, but that's a long way off, and we're planning to sail back to Hong Kong-"

"She'll love that," said Linda, smiling. "She always wanted to sail the seven seas... Christmas Island! It sounds so exciting! Will you be back by Christmas?"

"Yes, Linda. All being well."

It had gone better than expected. Ben only had one question which he wanted to ask Arthur in private. In some ways, it was a silly question for a 34-year-old to be asking in 2020, but Ben was determined to go through with it. He waited until the two of them were walking down the path to the taxi,

"Arthur?" Ben's heart was thumping. "If all goes well –

I mean, if Anna is on the Island – and I manage to find her – may I ask if I might have her hand in marriage? If she'll have me, of course. And once the divorce goes through-"

"My dear boy!" Arthur hugged him close. When the taxi driver sounded the horn, the two men parted and Ben climbed into the cab. As it drove away, he looked back to see Arthur holding his big red handkerchief in his hand.

17

For a Friday evening, Heathrow was not too crowded. Ben was grateful the Easter holiday rush had not yet started. He had arrived in good time, as he was anxious to confirm his first-class seat and make sure there wasn't any sort of mix-up. First class! he thought. They must be trying to butter me up.

He then made his way to the BA lounge – reserved for business and first-class passengers only – where he received an unctuous welcome from the uniformed receptionist. A gin and tonic and a handful of cashew nuts later, he decided to melt plastic at the duty-free shop which specialised in the latest electronic gadgets.

The camera expert on the evening shift asked him what he wanted the camera for. Ben decided to lie: "for taking photographs."

An exaggerated expellation of air emanated from the salesman's nostrils. "What *sort* of photographs have you in mind?"

"Er, bats at night," Ben replied. "So it must have a good flash. And a zoom."

"And how much does *sir* want to spend?" the assistant asked.

"Er, not too much, but it has to be good value," replied Ben, ever the economist. "And not too bulky or heavy. And waterproof, and with a powerful flash," he added.

The assistant sighed. "Well, if you're looking for *value*, you won't do better than this little chap. Flip-up flash, optical zoom of seventy-times, but you can also zoom in digitally on the screen once you've taken your photo. Of the bat." He smiled at a colleague who sauntered past and did a mock yawn as if to say we've got a right time-waster here. "It's got an optical viewfinder, stabilisation, a video mode, burst-mode and time-lapse, and an extra large tilting screen for showing your snaps to your friends. If you have any."

"What did you say?"

"If you have any photos you want to show to your friends. Otherwise, you can download them onto any computer: desktop, laptop, iPad or smartphone, or smart TV, or-"

"Can I try it out?"

"Of course, sir. I'll switch it on for you."

Ben was staggered by the zoom and the stabilised viewfinder. It was just like a telescope, but it didn't shake. He took a shot of the shop opposite on the far side of the mall, then zoomed in on the image on the screen and panned across. He could read the notice stuck on the side of the till fifty metres away, the bottom line, in very small print: *Cheques will not be accepted without a banker's card.* No need for a birding scope, he decided.

"I'll take it," he said.

"What?"

"The camera, and two spare batteries. And do you have a solar charger?"

"Certainly, sir. Do come this way, sir, and I'll put it

through the till. Perhaps you'd like to read about our extended guarantee while I get the batteries and charger for you, sir."

The sales assistant was still extolling the virtues of the camera when Ben walked out of the shop. Typical salesman, he thought. Can't stop himself, even after the deal is done. But Ben needed to get away as he had another important purchase to make, one which would set him back by much more than the £499 he'd paid for the camera.

The Dreamliner seemed almost brand new, and Ben couldn't help smiling as he boarded the aircraft and turned left. The first-class cabin was amazingly spacious, and each 'guest' had oodles of room around their chair-cum-bed and pull-out table. An impeccably turned-out female flight attendant with a broad smile revealing ultra white teeth offered him a glass of champagne, and a hot face-towel made of real towelling in case he wanted to wipe his hot face.

When he studied the menu card he was pleased he hadn't eaten seriously in the lounge, and when he gave in his order for the venison steak – sizzled in a jus of eastern herbs marinated in Chateauneuf du Pape – he was amazed and delighted it was still available.

After the meal, he scanned the selection of malt whiskies on offer and the long list of feature films available on his personal screen which twisted and tilted to suit any contortion a passenger might want to subject their body to. Luxury unlimited, he thought. Then he realised he had a problem: how to stay awake so he could enjoy it all.

Despite his valiant efforts, he succumbed while flying over Greenland, and remained tucked up in his horizontal bed, fast asleep, until the elegant white teeth gave him a gentle nudge and suggested he may like to prepare for the landing.

His four-hour stop-over in LA wasn't as bad as he thought it would be. The first-class lounge had showers and a gym, reclining chairs, a foot massaging service, a computer room and free wifi. He settled down at one of the desktops, put his phone on charge and emailed his accomplices:-

> Hi Cap'n and First Mate – at LA after super flight. Followed your instructions and bought a camera which will do the job – and will serve as binos!!! Got VAT off, too. Have a bit of a wait here for flight to Honolulu but will spend the time learning Morse. Any 'not before' date? No rush, as flight for CI is not till Tues morning. Should have good comms in Hawaii. Could discuss plans 'n' things.
> Bosun
> P.S. Thanks again for the sail – and all your help.

He liked his new nickname, even though there was no deck-crew to be responsible for aboard the *Juli-Emma*, other than himself. Moments later his phone pinged to informed him he had mail.

> Bridge to Bosun – good to hear all's well. Am working on dates and Einstein's learning Morse. Any clues would be good clues. Ring before you leave Honolulu. Might be your last chance. Godspeed.

The five-hour flight to Hawaii began well with breakfast being served shortly after take-off. Ben enjoyed the meal, even though his stomach was telling him it was time for afternoon tea. After landing and going through all the formalities, he took a cab to the hotel listed in his itinerary.

Although he was determined to stay awake until ten, local time, the testing out of the double bed in his room took several hours. The good news was he was up bright and early the following morning in time for a swim in the hotel's open-air pool before breakfast began at 5.30 am.

Ben had two fluffy pancakes, one topped with taro, coconut flakes, and sweet coconut sauce, the other with the green tea azuki riff, with fried mochi, red bean, ice cream, and a green tea sauce. And a large mug of coffee. Afterwards, he went to the information desk in the hotel reception hall to seek help in planning his two days in Honolulu.

At the top of his to-do list was to try out his new camera, and to take lots of pictures of birds to reinforce his cover story, should he and his camera be searched and interrogated. The next was to have a bit of fun – bearing in mind he was about to ride into the valley of death, or at least away from the delights and depravities of Western Civilisation. Last, but certainly not least, was to search for clues which might help Donnie and Sasha identify Gorith Island.

It seemed to Ben that anyone wanting to go to Christmas Island, or in that direction, would fly from Honolulu, so there was a chance that he might bump into someone going there or coming back. He would make a point of chatting to as many people as possible, and slip into the conversation that he was off there on Tuesday morning.

A quick chat with the helpful girl behind the information desk made him realise you need at least a week to scratch the surface of all the things that Honolulu and Hawaii had to offer. He chose three for his first day. Foremost was a one-day pass for the Waikiki hop-on, hop-off bus which would enable him to 'see the best of Honolulu from open-air trolleys and explore Diamond Head, Pearl Harbor, Sea Life Park, Waikiki, Bishop Museum and more!'. Just reading about it made him feel exhausted.

The next was just what he needed, a photo tour with a professional photographer-guide 'to discover Oahu's most photogenic locations, such as the Halona Blowhole and Makapu'u Point Lookout on the island's southeastern tip'. And, he thought, get to know how to work the new camera.

And finally, he included the enticing Waikiki Sunset Cocktail Cruise, on which he could 'watch the sun dip below the horizon as you take in Hawaii's beautiful coastline, sip on tropical Hawaiian cocktails with iconic Diamond Head and Waikiki Beach in the background'. And, he thought, meet some fellow sunset cruisers who might know a thing or two about the Line Islands.

That would do for one day, he reckoned, then on Monday morning he'd enjoy – according to the leaflet he was given – a '45-minute adventure hike to the summit of Diamond Head Crater, ascending 763 feet to reach the top for an incredible 360-degree panoramic view'. Then he would take it easy in the afternoon enjoying a two-hour Shark Dive off the North Shore.

All went well. The guided photo tour was fun and interesting, and he learnt not only how to use his camera, but how to talk the talk. He met lots of people over the two days, in his hotel, in shops, restaurants, coffee houses and bars, as well on his carefully selected tourist excursions, and each time he made an effort to bring the conversation round to Christmas Island. He had only two breakthroughs, but they were important ones.

The first was with a girl he met on the Waikiki trolley bus. She just happened to work for Fiji Airlines as a flight attendant, and on her last run to Christmas Island she'd opted to stay for a week, so she could answer the many questions she was often asked about the place. Ben seized his chance.

Yes, she said, lots of islands – and you can see many of them from the aircraft on the way down. No, they are not all inhabited, not since the Kiribati government started moving their people to islands less threatened by rising sea levels. Yes, a helicopter does meet the flight when it lands every Tuesday, and it takes people out to one of the southerly islands where they are, she believed, carrying out a project into saving the coral reefs.

His second breakthrough came during the Sunset Cocktail Cruise when he found himself conversing with an elderly English gentleman with a large white moustache.

"Christmas Island, eh? Know it well, from 1957. Was there as a lad. Six months, during my National Service. Don't suppose a young chap like you knows about National Service. Two years, it was. Everyone – or rather every man – had to do it. Unless they had some excuse, what! Then the bombs went off and we came home."

"Bombs?" Ben asked.

"Yes. Op Grapple, they called it. Testing out our H-bombs and things. All hush-hush, of course, and it didn't all go to plan, but that was covered up. They didn't really know about radiation then. I was one of the lucky ones. Down a big hole when the air-burst happened. You should have seen the place afterwards! Devastated – the whole island! And lots of others. Written off. Unsafe for years..."

"So are you on your way there now?" asked Ben.

"Ha! Just come from there, actually. Spent a week. Amazing how the place has recovered. Where are you staying?"

"I'm visiting one of the southern islands. There's a research station there, running a project on coral conservation. There's quite a team already out there, living on the island."

"What? Poor buggers. Those islands are wonderful for wildlife, but for humans they are hell. Relentless sun, no shelter, poor water supply, and the incessant screeching of seabirds. Desert islands! *A la Robinson Crusoe!*"

"Oh!" said Ben. "I rather assumed the island with the research station was habitable."

"Dear me, no. Very unlikely. The only one it could be is that one down on the equator, the one leased to the Japs some years ago. It was called Arikoras, in my day. Spelt A-R-I-K-O-R-A-T-I, because the T and the I togeth-"

"Yes," interrupted Ben, "strange, isn't it? Tell me, though. Why did the Japanese choose to go there?"

"Two reasons. One's top secret. The un-secret one is that they needed a satellite launch station on the equator for their space programme, as it's much easier and cheaper to chuck the things into space if they are launched at zero degrees of latitude." He paused, and Ben guessed he was waiting for him to ask about the secret reason.

He thought he'd better oblige. "Interesting. Can you tell me anything about the other reason?"

"My dear chap. Couldn't possibly. Anyway, I hardly know you!"

"Sorry, I'm Ben," He held out his hand.

"Blenkinshaw. Howard Blenkinshaw. How d' you do. And this is my wife, Dot."

After the introductions, Ben continued to press Howard on why the Japanese chose Arikoras. Both the men had consumed their two free Hawaiian cocktails, and Ben noticed that Howard had helped Dot out with hers.

Howard looked from side to side, leant forward towards Ben and lowered his voice. "All right, then. Back in 1957, I was a part of a Royal Engineers well-drilling team, and we were working on Arikoras."

"Drilling for water?" To Ben, it didn't seem to be very secret at all.

"No," the man said in a whisper. "A deep vertical shaft for an experimental ADM!"

"Really? What's that?"

"An atomic, demolition, munition." He said it slowly. "We were proud of that, us sappers, I can tell you! You see, all the bombs being tested – and there were quite a few of them – were designed to cause death and destruction, But an am...aton... an ADM was for peaceful purposes, like earth-moving; for example, making a cutting for a canal, or moving a mountain out of the way. And mining, and things. Anyway, that was the idea."

"Didn't it work, then?"

"No. Or rather it worked too well. They were too ruddy powerful. The one they popped down our hole moved earth all right – fifteen million tons of it! Formed a crater 500 feet deep and 2000 across! Changed the island completely. It looked like the atoll had a volcano plonked down in the middle of it.

"Of course, it was uninhabitable for years because of the radiation. But the Japs moved in there in the nineties and built all manner of things, apparently. Constructed a roof over the crater, just like in that James Bond film, er – forgotten it. Didn't open, though. Made out of solar panels, which collected rainwater. Damn clever, if you ask me. And the space underneath provided offices, laboratories, living accommodation and workshops."

"Are they still there?"

"What? The facilities? I assume so. Who would move them? I didn't get down there myself. A hundred and fifty miles! I'm a landlubber, I'm afraid."

"But I gather there's a helicopter that goes down there?" said Ben.

"Helicopter? You'd never get us in one of those, would they, Dot?"

The two men continued to natter, but with Howard doing most of the nattering. Ben gleaned that the Japanese had moved off the island when their space project was abandoned in 2003 because of the country's economic stagnation. There had been a string of failures, and the emphasis changed from supporting the International Space Station to launching small spy satellites which could keep an eye on North Korea.

Finally, the cruise came to an end with the catamaran depositing its passengers on the jetty which had been wheeled out from Waikiki beach for that purpose. Once ashore, Howard and Dot wished Ben a good night and a safe journey.

"And you too," said Ben, "it's been great talking to you. Just one more question, if I may, Howard? Does the name Gorith mean anything to you?"

Howard frowned and slowly shook his head. "No, I don't think so."

"Yes you do, dear!" It was Dot. "The butcher!"

Ben's heart missed a beat.

"You know," said Dot, "the one in the village!"

Howard sighed. "Gareth, dear. His name is Gareth."

Before he left the beach, Ben decided to carry out his experiment. This entailed selecting the time-lapse mode on his camera with an interval of three seconds, flipping up the flip-up flash and setting the thing on a rock.

Having ensured it was working – losing his night vision in the process – he ran along the beach intending to stop when he could no longer see the flashes. After about half a mile, he gave up, as the flashes seemed as bright as ever, and he turned around and ran back to his camera before anyone pinched it.

The following day, he decided to take his heliograph with him on the Diamond Head trek, and when no one was looking, he tried it out. He needed practice, as he found it difficult to pick up the target, and to hold it steady once acquired.

By the time Tuesday morning came round, he reckoned he was more physically fit than when he arrived, despite the aching calf muscles, and he felt confident he could fight off any sharks he might meet when swimming through the surf with Anna to the *Juli-Emma*.

18

It was Tuesday, 31st March 2020. Ben had to be careful to get his days and dates sorted out, as he was about to go forward in time when he crossed the Date-Line. He wondered if he would be a day older – and, if he continued travelling around the world in a westerly direction, whether he'd end up in the middle of the following week. But his main concern that morning was making the phone call to Donnie and Sasha, before any possibility of contacting them was lost for ever, or at least until he'd mastered his heliograph.

Hearing the rings reminded him of his call to Uplands, just a couple of weeks ago. How my life has changed since then, he thought. Would Donnie pick up? It was 3.30 pm in England, so unless there was a problem, he would soon be discussing the forthcoming operation.

Not a doddle, he thought, by any means. To rescue a girl, possibly brainwashed and held captive by an evil cult on an island somewhere in the Pacific, and get her on board a yacht – without any of us knowing where anyone would be at any particular time.

"Bosun! Good afternoon! Or should I say good morning? How *are* you?"

"Fine thanks, Donnie, and you – and Sasha, and *Juli-Emma?*"

"All of us are fine. Under sail, having a final shakedown around the Isle of Wight. Wish you were here, as they say! Now, down to business. When do you take off?"

"Late this morning."

"And you arrive at Christmas Island when?"

"Er, got the ticket here on my phone. 15.29 pm local time, Wednesday."

"What? That's a heck of a long flight. You going by balloon or something?"

"No, Donnie. The flight crosses the Date-Line."

"Ha! Got it. Sorry, I was being thick. I have a date for you."

"Great. Fire away!"

"Taking everything into account, we reckon we'll arrive not before mid-August and no later than the 7th September. It's a big window, and we've got to allow time to find your island-"

"I've good news on that, Donnie. I had a pretty good steer on where it might be."

Ben related the information Howard had passed on to him about Arikoras, explaining that it was the only island, apart from Kiritimati, which could support a community of five hundred. It was about 150 miles away from Kiritimati and on the equator with an extinct volcano on it, a small one.

Donnie thanked Ben, saying that all made sense, given that Kiritimati was at 1° 52′ 0″ N, which in old money meant it was 144 miles north of the equator. Donnie said he would plot the two possible positions of Arikoras on the chart.

"Two positions?" Ben asked.

"Sure. Compass point of Christmas. Radius of 150 miles. Cuts the equator in two places."

"Agreed. But I doubt if there are two small atolls each with a big crater on them. Perhaps you could google-earth them both and see which one it is."

"Sure, Ben. Hang on, just putting you on speaker phone, so I can do some plotting. Wait one…

"The westerly option doesn't exist! Zooming in some more… Nothing there at all. Even if Howard's distance is a bit out, there's nothing for miles. Checking the easterly one… could well be… A bit further than Howard's 150 miles, but smack on the equator!"

"Great. That's progress. So, how are we going to meet up?"

"Well, you're going to be on that island from this evening onward. Or tomorrow evening. So when we arrive you will definitely be there, if you're still alive-"

"What the-"

"A joke, Ben! Me being silly. What I'm getting at is that we know you'll be on that island when we arrive in the area, so somehow *we've* got to let *you* know we've made it. Without giving the game away."

"How about sending up a flare?"

"Good idea. Our rocket flares go up to about 300 metres and last for about thirty seconds. That would allow us to hold station well clear of the island, as those things can be seen for miles especially at night – if you happen to be looking in the right direction at the right time."

"How will I know what direction to look in, and what will be the right time?"

"Okay, Ben. Let's think about this. Every night, after 7th September, you look along an agreed bearing at a certain time until you see our flare. But I don't see how you can let us know that you have seen it."

"Er... My heliograph?"

"Brilliant, Ben. But at night?"

At that moment, Ben heard Sasha's greeting. She explained she'd been listening to the speakerphone while keeping watch. "Sounds as if we a problem, Houston."

"Damn right, Sasha," said Ben. "Do we hope for a bright moon?"

"What about... a flare at night, then use your sun-thing the following morning?"

"Good thinking!" The boys said it almost together, even though Ben was many thousands of miles away on the end of a phone.

"Okay," said Donnie, "listen up, you two. Getting the time right could be a problem, and it might be difficult for you, Ben, to look down a particular bearing, so why don't we keep it simple? We'll fire a flare every evening at say, exactly one hour after sunset, from a position on a line between the island and where the sun sets, probably about 20 kays out. Clear so far?"

They nodded.

"You, Ben, will then make contact with us using your shaving mirror at noon the following day. Noon is best, as any sea mist will have cleared by then. And if our clocks have gone haywire because of the Date-Line, let's make it sun-time. Easy on the equator. You should have us visual at 20 kays, and we'll have our binos trained on the island ready for you. We can then talk. You're not the only one with a shaving mirror! Questions?"

"Sounds good to me," said Ben.

"I'm up for it," echoed Sasha. "No questions, just a suggestion. Why should Ben sit around waiting until noon? I mean, if he sees us, perhaps through his telephoto lens on his new camera, even before 7th September, could he not take out his thing and flash us? We might see him." said Sasha.

"Hope not!" said Donnie. Ben heard an exaggerated yelp from him down the phone and guessed what had happened. "But seriously, that's a good idea, Ben. If you see *us at any time* during daylight hours, just..." Ben could hear him laughing. "Just get out... just get..."

"All right. Joke's over," said Sasha. "Pull yourself together! Don't be so childish."

"Okay," said Donnie, clearing his throat, as if that would stop his giggles. "Let's aim to have the first flare up on the evening of 7th September – taking the Date-Line into account, guys? That'll give Sash and me plenty of time to get into the general area. If we're early, we'll just swan around a bit and enjoy the islands, while you languish in that commune."

"Oh, thanks!" said Ben.

"And, Ben. In the meantime, can you recce a good landing spot for the rib? You know the requirements."

"Aye-aye, Cap'n." He looked at his watch and realised he needed to get going. "Well! See you guys on Gorith Island!"

"Have a nice flight!" said Sasha, "and a nice holiday with Gorith and his gang. And good luck in finding Anna!"

"And Ben," called out Donnie, "don't get brainwashed!"

It was a sad moment for Ben when he heard the click. For the first time since he landed at Heathrow, he felt truly alone. Despite the tragic news from Arthur, he was pleased to have met him again, and Linda, too. He was so relieved to see that a bit of her old self had emerged at their last meeting: the feisty fighter, just like her daughter.

And Ling. What a rock she had been. And good company, at the hotel, the little Italian restaurant in Hammersmith, at St Paul's, at the pub, and of course at the wedding. Now she was gone. At least she had introduced him to his new sailing buddies. He loved their sense of fun, their professionalism and their can-do approach. He just hoped he wouldn't let them down.

As he boarded the Fijian Airways plane, his stomach told him that his adrenal glands were doing their job, preparing him for the flight or fight which his subconscious was anticipating. A bunch of daft loons, he said to himself, who believe in peace and freedom for God's sake. Why should I be frightened of them?

It didn't work. Those glands kept doing their stuff. The flight attendant must have sensed there was something wrong because she offered him a boiled sweet. It was the best she could do. First-class was demarcated only by a curtain, pulled across the aisle when all twenty-one passengers had taken their seats.

His only consolation – apart from the boiled sweet – was the fact that with every air-mile flown, he was getting nearer to his Anna. He felt the little box in his pocket. Not long now, he thought. Not in the scheme of things. It'll be how it was always meant to be. He had his fingers crossed.

The landing was bumpy even before the aircraft had touched down on the cracked tarmac, drained of its resilience by the relentless heat of the equatorial sun. His relief that they had landed safely seemed to be shared by everyone else, including the flight attendant and the pilot who beamed back at the passengers behind him when he heard their applause.

It was mid-afternoon, the hottest part of the day, and the dark grey surface of the path leading to the terminal building shimmered. Customs and immigration seemed to take ages, and Ben felt the sweat trickling down the centre of his back and the sides of his chest as he waited in the queue. Finally, it was his turn. He noticed that the official was writing down by hand every single detail in his passport. Why? he asked himself. Haven't they heard of photocopiers? At least he didn't have to wait for hold luggage.

The arrivals building was hardly more than a corrugated iron shed, but at least it provided shade. There was no line of taxi drivers holding up cards with people's names on them, and Ben felt the butterflies waking up. Then he heard a woman's voice.

"Meeter Ben Berramy?"

He swung around and saw her smiling face. He lowered his head to allow her to put the lei of jasmine blossom around his neck.

"Wercome to Kirisimas! Would you forrow me prease?"

He did as he was told and found himself being led out of a side door across more shimmering tarmac to a helicopter. The door to the passenger compartment was open, and a short flight of wooden steps had been placed below it.

Prease, Meeter Berramy. Take your seat, ten fassen your safey berit... Enjoy your fright!"

Normally, the mis-pronouncement of that word would have made Ben smile, but the aptness of it in the circumstances in which he found himself made him shudder. The door thrumped shut. Opposite him was a small window through which he could just see the top of the corrugated iron terminal building. He heard a soft whine which slowly got louder until it became a roar and then a rapid whop-whopping.

He was the only passenger. No crew members were visible. The aircraft began to shake. The faint smell of paraffin would not have normally turned his stomach, but it panicked the butterflies. He remembered Howard expressing his feelings about these machines, and reckoned he had a good point.

The extra tug of gravity told him the thing was airborne, and he watched as his view of the wriggly tin roof slid away revealing a clear, azure-blue sky. He felt a light, cool breeze on his face when the air-conditioning kicked in. As the pilot banked to port, Ben saw below him Christmas Island in its entirety. It was getting smaller as the helicopter climbed, taking him further away from civilisation. There was no turning back.

19

Ben felt the power easing off and looked at his watch. He'd been airborne for just over an hour and had spent most of the flight worrying about how to behave and what to say when he arrived. His original idea of demanding to see Gorith and insisting he released Anna wasn't going to work; he couldn't imagine remaining among them for several months after such a showdown, waiting for *Juli-Emma* to show up on the horizon.

He would have to be more cunning and bide his time. He'd play along with them, humour them. The time would not be wasted. Hopefully, he'd find Anna soon and take care of her. If she had been brain-washed, or 'guru'd', or got at by Gorith himself, he could gradually help her to recover.

He hadn't forgotten his other task which was to select a suitable landing site for the rib. He reckoned his camera would be invaluable, as he could take a quick shot of a likely place then zoom in on it on the screen later and study it in detail. And his recces could all be done under his cover of being an avid bird-watcher.

His final task would be to collect as much evidence on the cult as he could so that once he got back to England, he could persuade the Foreign Office to mount a military operation to rescue all the other victims and close down the commune for good.

He thought the best way of achieving all this would be to gain the confidence of the community by acting as the willing student. He hoped that over the months they would share their secrets with him. He would have to be strong, but the bonus would be that his experience of their mind-bending techniques and methods of persuasion and hypnosis, of what Anna had already been through, might help him nurse her back to health before the cavalry arrived.

A problem was deciding when he would confide in Anna and tell her the plan. He didn't like the idea of lying to her, but if he did tell her the truth while Gorith still had her in thrall, she might spill the beans and wreck the mission.

He felt a bump, and the gentle whop-whopping above his head diminished to a whoosh-whooshing which gave way to a dying whine. He had to shield his eyes from the sun's glare when the door suddenly slid open. He realised he must be facing west, as before him he could see the silhouette of a robed figure, about fifty paces away, against the early evening sky. Gorith! he thought.

Hands on each side of him helped him down from the helicopter, and a smiling face said welcome to Gorith island as its owner placed another lei over his head and kissed him on the cheek. He could smell orange blossoms. Someone took his cabin bag for him, and the robed figure gestured with an outstretched hand that Ben should proceed towards the open grass-roofed building at the side of the landing pad.

There, another figure, a man in a long cream robe, was holding a silver tray on which there was a glass of what looked like fruit juice, with a slit slice of pineapple sitting on its rim and two ice cubes clinking together on the surface. Probably drugged, thought Ben, but I'd better play along.

The man smiled when Ben raised the glass to his lips, and he asked Ben, in perfect English, if he would care to take a seat in front of the reception desk. A few formalities to go through, he said, then you will be free to go to your accommodation. Ben was surprised the drink had no effect on him, apart from being refreshing and delicious. When the man asked for his passport, he provided it, and in return he was given a watch.

"This, sir, is your room key. Have you ever skied?"

"Er, yes," said Ben, finding it hard to guess the relevance of the question.

"For the moment, think of this watch as a ski pass. It will give you access to all the public spaces and your own accommodation."

Ben thanked the man. It reminded him of the latest Apple smartwatch, selling in their thousands in Hong Kong but not yet in London. It had a chunky but attractive body with a black square screen and a white strap. He noticed that the man was also wearing one.

Ben removed his own watch and fastened the white strap of his new one around his wrist. The screen sprang to life showing an analogue clock face which told him it was 6.17 pm. He thanked the man with a smile.

"Sir, the main dining hall is through the door to your right. Dinner is served from six thirty."

"Thanks," said Ben with a smile. "And, my accommodation?"

The man smiled back and told Ben to look at his watch. The clock face had been replaced with a little map on which a red dot was blinking. At the top of the screen there was a blue arrow, and Ben noticed that if he turned his wrist, the arrow would keep pointing in the same direction. Just follow the arrow, the man said.

Ben had often used his mobile as a satnav, both in a car and on foot, so the technology wasn't new to him. And with over thirty geostationary satellites to choose from, he knew that these little beasts could be accurate to within a few centimetres.

He followed the arrow from the reception hut down some steps and along a path which wound its way between some trees. Darkness had rapidly descended, which was no surprise to Ben as he knew the earth's surface moved faster at the equator, making dawn and dusk much shorter than in temperate climes.

His route was lit by tiny lights at ground level which came on as he approached them. He smiled. Nothing magical about them, he thought. Infra-red sensors and LEDs had been around for years. He could hear in the distance the familiar sound of waves breaking lazily on a shore; and ahead of him, crickets were chirping their mating call, only to fall silent when they sensed his presence.

After about five minutes, the blue arrow told him to take a right turn, and, lo and behold, in front of him was a short path leading up to some steps, at the top of which was a platform with a door beyond it. The automatic light above the door switched on for him, but it wasn't bright enough for him to make out much of his surrounding, or work out what sort of building it was.

When he reached the bottom step, his watched pinged. He looked at it and saw the arrow had disappeared. This is it, he thought. My home for the next six months. Play along. When his hand was about a metre from the door handle, he heard a click, and the door swung slowly open. The soft, subtle interior lighting came on gradually, allowing his eyes to adjust.

The interior of the building reminded him of one of those luxury caravans which huddle together in groups, blighting British coastlines and beauty spots. The door slowly closed behind him. It didn't take him long to explore the inside: just the one main room with a bed on one side, a sofa on the other and a low table between them. At the far end, there were two doors with a big flat-screen TV between them. On the screen was a message:

> A warm welcome to our world and Villa Rosalind. Your introduction to Gorith Island will take place here, at one hour after sunrise tomorrow.
> Bless you,
> Gorith

No long lie-in, he thought.

The left-hand door revealed a kitchenette, complete with sink, hob, microwave and mini-fridge. Inside the fridge were milk, fruit juice, two bread rolls and two eggs. On the small worktop next to the hob was a basket of fresh fruit, an espresso coffee machine and four capsules.

In the cupboard above the hob he found glasses and crockery, and in the draw to the left was cutlery – four of everything. I can have a guest, he thought. He wondered if the sofa might be one of those convertible jobs, and he imagined Anna joining him in his little nest in paradise.

The right-hand door opened into a bathroom with a roomy shower, a large basin and a proper loo – and with a built-in washing machine. We'll soon test that out, he thought, stripping off his sweat-sodden Hawaiian tee-shirt, shorts and underpants. Having popped them in the machine and pressed 'go', he had a shower and treated himself to the clean and dry but creased clothes from his cabin bag. He was ready for dinner.

Then it happened. His worst fears. He tried the door handle again. It didn't turn. He pulled as hard as he could. He noticed there were shutters over the windows, the roll-down type designed to keep out burglars, or prisoners in. His heart raced, as he realised he was trapped.

He tried the door handle again, and he noticed that is wasn't a typical caravan door which you could kick your feet through, but more like a security door, metallic with strong hinges.

What an idiot, he thought. On my first day! "Fuck", he shouted out loud at the TV screen which was still showing the welcome message. He sat down on the bed. Keep calm, he said to himself. Breath deeply. What would Ling do?

He felt even more of an idiot when the front door of Villa Rosalind swung slowly open as he approached it – this time wearing his new watch which he'd left in the bathroom. It got me in, he thought. It's got me out.

He stood for a moment on the small veranda outside the door, breathing in the cool night air. He saw the stars above him and gasped at their beauty. For the first time in his life, he saw the magnificence of the Clouds of Magellan and the thousands of constellations denied to Western eyes by light pollution. The word that sprung to his mind at that particular moment surprised him, bearing in mind he was now in the heart of the enemy's camp. It was freedom.

As he made his way back to the reception hut and the dining hall, he couldn't help thinking that he'd fallen on his feet. Gorith Island was not what he'd been expecting, no *Camp on Blood Island*, not a French penal colony. More like a hotel, he thought. One of those resort hotels you get in places like The Maldives. Must have cost a bomb. Howard's words came back to him, and he found it ironic that the island had once been the site of a nuclear explosion.

The large dining hall was divided into sections, each with a different theme, and, he assumed, different fare. Being a bit of a coward about such things, he chose the Western Grill and took a seat at one of the tables for two. The place was beginning to fill up with Gorithians, all dressed in long robes and looking very smart. He was the only one in a creased shirt and shorts, but at least they were clean. People smiled at him when they passed, but it was a relief to him that no-one asked to join him, enabling him to take in his surroundings and observe what happened.

All the food was from self-service buffets, enabling him to help himself to whatever he fancied and control the portions. It was all beautifully displayed on large rectangular dishes with glass lids, well illuminated so you could see what you were getting. He watched other diners before making a move himself.

They would go up and take a plate, survey the culinary delights on offer, then lift up the hinged lid over their selected fare and return to their table. He noticed that the lids closed automatically. Neat, he thought, as it keeps the food warm and stops contamination from sniffles and sneezes.

Got it, he thought, and feeling self-conscious in his western clothes he went up to the tables and surveyed their wares. Having chosen tenderloin of pork, he felt embarrassed that he couldn't open the lid. He tried hard, but it wouldn't budge. Then a light bulb went on in his head. Ah, he thought, remembering his ski pass on his left wrist, and he changed hands.

The quality of the meal confirmed his assessment that the place was more like an upmarket hotel, and he awarded the kitchens five stars. He was pleased he wasn't having to pay for it. Having polished off a dessert of two slices of fresh mango and one thick slice of pineapple, he made his way back to his quarters, longing for daylight to come so he could explore his new surroundings. And start his search for Anna.

20

He was woken by the quiet hum of an electric motor, and he watched as the window shutters slowly rose allowing the early morning sunlight to stream in. He leapt out of bed and into the bathroom, aware that soon someone would be coming to give him his 'introduction', whatever that entailed. He hoped they would tell him a little bit more about his smartwatch and any other tricks it had up its sleeve.

Not that he couldn't work it out for himself, having had a smartwatch in the past. They were good and could do most things a mobile phone could do, but if you are a hedge-fund trader, you have to wear a Rolex. If you don't, potential clients will think you can't afford it, and if you can't afford one, they reckon you're not worth knowing.

But the ping-pong sound surprised him. He looked at the screen and read the message: you have a visitor. Shit, he thought. He opened the door, with the correct hand, and saw a person standing there. It was the mysterious figure waiting on the edge of the landing pad when he'd arrived. Now he could see him clearly: the flowing white robe, the sandals, the hooded eyes, the long grey hair, the beard, the large silver crucifix hanging from a long chain around his neck, and the smartwatch on his left wrist.

"Gorith?"

"No, but Gorith has sent me. My name is Asba. He has appointed me to be your learning servant."

"Hi, you'd better come in."

"Thank you," said Asba. Ben heard his smartwatch click.

"Please, take a seat... Er, would you like a coffee?"

"I will not, thank you. But please, have one yourself."

Ben went to the kitchenette, placed a capsule in the machine and pressed the button. A few minutes later he returned to the living room with a mug in his hand. "So, a learning servant, eh? What on earth's that?"

"Well, you are here to learn about our community, and I am here to help you."

"So, are you a... teacher?"

"No. I am an aide, an assistant. My purpose is to answer your questions, to explain things. You choose what you wish to learn, how you wish to learn it and when. It is up to you. You are the master. I am the servant – slave if you prefer."

"That's very strange."

"Perhaps to you. Our way is different. Why try and teach somebody who does not wish to learn? Even if knowledge is successfully imparted to an unwilling recipient, he or she is hardly likely to use it to any great effect. And people learn best if they go at their own pace rather than that of the teacher."

"So, are you an expert on all things Gorithian?"

"No. I have been here for three years, so technically I am a graduate. My servant said I'd done well, but I know I have much still to learn. As they say in your world, you learn a subject properly only by teaching it, and I will learn by serving you. We will learn together. I will accompany you on your learning journey. You are my first master."

Although Ben found Asba's words puzzling, he seemed to be making sense, and Ben felt he could get along with him. "So, Asba, you're here this morning to give me an introduction." Ben remembered the Rajneesh sect in Oregon. He saw a striking resemblance between their leader, Bhagwan Shree, and Asba. Be strong, he said to himself. He sipped his espresso. "I trust it isn't going to be more of an indoctrination?"

"No. I am not here to indoctrinate you. If anything, I hope to *un*-doctrinate you – if you are willing to review your beliefs, values and perceptions which you might hold dearly. I warn you; it is a difficult path to tread."

"Sounds like brain-washing to me," said Ben.

Asba smiled. "It is an unfortunate term, brainwashing, as it implies a cleansing process which it is not. All Gorith hopes you will do is to *review* your thoughts and philosophy, your outlook on the world, nature, humanity, morality; on life – and on death. Only change your views if you wish to do so."

Fair enough, thought Ben. At least we've cleared that one up. "So, Asba, do please continue with your introduction."

"Thank you," said Asba, "but I have finished."

"What? Aren't you going to, er, show me around the Island?"

"Yes, if you wish. You could do that yourself, on your own. Go where you choose to go. Do what you choose to do. You will learn more by discovery and experience than by me telling you things. But it is up to you. We can walk and talk, and I can try to answer any questions which may occur to you on the way. I am in your hands."

Ben thanked him. He felt in control. "Yep. Let's walk 'n' talk. First of all, this watch thing. Can explain how it works and what it does?"

"My role is to help you with the difficult questions, not the easy ones. The watch is straightforward. It is like any smartwatch, but with a few of our own applications. I would not wish to rob you of the surprise and joy of discovering them for yourself." He smiled and stood up. "I am ready when you are."

Ben gulped down the remains of his coffee and rose to his feet. "Asba, please lead the way."

The door closed slowly behind them. Ben turned around to lock the door but then remembered there was no key to carry around, to lose or forget. He noticed that the walls of Villa Rosalind were clad in palm fronds, and the luxury-mobile-home part of it sat on stilts rather than little wheels, under a pitched roof also covered with dried palm leaves.

The compacted earth path was wide enough for them to walk side by side, and Ben was aware that they were retracing his steps of the previous evening. To his right, there were tantalizing glimpses between the trees of white sands, a strip of light blue water, then one of white surf with the deep blue of an ocean beyond.

"Wow!" said Ben, turning to his companion. "That looks inviting. Is it safe to swim off the beaches here?"

"It is safe to swim in the lagoon, but not in the open sea. There are sharks out there, and over the centuries they have acquired a taste for human flesh. You see, the early inhabitants of this island used to dispose of their dead by floating them out to sea on rafts of copra. And although we do not dispose of our dead in that way, the sharks' instinct remains. We do not swim in the open sea."

Got that, thought Ben.

Soon, they arrived at what Asba called the hub. Ben recognised the landing pad but noted there was no helicopter present. Asba led him through the reception hut and suggested he might like to visit the shop. When Ben protested he didn't have his wallet with him, Asba smiled.

"Just select anything you want, and it will be debited to your account. For example, you may wish to acquire a couple of djellabas." Asba must have noticed Ben's raised eyebrows. "Like mine," he said, holding out his arms sideways and looking down at his loose-fitting robe.

"They are very practical on the island, being made of lightweight cotton. Not only do they shield you from the sun and keep you cool, but they also dry quickly. And you can carry things in the hood; it's like a small backpack." He turned around to demonstrate this feature. "And you will not look quite so much like a whitey."

"Whitey?" asked Ben. "Sounds a bit racist!"

"Not at all. It is just a term we use here for new-comers – those who have yet to acquire a tan. It was used to refer to the young soldiers who came to these islands from your country during the tests." He looked at Ben as if he expected a response.

"Yes. The nuclear bomb tests. I heard about that. And that the Japanese-." Ben stopped himself. "Yes, I would like to buy one, or at least look at them."

The only other person in the shop was the sales assistant, a young girl, well tanned with long dark brown hair and green eyes. Ben reckoned she was in her early twenties, possibly doing a gap year after university. She was wearing a pale green robe with white embroidered trimmings. And a smartwatch. Asba gestured to the girl that Ben was the customer, not him.

"Good morning, sirr!" The accent was French. "'Ow can I 'elp you today?"

"I would like to see some, er... of these robes, please."

"Djellabas. Of course, sirr. Over 'ere."

Ben started looking through the rack.

"If I may say, sirr," she said, "I would recommend for you a long-sleeved one, to protect your skin from zer sun, but not too long in the body, as you might trip on it."

But I don't want burnt ankles, thought Ben. In the end, he chose two pale blue ones with black trimmings and took them over to the counter. "I'll take these, please," he said. His smartwatch pinged.

"All done, sirr," the girl said, removing a small tag from each garment. She folded the robes up and gave them to Ben. "Thank you, sirr."

His watch pinged again. "And many thanks for your help," he said, and he heard a faint ping from her smartwatch.

As they walked out of the shop, Ben turned to Asba. "I don't get it. I didn't sign anything. And she didn't write anything down. How can my account be charged? Surely they must keep records of some sort?"

"They do. Or, should I say, it does. The system. It is simple. The electronic tag on each djellaba was sensed by your smartwatch. Rather like the door to your villa reacts when you approach it. When you said 'I'll take these', your watch – and hers – heard those words and the transaction was completed. You'll find a record of it on your purchases file-"

"Hang on, though. Supposing I hadn't said those words. What if I'd just said 'okay'?"

"The system is happy to accept any words or phrases which imply a trade has been agreed and carried out. You could have said, 'it's a deal, I'll have those, yes that's fine, I want them' or perhaps a hundred other combinations of words which have that same meaning. The system also takes the context into account. It knew from the GPS of your smartwatch that you were in the shop-"

"Okay. That's clever." Ben liked the relationship between him and his 'servant'. He felt he could interrupt him without him getting all stuffy about it. Not at all like his teachers at school, or his supervisors and tutor at uni, who had to be treated by the students as if they were gods.

"I understand how all that could work, but what's all the pinging for?"

"A number of circumstances will cause your watch to emit that sound – to let you know it has carried out a function. You heard the one which signified that the transaction had taken place. When it did it a second time, it was telling you her 'thank you' to you had been registered on your file."

"Why on earth would it want to do that? She just thanked me for shopping there."

"Little words," said Asba, sighing, "little words. But their importance is huge. They oil the cogs of human interaction. They cost nothing to give but mean much to the receiver. Gorith wants to encourage his people to use them. That's why they are recorded. Have you ever read newspaper articles online?"

"Yeah. Often."

"In that case, you will be aware that many invite comments which then appear after the article, and readers are invited to 'like' a comment, or dislike it, by selecting a tick or a cross, a smiley face or a grumpy one. Gorith does not encourage negative feedback, so the system only records words of thanks. We call them 'likes'. When you receive one, your smartwatch pings."

"Does it matter how you say them? If I say 'thank you' or 'thanks'."

"No. The important thing is what is in your mind and in your heart when you say it. So the system recognises all terms of gratitude: 'thanks a lot, many thanks, cheers, most grateful, that's kind, much obliged'... Whatever one you can think of, you can be sure the system has already thought of it."

"Ah! I get it. Good system! But surely it's open to abuse. I mean, you and I could spend the whole day thanking each other and clock up loads of likes."

"No. While an individual can award as many likes as they want to, the number received by one person from a particular individual is limited to one each day. The system also takes context into account, and the words of thanks must be said in earshot of the person – or rather their smartwatch."

Asba led Ben into the next building which housed the Island's library. Ben was surprised at the number of books it held; real ones, but mostly paperbacks. About half a dozen Gorithians, all in djellabas, were browsing the well-filled shelves, sampling what was on offer and carefully replacing a book if it did not appeal to them.

Ben did the same. He noticed that the other people in the library all smiled at him, but he was relieved that none spoke to him. He didn't feel ready to converse with them, while still wearing his creased shirt and baggy shorts; he felt very much a whitey.

Asba explained that all books were available in e-format as well, on the screen in his villa, but some people still preferred a printed version which they could take to the beach or read while sitting on their veranda. Please, he said to Ben, take a look around.

Ben noticed that in many cases there were two copies of the same book, side by side on the same shelf. After a while, Ben selected one of the copies of *Tai Pan*, written by James Clavell. It was a book he'd read ten years previously when he was first posted to Hong Kong. His line manager said it was required reading, as it gave the reader a good insight into the founding of the province in the 1840s, the competing trading companies and the character of its people. Perhaps he was missing them, or some of them, he thought. He knew he would enjoy revisiting that world – hopefully with Anna, and he would introduce her to Ling. He had a feeling the two girls would get on.

He signalled to Asba that he would like to borrow the book, and Asba pointed to the unmanned check-out desk. Ben watched as a woman ahead of him swiped the barcode on the back of her book over the scanner and continued on her way.

Once the two men had left the library, Ben said, "That was simple enough, but how long can I borrow the book for?"

"There were two copies, so you can have it as long as you like. Had there been a single copy, Gorith prefers it if you return it within two weeks, although the system does order a replacement straight away."

"So there's always at least one copy of a book on the shelves?"

"That is what we hope. At least for most of the time."

"Clever," said Ben, "but expensive."

It was the economist in him. He was wondering who was footing the bill. Not that library books cost a great deal, but when you added it all up, the systems, the software, the buildings and staff costs, you're talking serious dosh. He assumed he would get presented with his bill on checking out, then he remembered he would not be checking out at all. He'd be fleeing, possibly at the dead of night, with Anna. It needed more thought. Fortunately, time was on his side.

21

As the two men left the library, Asba said the next stop would be the art gallery. Ben was intrigued, but he couldn't imagine buying a picture, not for himself. It would be difficult enough escaping with Anna, let alone with a painting under his arm. He allowed Asba to lead the way in.

It was a similar building to the library, walls of palm fronds on a stout wooden frame supporting a steeply pitched roof. Hanging on the walls were several pictures varying in size and different media. Some were portraits, others still life, but Ben preferred the seascapes. He thought of Donnie and Sasha, sailing across the ocean aboard *Juli-Emma*, and he longed for the day when he would spot her on the horizon, in full sail coming to rescue him and Anna.

"Please notice that we have some remarkable artistic talent on the island," said Asba, "and look at this pottery," he said, pointing to the exhibits on tables running down the centre of the room. "And these ceramics. All made here. On the island."

"They are remarkable," said Ben. "Are they for sale?"

"No. The artists display them here for all to see and

enjoy. They hope they will give visitors, like you, pleasure in seeing them. And in the case of the sculptures, of touching them, feeling them. Please take your time. Enjoy them."

Ben had a good wander around. "I must say, Asba, I do like that one." He pointed to a large oil-on-canvas image of a coral island, shimmering in the heat of the day; a fisherman in the foreground casting a net which seemed suspended in the air by magic.

"In that case, may I suggest you show your appreciation of the work by pressing the button on the little box below it. This will be recorded on the personal file of the artist as a 'like', in the same way as a 'thank you' would be. It is a way of saying to the artist 'well done'.

"If they were here, of course, you could say the words directly to them, and your praise would be similarly registered. All terms of appreciation are recognised, such as 'bravo, good on you, that's nice, good job, cool, great work'... Gorith says it is important to give positive feedback if someone has done something well which you appreciate. He says that recognition of effort is a reward which provides motivation for future tasks."

"So," asked Ben, "if I say to someone 'well done', they get a 'like' from me. But if they then said 'thank you', because they were pleased to get the praise, would I get a 'like' back from them?"

"Certainly. Gorith wants people to praise each other, when it is deserved. It encourages self-worth and binds our community together."

"So what happens to all these 'likes' which are recorded? The number must keep on rising."

"That, Master, is a question for another day... Let us

have some lunch together. Then after lunch, I will take you back to your villa, and we can name you."

"What? But I have a name. Why would I want another?"

"Because, while you are on Gorith Island, you will wish to use a Gorithian name. I will explain later."

Lunch was a light affair, compared with the meal the previous evening. Asba explained that all the dining rooms served the same at lunchtime, a varied selection of tasty salads with a wide choice of dressings, followed by fruit and cheese. Both white and brown bread rolls were available, and jugs of fruit juice and iced water were provided for people to help themselves.

Ben remembered to lift the glass lids with his left hand, but couldn't understand why they should have gone to the trouble of automating them in this way. Having helped himself to a generous portion of salad, he returned to his table to join his learning servant.

"A question for you, Asba. Why won't the lids above the food dishes go up if your smartwatch is not close to the handle?"

"Two reasons. It is a principle of Gorith's that – where possible – the facilities he has installed on the island are only available to those who have the Gorith watch. The second reason is that he is very concerned about all of us, about our safety on the island and our health. You may notice that there are few obese people here, and this is because of his programme of diet control."

Ben listened, as he tucked into his rather large portion of avocados, sliced tomato and potato salad, drizzled over by a generous amount of thousand-island dressing. He let Asba continue.

"You may have noticed the rubber mats on the floor in

front of the buffet tables. They are able to measure your weight and record it on your personal file. If the system detects a worrying increase – or indeed decrease – in a person's weight, it is able to adjust their diet accordingly by controlling that person's access to certain foods.

"Of course, they are given a diet to follow, but should they be tempted to break it, the system helps them out. And, those mats are able to weigh the portion of food you choose to take by comparing your body-weight before and after you have helped yourself. If the system thinks you are overdoing it, even if you are not on a diet, your smartwatch will warn you."

"Asba. You amaze me. That is serious control! I thought one of Gorith's principles was freedom."

"It is, but not if it does you harm. Gorith says he finds it difficult to strike the right balance. He loves us all, and he is adamant he does not want to lose any of his subjects. And so far, he has not.

"You may have noticed the two gold studs on the back of your watch, and the tiny camera in between them. They are there to monitor your pulse rate and blood pressure. Should something abnormal happen to your heart, your watch will alert you and advise you what to do. And, like other smartwatches, yours will record your physical activity, distances run or walked, steps climbed. Gorith wants us to keep fit so we can enjoy this paradise he has created for us."

After lunch, the two men strolled back to Villa Rosalind. Despite the tree canopy covering the path, it was hot, and Ben felt his shirt becoming clammy. His brand new djellabas were hanging uncomfortably over his right arm, and he was very much looking forward to slipping out of his restrictive western garb and into one of those loose-fitting, flowing robes.

He led the way up the steps and, as his front door swung open, he felt a delightful waft of cool air from the main room. Wonderful, he thought. Air conditioning. I'll give this place another star on Trip Advisor. Having offered his servant a seat, Ben disappeared into the bathroom for a few minutes then returned freshly showered wearing one of his djellabas.

"If I may say so, a good choice," said Asba. "The colour suits you and it is the right size. We will now complete the process and name you. Then you will have become a true Gorithian."

Asba demonstrated how the smartwatch could serve as a TV remote control, and he summoned up the app which would, he said, help Ben choose his new name. A list of trees appeared on the screen.

"All Gorithian names comprise the names of two trees if you are male. Or, if you are female, two flowers. Or if you are not sure about your gender, your name can be made up of a tree and a flower, or a flower and a tree, depending on how you feel about it. My full name is Ash Banyan, but the shortened form of all Gorithian names takes the first two letters of the full names. We choose our names ourselves, and now I invite you to choose your names from the list on the screen."

"Why, though?" Ben thought it quaint and childish. And sexist. "What's the point?"

"In your world," said Asba, "when you see someone, you can usually tell their gender at a distance. Their height, their shape, the clothes they wear, the style of the hair. Of course, it is getting more difficult for you, as the gender gap in all things is diminishing. One could argue, does it matter? But it can lead to awkward, uncomfortable situations and misunderstandings.

"Here on Gorith Island, you will not have that problem. If someone comes within a few paces of you, your watch will sense their presence, and the screen will show you their name. That in itself is useful – and it avoids lengthy introductions – but it tells you their gender and gives you an insight about how they feel about themselves."

Ben cast his eye down the list. All the usual ones were there, oak, ash, beech, birch, and many he didn't recognise. Being the rugby player, he wanted to choose something that was both supple and strong, so after some soul-searching, he selected Willow and Cedar. He was relieved to see on the screen that this combination had not been taken, but not so happy when Asba pointed out that his short name – the one everybody would know him by – would be Wice.

Asba must have noticed Ben screw up his face. "You will get used to it. It is a good name. Think of Nice and Wise."

"Hmm," said Ben. "As your master, I insist on you calling me Wice from now on. In that way, I might just get used to it."

"Come!" said Asba, smiling. "Let us explore the island. Wice!"

Master and servant turned right when they joined the main path, leading away from the hub, the dining hall, the shop, the library and the art gallery. Ben noticed the trees were becoming more sparse, and his view of the coastline to his left was clearing. He could see the rollers coming into the shore, having broken on the coral reef beyond. How sad, he thought, that the coral is dying and that the reef out there is crumbling away, that this very island is under threat.

"Wice! Look now to your right! Through the trees!"

Ben did what his servant told him, and he saw for the first time the outer wall of the Great Crater, rising up above the treetops. He remembered Howard telling him how it was formed. He saw the vegetation on its slopes, trees at first, then scrub, followed by grass and then bare rock, rising high into the sky perhaps to 300 metres, he thought.

"See that?" Asba asked, pointing to the crater's rocky rim. "That is why we are here!... Those concave slopes cause air currents – from any direction – to rise, to cool, and deposit on our island their precious cargo of fresh water. Some day, you will see – you will walk in – the Great Crater, in which the water collects. And that is the water which sustains life – our lives – on Gorith Island..."

Ben didn't know how to respond. He was overwhelmed by the thought that some dreadful experiment some sixty years ago had somehow made Gorith Island habitable.

"That is right," said Asba, as if he were reading Ben's mind. "The irony, that a nuclear explosion should have created our Great Crater and produced a life-supporting environment. It enabled the one nation in the world who had suffered from the devastating effects of two atom bombs, to send some of their number to come here and work and live on this island. They turned it into what it is today."

"Asba, I know the Japanese built a base here, in the nineties, but how much work did they do? I was told they constructed a floor across the crater and installed a solar farm there. Is that right?"

"It is – but they did much more. Of course, it was a

closely guarded secret. Much of their work was to do with defence. But they did build a community here. This was their NASA. Their project, the overt one, was to support the International Space Station, and they designed and built spacecraft here to do just that. Factories, workshops, officers – and accommodation to house all the people who worked on the project, and the crews who would be transported in the spacecraft to the Station."

"So how much work has, er, Gorith undertaken since the Japanese left?"

"They left fifteen years ago, and we took it over a year later. There was much work to be done, to repair, maintain and improve the facilities which they had constructed. Your villa is one of the originals, installed by the Japanese. They were designed to withstand an explosion in the event of a failed launch. Gorith then added the sloping roofs and the natural cladding.

"A lot of work was carried out, but Gorith saw it through. This is what you see here today. It was a great achievement, and I think we can all be proud of what our leader created. A world within a world, able to hold its own place on the international stage, to survive without handouts, without selling its soul to the superpower hegemony... A community which empowers its members rather than exploits them, a society-"

"Great speech, Asba." Ben felt he didn't have to kowtow to his servant. "But who funded it? Who paid for it all? Okay, I understand you inherited a few huts from the Japanese, and their water collection system and solar generators, but the cost of just running this place today must be huge. Where, for f... for Heaven's sake, does it come from?"

Asba smiled. "I am sorry. I am jumping the gun. All will

be revealed, I promise you, but it is your first day. You would not... understand."

Ben felt cross for the first time since arriving the previous evening. He wanted to yell at Asba. Look here, you, er, cross between an ash and a banyan tree, I studied economics at Cambridge University and I'm a successful hedge-fund manager. Please do NOT tell ME what I do and do not understand when it comes to matters of investment. But he remembered the strategy: humour them, gain their confidence.

"Okay, Asba. Just tell me when you're... when you think I'm ready."

The two walked in silence for a few minutes. It was broken by Asba. "You may like to take a walk up there one day, to the crater. It is beautiful up on the rim. Wonderful views. Always a breeze."

Yes, thought Ben. I must do that. A wonderful observation post for spotting *Juli-Emma*, in a few months' time.

"Perhaps we can do it together," said Asba.

Yes, thought Ben. Good cover, to have my servant with me.

They walked on for some time before turning back. Asba said he was anxious to make it back to Ben's villa before nightfall. He pointed out interesting features, the plants and rocks, shells and insects which they came across. He drew Ben's attention to the two fishermen standing up to their waists in the lagoon trying to lure the tuna onto their lines. He stopped when he heard a bird-call and begged Ben to listen. Then he whispered to Ben what it was and smiled when Ben nodded.

When they reached the turning to Villa Rosalind, Asba stopped.

"Same time tomorrow?" asked Ben.

"No. I advise you to reflect on today, read your book and enjoy the island. I suggest that I return in one week's time. We can go on an expedition and explore more of the island, and at the same time discuss some of the issues which are on your mind."

Ben felt sorry he would not be seeing Asba the following morning, but he had to concede that Asba had a point. There was much to reflect on, and he guessed that many questions would arise in his mind by the time they next met.

The last thought he had before drifting off to sleep that night made him smile. He had survived his first full day on Gorith Island. They had not brainwashed him or even tried to do so. Indeed, he felt empowered, in control, and happy. All he needed to do was to find Anna.

22

A wave of loneliness washed over him as he woke up realising he would be on his own for the next six days. But he had to agree with Asba about time for reflection. There was much for him to get his head around, and it was also an ideal opportunity to relax and enjoy the place. It was a strange world, but a benign one. Or so it seemed, so far.

He began the day by making his own breakfast, then he finished his book, *Shōgun*, and had a play with his Gorith watch. He enjoyed discovering how these gadgets worked, and Asba was right to leave him to explore its capabilities.

He introduced himself to Gaston, the Gorith Island equivalent of Siri, and tested him on a few simple questions. The avatar was able to answer most of them, but Ben decided to keep the more complex ones to ask Asba next time they met. He wanted to hear more about 'likes' being logged. It wasn't something he'd ever come across, and it intrigued him. He gave it a new name: 'non-monetary motivation'. He was quite proud of that, and he decided that when he got back to civilisation, he might blog about it.

Back to civilisation, he thought. More like from civilisation. Back to the rat-race, the corruption, the crime, the sheer depravity of the world he knew. Enjoy Gorith Island when you can, he told himself.

On his way to lunch, on that first day on his own, he met a couple of fellow Gorithians – a man and his wife – and they invited him to join them. Ben knew he had to be careful what he said about himself when he remembered how easily it had been for Ling to wheedle out of him the sorry tale about Anna during his first meal with her at the airport hotel.

But Bero and Roma were very pleasant. They did not intrude by asking him lots of personal questions, yet were polite enough to ask him about his interests and hobbies. He reciprocated, and the three of them had a delightful and harmless conversation about fishing, photography, snorkelling and stone polishing. Roma asked if he would like to see the necklaces she had made, but Ben said they could hardly be more beautiful than the one she was wearing.

He hoped he might see the couple again and he asked them how long they were staying on the Island. They looked at each other and frowned as if Ben had asked them a difficult *Trivial Pursuit* question.

"But we live here," said Bero. "This is our home. Until we decide otherwise." He put his hand on Roma's, across the table, and they smiled at each other.

After lunch it was hot, and Ben was grateful for his loosely flowing djellaba as he sauntered back to his villa. He was particularly pleased with the hood. Not only did it protect his head from the sun's rays, but the trimming around its edge stiffened it enough to form a peak which shielded most of his face, leaving just his jaw exposed.

There's a solution to that, he thought, and he decided to grow a beard. In fact, he wouldn't shave at all, from now on. It would save all that messing around with sun-cream.

He noticed that someone had been in the villa while he had been at the hub. The towel had been put back on the rail in the bathroom, and his other djellaba – the brand new one – had been hung up in the small fitted wardrobe at the end of his bed. The jug of fruit juice had been replenished, and the used coffee capsule had been replaced with a new one.

While he was grateful for room service, he did wonder if it was wise to leave his valuables in the villa: his Rolex, wallet, iPhone – not that it was any use here, he thought – new camera and the little box. They were all there, in his cabin bag, but he made a mental note to ask Asba if he should make other arrangements to keep them safe.

For Ben, the first few days dragged by. He started on *Tai-Pan*, and that did help to pass the time; whenever he read the name May-May – the main character's Chinese mistress – he pictured his good friend Ling. He often wondered how she was and whether her operation had been a success.

He enjoyed his siestas after lunch, his half-sleep, sprawled out on his bed under the air conditioner. But the downside was he would wake up at two o'clock in the morning and couldn't get back to sleep. He would invariably drift off shortly before the shutters would go up, and the bright sunlight would prise his eyes open again. By lunchtime he would be feeling a bit sluggish, and by the time he returned to his villa after the meal, he would be ready for his siesta. It was a vicious circle.

He met Bero and Roma a couple of times – and each

time his watch informed him that their full names – Gorithian ones – were Beech Rowan and Rose Marigold. Nothing to worry about there, he thought. He met others, but it seemed that while all Gorithians were delightfully charming and polite, none of them seemed willing to stray into any waters unchartered by the usual small-talk. Just as well, he thought, but he did miss the verbal exchanges with Asba and the frank answers he gave.

A luxury which Ben much appreciated was Fliction, a film service like Netflix which he could summon up on Villa Rosalind's screen. There was a good selection of films, and he had enjoyed a couple of them, but what he had found more interesting were the documentaries.

One he watched was about the Davidians, the religious cult led by David Koresh and based in Texas, near the small town of Waco. The siege was famous, but he wanted to learn more about cults, their leaders and what drives their followers, as it might help him understand what Anna had got herself involved with.

The first thing he picked up was the meaning of the term 'cult'. Koresh claimed that Christianity was a cult, and in the early days it probably was. Some say the Mormons used to be a cult but are now a religion. And the smart answer to the question, what is the difference between a cult and a religion, is about a hundred years. Ben wondered if the Gorith Foundation could be classed as one, so he set about doing a 'compare and contrast' exercise on the two: what Gorith was up to here on his tropical island, with what went on at Waco.

Koresh was a strict authoritarian and believed in harsh discipline. Gorith, on the other hand, claimed he believed in freedom and choice. From what Ben had seen so far, this seemed to be the case. Gorith motivated his followers with praise, whereas the regime at Waco was one of threat and fear. At Waco, there were several children who were abused and ill-treated by Koresh and his followers. Ben had not seen any children on Gorith Island, so that was one major difference.

Finally, all reports of Koresh, from both his followers and the authorities, say that whoever Koresh actually was, he himself truly believed he was the Son of God, the Messiah, the Antichrist, and that he could do anything in the name of God. Ben wondered who Gorith thought he was, and he made a mental note to meet him and ask him that very question.

Although Ben's watch was able to tell him the day, the date, the month as well as the hour, minute and second, he lost track of the days. Perhaps they skipped by because he was enjoying himself. Or was it because they were similar? He had to admit his daily routine hardly changed from one day to the next.

He would wake each morning at sunrise – or rather shutter-rise – and go for a dip in the lagoon, a ten-minute jog away. After showering – but not shaving – he would prepare his breakfast: one boiled egg, a brown bread roll and a glass of fruit juice. He would then sit on his veranda and read until it got too hot to concentrate.

A wander to the hub would follow, and he would repeat the visit he had made with Asba by going to the shop for a browse, then to the library to look at the 'new releases' shelf. He was pleased that when he'd put his dog-eared copy of *Shōgun* on the donations table, his watch clicked.

Next, he would pop his head into the art gallery to click on any new masterpieces he liked, and that always got a click back. After lunch, he would return to his villa for his siesta and remain in the air-conditioned environment until it became bearable enough to sit on the veranda again.

Naturally, he kept his eyes open on his travels, hoping to spot Anna. But he worried that he might not recognise her. Perhaps she'd cut off her long blonde tresses, or put some weight on her slender frame. And if she wore a djellba with the hood up – as he did to keep off the sun – he wondered whether the two of them might pass each other by without realising it.

He was outside reading one early evening when he heard the sound of a helicopter. He realised it must be Wednesday, the day the flight from Honolulu landed at Kiritimati. It reminded him of his arrival exactly a week previously. It occurred to him that perhaps he was no longer the new boy, and his curiosity prompted him to dine early that evening so he could spy any wide-eyed arrival who might enter the dining hall.

It turned out to be a couple, probably in their sixties, and, judging by the hand-holding, an item. Their clothes and hairstyles were western and indicated they were male and female. Ben wondered what had brought them to the island – apart from the helicopter – as he could not imagine they were here to do the graduate course.

On his travels – so far – he'd come across few people whom a thirty-four-year-old would call elderly, so he'd got the impression the place was generally populated by adults of a working age. That's another question for Asba, he thought – and he smiled when he realised that his learning servant would be at his door an hour after sunrise the following morning.

When he got back to his villa, Ben decided to make

a list of all the questions he planned to ask Asba in the morning. The trouble was there didn't seem to be any paper around. He asked Gaston, the Siri sound-alike on his smartwatch, to switch on the notebook app, the one that thinks it's a dictaphone. He took a deep breath – then stopped. He did not like the idea of Gaston listening in. Of course, Gaston was not a real person, but just a voice analyser and search engine installed onto a supercomputer somewhere. Even so, he preferred to keep his questions for Asba private.

23

Knowing it was Thursday, and that Asba would be arriving one hour after sunrise, Ben cut his lagoon swim short and sprinted back to Villa Rosalind. After a cold shower, a three minute boiled egg, a brown roll and a cup of coffee, Ben was ready for his visitor.

"Asba! Come in!" he said, with a huge smile on his stubbly face.

"Thank you," said Asba. Ben's watch clicked. Asba looked around him. "So, is Villa Rosalind starting to feel like home?"

"It certainly is. Do take a seat... I'm going to miss this place when I leave. "

Asba frowned. "But that's not going to be for another three years, is it?"

"No, Asba – unless I get chucked off the course," said Ben. He tried to make light of his error and quickly changed the subject. "A question, if I may. Is it safe to leave valuables here?"

"Yes. There is no crime on Gorith Island. Why would anyone steal anything? What would they do with the loot? There is no pawn shop around the corner, no fence to meet in the pub. Even if they did manage to flog the swag, what would they do with the money?

"The room service personnel are tracked by the system, through their watches, so it knows where a particular member is at any time. And all members wear body cams. You might have noticed that each wears a little brooch clipped onto the front of their djellaba. It is blue-toothed to their watch-"

"You're going too fast, Asba. Who or what are members?"

"I apologise. You would call them employees. They are the people who work for Gorith and run the practical aspects of the island."

"Are they Gorithians?"

"Yes. We all are. When we help run the island, we are members. When we help people to learn – a trade or skill or the Gorithian philosophy – we are learning servants. At the moment, you are simply a Gorithian. If you chose to teach, you would become a learning servant. If you chose to take on work, you would become a member."

"What work would I do? You say I could choose-"

Asba held up his hand. "Let us deal with that matter in due course."

"Going back to the body cams, what are they for? What happens to the footage? Who looks at it? I mean, who on earth would be interested in looking at a maid – a member – cleaning a room?"

"Steady, Wice. Think of those body cams as dash-cams, those little recording devices on cars these days. They are on all the time, but nobody looks at the footage unless there is an incident."

"But there's hardly likely to be an incident when cleaning a room."

"You are right. But if there was a complaint of any description – for example, a personal item had gone missing – the system could examine the footage and deal with the member accordingly. All members have them, whether they work in Domestic Services, on the farm, are fishers or maintenance staff."

"Are they happy to be monitored like that? To have the system spying on them in case they do something wrong?"

"Yes, they are quite happy. The purpose of the monitoring is not to catch them out when they do something wrong, but to enable Gorith to reward them when they do something right."

Ben smiled. He'd never thought of it in those terms. "So does Gorith spend his days going through dash-cam footage?"

It was Asba's turn to smile. "No, Wice. The system copes with that perfectly well on its own. The pattern recognition software is very reliable these days, and fast. In some ways, it is similar to the facial recognition programs of old, but the routines today analyse each frame and can identify unusual incidents. It can tell if a member has done well – and reward them appropriately. If they have failed, a servant can be tasked to point out to them their error and help them put it right.

"There is, of course, a third purpose. And that is to make the member *aware* that his work is being monitored-"

"A sort of deterrence? 'If I make a mistake I'll be punished', that kind of thing?"

"No. More like, 'If I make a special effort I'll be praised'. Often, in your world, effort goes unrewarded. If a worker thinks that any extra effort goes unnoticed, he is less likely to make it, and his standards gradually slip until he has to be reprimanded. Then he loses all pride in his work and his self-respect and the respect of those around him.

"Now, may I suggest we have a hike up to the Great Crater? It is best to make a start before it gets too hot. You may wish to take your camera."

Master and learning servant set off side by side following the path winding through the palm trees and low scrub. Asba took the opportunity to explain to Ben how the underground nuclear explosion which caused the crater had also produced an interesting side effect.

Many of the islands of Kiribati were arid and desert-like, even though they did have rainfall. The problem was the ground. Being principally limestone and porous, the water would soak into the subsoil rather than form ponds, rivulets and streams. However, the extremely high temperature created by the nuclear device melted the rock in which it was embedded. When the molten rock solidified, it formed an impervious lining to the crater producing a circular reservoir to catch the rain.

He told Ben that the Japanese retained the reservoir but constructed a floor above it supported on pillars. High above this floor, they built the solar roof which to this day provides the island's electrical power, well in excess of its needs. Rainwater falling on the roof is directed into the reservoir which had become, in effect, an underground lake. In times of drought, power from the solar panels drives reverse-osmosis installations on the shore-line to produce fresh water, and this is pumped up to the reservoir.

There were several questions Ben wanted to put to Asba, but as the path became narrower, they were no longer able to walk side by side. As they began to climb,

Ben found he didn't have the breath to talk. The path became steeper, and he was pleased Asba was leading, warning Ben of tricky sections and advising him of handholds when the walk became a scramble.

The vegetation, a mix of stunted trees and undergrowth, gradually gave way to desert grass and other sparse plants, struggling to survive among the rocks and stones. After a few minutes in the open, Asba stopped and turned around. "Wice. Look behind you!"

Ben turned and looked over the top of the trees below him. The view took his breath away. He was reminded of Keats famous lines: 'He stared at the Pacific. And all his men look'd at each other with a wild surmise – silent, upon a peak in Darien'. He felt a fresh breeze on his face and he blamed it for his watery eyes. The classified advert in the magazine came back to him. 'Paradise is now here'.

He wondered how far he could see. The air was gin-clear, so his vision was only limited by the curvature of the earth. Let's test this magic watch, he thought. "Gaston, what is my height above sea level?"

"You are one hundred and twelve metres above sea level," was the metallic reply from the small speakers.

"Gaston. If I'm a hundred and twelve metres above sea level, what is the distance to the horizon?"

"Thirty-seven point eight kilometres."

"Gaston. Many thanks!"

That's a long way, he thought. Would I recognise *Juli-Emma* from up here? Perhaps my camera would. He took a photo, even though he saw no ships.

"Wice! Let's go to the top!"

Ben stood up, and, being careful not to catch his foot in his djellaba, he followed Asba up the narrow, stony path to the rim of the crater. From the ground, it looked like a sharp, jagged edge, but up there it was more like the brow of a steep hill. The two men looked down the concave slope into the crater. Ben saw two helicopters parked beside a landing pad. It wasn't like the one he had landed on a week ago, but an industrial-sized one, a heliport. The helicopters were heavy lift ones, and to one side of the pad was a stack of ships' containers, the ones with grills on the sides indicating they had built-in refrigeration units.

"See those?" said Asba. "They bring in all our supplies. Those we cannot provide on the island. And the surface you see is made of clear poly-carbonate from recycled water bottles, hot-poured over the solar cells. There's a one in two hundred gradient sloping down from the centre to the edges allowing the rainwater to drain naturally into the reservoir below the floor."

"What's between the roof and the floor? I was told the Japanese used it for all sorts of things to do with their space programme, so is that where Gorith lives?" Ben imagined an underground palace with every form of luxury money could buy: marble swimming pools, health spas, a golf range, pool tables, a velodrome and cinemas. Or perhaps it housed the headquarters of the Gorith Foundation whose tentacles stretched from its nerve centre here right across the globe.

"No. Some of it is stores and workshops, but we use the main hall for The Gatherings."

"Gatherings. What are they?"

"That, Wice, is a question for another day. Come! I would like to show you something."

He led Ben back from the edge and asked him to walk towards a rocky outcrop about twenty paces away, off the path. As Ben approached it, he felt a strange sensation on his left wrist. He stopped and turned to face Asba.

"Go on, Wice!"

Ben obeyed his learning servant and continued to walk away from him. "Ouch! What the f- was that?"

Asba was laughing. "Come back here. I'll explain."

Apparently, there was a dangerous drop-off beyond the outcrop. Ben's watch had warned him about it by administering a mild electric shock through the electrodes on the back. When he had continued to approach the hazard, the watch had increased the voltage. Saves us having to put up lots of fences, said Asba.

"So, let me get this right, Asba. The watch stores all the dangerous areas on the island and when the watch gets close to one it electrocutes me?"

"Nearly right. There must be something wrong with yours, though, as you survived."

Ha, ha, thought Ben, but he smiled at Asba's teasing.

"Actually, the watch does not store them," continued Asba. "Its GPS is continuously sending your position back to the system which checks its digital maps of the island. If you are about to walk into danger, it sends you a warning through your watch. And if you take no notice, it gives you a tap on the wrist.

"It is better to have the out-of-bounds areas stored centrally, as they do change, particularly in bad weather. There are some coastal areas where a wave can sweep you out to sea, and sometimes a nuclear hot-spot can occur if there has been a landslip. Gorith likes to take care of us... All of us... He..."

Asba hesitated. "He... loves us."

The two men made their way down from the crater and

along to the hub. Ben asked his servant if he would care to join him for lunch and Asba accepted. Few people were around, but each time they passed someone, Asba would greet them with a nod and a smile, and they would do the same.

Over their tabbouleh and feta salad, Ben decided to tackle Asba about the 'likes'. He'd thought about it in the night, during one of his two o'clock sessions, and he couldn't get his head around the fact that 'likes' were constantly being created. Surely, he thought, their value and meaning must be being eroded – a process similar to monetary inflation.

"So what happens to all these 'likes', Asba. Do they just sit there, on one's personal file?"

"Ah, the first point I need to explain is that they are 'likes' when they are given, but when they are received, they become 'kiles'. A kile is a unit of currency, and in certain circumstances it can be traded and donated. You can use them in the shop – as you did last week – although you probably were not aware of them then. Members are paid in them, and all Gorithians are taxed on them."

"What? Income tax?"

"No. Gorith does not believe in taxing income."

"He has a wealth tax?"

"Yes, and no. It is a wealth tax, in that it is related to the total number of kiles a person has in his account, but it is only levied on what they spend. For example, your djellabas each cost two-plus-two kiles. The first figure is the basic cost. The second one is a retail tax and is a percentage of the buyer's total wealth, always rounded down.

"So, in your case, you paid no tax because two percent of your total wealth – at least when you made the purchase

– was less than one kile. If your wealth at the time had been a thousand kiles, you would have paid the basic price of two, plus the tax of two percent of your wealth, giving an overall price of twenty-two kiles."

"Wow, that's a big difference!"

"In monetary terms it is, but the more wealthy a person is, the less value a unit of currency has to them. The idea is that each person, whether they be wealthy or poor, pays the same in terms of *value to them*. Our tax system has two functions. To make life fairer, and to prevent inflation of the currency."

"Surely, though, the system could be abused. For example, I could pay two kiles for a djellaba, then sell it to a wealthy person for half the price they would pay if they bought it in the shop."

"No. You would be free to sell it for no more than you paid for it, and the buyer would pay the tax due on the item. So, neither you nor that wealthy person would profit from the transaction. It sounds complicated, but the system handles it all and does all the calculations. Look how simple it was for you to buy your djellabas, both for you and the sales assistant."

"True. But setting prices and the tax rate must be quite tricky, getting it right. Who decides on the tax rate, and indeed on the basic cost of an item in the shop?"

"Well," said Asba, sighing. "There is a committee who set prices and tax rates, but we do have data processing resources to assist."

"So, Asba. Who's on this committee? Are you?"

"Yes. And so are you. Every Gorithian is on the committee – and on all the other committees, those for farm produce, menu planning and so on and so forth. But that does not mean they attend every meeting of every committee. They choose, depending on the agenda for each meeting and their particular interests. It works well. All meetings are held over the Mesh – our own internet – so people attend remotely, remaining in their accommodation with their big screens in front of them."

Ben was fascinated. He needed to think about that. And about likes and taxes. But he had one more question. "Asba, who governs this island? Who's in charge? Who's the top dog? Is it Gorith? Surely he can't manage everything."

"All in good time, dear friend."

24

By the end of the third week, Ben felt he had changed. So far, it had been a luxury holiday for him, in a tropical paradise – all paid for by someone else. He'd enjoyed himself, kept fit, eaten well and met some nice people. He'd read three books, watched four good films and amused himself by talking to Gaston on all sorts of subjects.

Ben reckoned Gaston knew as much as Google. But he realised Gaston was merely the personification of a search engine – probably Google anyway – with a voice interface. Ben had learned by trial and error some useful commands, like saying 'Gaston, *tell* me about such-and-such'. Gaston would then tell him, through the little speakers in the side of his watch. If Ben said, 'Gaston, *show* me such-and-such', and he was in his villa, the search results would be shown on his big screen.

So far, the claims of the Gorith Foundation, of creating a community where peace, freedom and tolerance reigned, continued to be valid. However, and it was a big however in Ben's mind, his faith and trust in the world he'd left behind had been shaken. He'd come to realise that there are better ways of doing things, of organising a society so that self-belief and mutual respect empowered individuals equally.

He recalled Asba's words, when they first met, that he hoped to un-doctrinate him. And in some ways his learning servant had achieved just that. Ben was no longer convinced that his mother country had the best governmental system in the world, or was even a true democracy. Nor was he sure about the universality of the fundamental economic laws of supply and demand, diminishing returns and competition.

He realised that many societies have struggled over the centuries to come up with a better way of doing things, and the Gorith Foundation – whatever it was – wasn't the only organisation to experiment. The edge they have over all the other groups who had tried it was information technology. He was no expert on the behaviour of electrons in a silicon matrix the size of the proverbial pinhead, but he understood what Gorith was achieving with IT. He was impressed.

He knew he still had a lot to learn, and he wasn't surprised that his course – whatever that meant – was three years. He appreciated his time was limited, and he would never become a learning servant, yet he wanted to continue the journey and to climb the mountain as high as he could before leaving with Anna to rejoin the so-called real world.

But before that happened, he liked the idea of becoming a member, of doing some work while on the island, of contributing something more tangible to their world, rather than sitting around reading and watching films and strolling around the place.

He wondered if it would be possible to fit it in with his mission. He had done some exploration of the coastline, without going out of bounds, and he had recce'd a couple of good observation points up on the rim of the Great Crater. But he had made no progress in finding Anna. He was always on the look-out for her, but nobody, even at a distance, had come anywhere near looking like her.

A positive aspect of his time so far had been the developing relationship between him and Asba. He had given Ben so much to think about and reflect on, that his influence had been far greater than their time together would suggest. Ben wondered if Asba might help him find Anna, but he would have to be careful how he brought the subject up.

He wondered how he would feel when he spotted *Juli-Emma* on the horizon, come to rescue them from this utopic paradise. He remembered Bero's and Roma's astonishment when he had asked them how long they were staying. It's our home, they'd said. He should have asked them how long they had been Gorithians.

Ben's third week had been a success, in that he had become a member. Asba had shown him the alternatives, the farm, the medical centre, the emergency and rescue centre, the repair and maintenance department, the kitchens and the domestic services. All of them had attractions. He liked the idea of being part of the emergency and rescue team. It reminded him of the TV series *Thunderbirds are Go*, a remake of the 1960s series of which his father had been a great fan.

But the Gorith Island version had very limited resources. While it did boast a fleet of search drones, it had only three rescue vehicles, basically electric quad bikes each with a stretcher rack and climbing equipment for cliff rescue. There was also a fire trailer and an inflatable life boat, but none of the facilities of the Gorith Island Emergency and Rescue Service had ever been used in anger; only for training. Ben guessed that the island's system of invisible safety fences did much to prevent emergencies happening in the first place.

The farm appealed. It was more of a small-holding growing vegetables and fruit, but with a noisy herd of pigs and a large chicken coup. The irrigation system intrigued him, but he wasn't keen on being on the far side of the island – and the half hour walk to get there.

He was surprised to hear there was indeed a research station on the island – also on the far side – but not being a scientist of any description he decided to strike that off his list, too.

Service in the kitchens did not appeal to Ben. If you don't like the heat – or rather even more of it – get out of the kitchen. As for repair and maintenance, DIY had never been a favourite pastime.

Domestic services did appeal, not because he had always wanted to be a waiter or a cleaner, but he thought that working in the main dining room would give him a better chance of finding Anna. Surely she would come into the hall at some stage during the next five months, he thought, assuming she's still here.

The job was not waiting at table, as it was all self-service, but he would be responsible for topping up the serving dishes, and for clearing away the plates and things and wiping down the tables, and being nice to people. His tips would be in likes which would magically turn into kiles and swell his Gorithian bank account. Not that he cared about amassing lots of electronic cash, but there was something very satisfying about hearing the clicks.

His hours of work suited him and his adopted lifestyle.

No morning work, as breakfasts were taken in villas; and lunch customers were usually clear by early afternoon. The main hours of duty were from six in the evening until ten. Asba showed him how to register, and when he turned up the following day, his dining hall robe – complete with little brooch – was waiting for him.

Thursday mornings became the highlight of his weeks. He would wait anxiously for the sound of the doorbell, and when the two men greeted each other, it would be with a hug and a smile. They had become close friends. Sometimes they would have a coffee together in Villa Rosalind before deciding where they would take their walk. At other times they would start their expedition straight away so Ben could make sure he was back in time for his lunch-time duties. While they enjoyed each other's company and their perambulations around the island, it was their discussions which thrilled Ben. For him, they explored uncharted territory and took him where no man – at least from his world – had ever been before.

In early May, Ben managed to get out of Asba the answer – or rather an answer – to the big question. It started off simply enough, as they were walking slowly side by side along a path that skirted the lagoon.

"Asba, who's in charge, here? Who runs the place, calls the shots? Does Gorith do it on his own? Is he some sort of benign dictator? Does he have a coterie of generals to advise him?"

"No. We have a government. We call it the Council. They make the decisions, again with the help of the system which is able to run simulations for them so they can stress-test proposals before they are implemented."

"And am I represented on the Council?"

"No. You and I and everyone on this island are on the Council. The idea of representation stems from the early days of democracy in countries like yours when the governments had to physically meet, clearly impossible for an entire population. And of course, few people had the means to travel to, say, London, even if Parliament had space for them. Representation was the only option.

"Here we have the Mesh – our version of the web, you will remember – so it is easy to meet. And everyone, all of us, can have our say. We can choose to become involved, or simply leave it to others. There are no political parties; no-one is forced to vote against their conscience. There are no protests because each Gorithian enjoys equal power. There is no elite exploiting the masses.

"Many issues are decided by referenda, in which we are invited to choose one of perhaps three options. It's very simple. Some matters are subject to a rolling referendum, so if the facts change, people can change their minds. And anyone can launch a petition."

Ben smiled at Asba's reference to the words of the great economist John Maynard Keynes who had a reputation of changing his opinions over the years. When a critic accused him of being inconsistent, he reportedly replied: 'When the facts change, I change my mind. What do you do, sir?'

Oh well, Ben thought. Perhaps I should change my mind about this place.

"Asba, I'd like to meet Gorith. Any chance of fixing that?"

"Hmm. You want to go to Gorith?"

"Yes, I do. I really want to."

"Wice. It is not enough to want to go. He has to invite you."

"Well, can you get him to invite me, please?"

Asba's eyes avoided Ben's. "No. I cannot. The time has to be right. Only you and Gorith can decide that."

"But I've decided! I want to meet him!"

"You must decide together."

Ben could feel his learning servant's discomfort. "Look, I don't want this to be embarrassing for you, but how can he and I decide together if I don't meet him?"

Asba remained silent.

"He is a he, isn't he? Or is he a she? Or an it?"

Asba stopped walking and Ben did the same. "Wice. Do you have a religion?"

Ben was puzzled. The question of religious beliefs had never come up previously. "No, Asba, I'm not religious – in the sense that I don't go to church. I was brought to be Church of England, and that's what it says on my birth certificate."

"Do you believe God exists?"

"As a man in the sky with a long white beard? You must be joking. Hey, Asba. You're not trying to tell me Gorith doesn't exist, are you? Look around you! This island! This commune he's created! His foundation! This project! The whole damn thing-"

Ben stopped himself when it dawned on him what he was saying. He just looked at Asba and raised his eyebrows, waiting for guidance from his learning servant.

"Wice. Gorith is very real. Like the weather is real. The evidence is all around us. But what we term artificial intelligence is a hard concept to grasp. It is easier for us to understand and accept it if we personify it. Like the ancients did with their gods. Amun, Ra, and Amun-Ra – the Ancient Egyptian gods of Sun and Wind. Or the Greeks with theirs. Poseidon for example. God of water, horses, and earthquakes. Someone to blame for shipwrecks and drownings and no doubt other unexplained disasters.

"Today, we understand much more about the forces that affect our planet, and we do not need to think of them as people living in the Heavens or the Underworld. But when we are dealing with machines that listen to us and talk back to us, we humanise them. We give them names, like Siri, Alexa and Gaston.

"Gorith is not a physical being, not a person. But he is alive, and he thinks. He comes up with ideas. He solves problems. Call him an 'it' if you prefer, but it will not help you to understand him or his ways. Most people on the island, including me, find it easier to think of Gorith as a him – and Mother Nature as a her." Asba smiled and held out his upturned palms towards Ben as if he was offering something to him.

"Thanks, Asba."

Teacher and student walked on in silence. Eventually, Ben was the one who broke it. "So this, er, intelligence. Is he some sort of super-computer? I mean, does he have a physical presence? Is it like Hal in that film, *A Space Odyssey?*"

"No. Things have moved on since 2001. We have had 'the cloud' for many years; now AI is no longer the hardware. It is the software. It does not have a physical presence. If a computer is the body, the program is the spirit. It can be anywhere and everywhere.

"Nowadays it interfaces with human intelligence. The two work together. In a way, you and I are part of Gorith, in that we contribute to the system which runs our community through our work as councillors and committee members. Next question, please!"

Ben laughed. He had enough to be going on with for the moment. But he knew he had a long way to go, up the steep learning curve ahead of him. He realised that the more questions he asked of Asba, the more remained.

The men resumed their walk. Asba smiled and turned to Ben. "Wice. You are doing well."

Ben's watch clicked and he smiled back. "Thank you, Asba, for your kind comment – and for the kile it's produced." He heard a faint click from Asba's watch.

"All these clicks!" said Ben. "Do students like me ever get the opposite? Is there such a thing as an 'unlike' perhaps? Or a 'dislike'?"

"We call it a rap. On the knuckles. But it is very rarely used. Only the system is able to administer it, and only in exceptional cases."

"Okay, Asba. Give me an example of an exceptional case."

"You may have noticed that personal freedom is a cornerstone of our philosophy, but there is a limit-"

"Like crossing into an out-of-bounds area?"

"No. Not at all. We have out-of-bounds areas to keep us safe, allowing you the freedom to wander anywhere else. And we are allowed to do anything we wish, and say anything we like, with one important proviso."

"And what's that?"

"Gorithians must not cause offence. Of course, it is easy to say that, but what does it really mean? Probably different things to different people. What is offensive to one person may not be to another. Calling a black man a nigger is clearly highly offensive. Calling a white man a nigger is not. It is also dependent on who is causing the offence. Using the nigger example, it does not generally cause offence if one black man calls another black man a nigger.

"The 'f' word is another example of the difficulty in defining offence. It used to be extremely rude to use it any circumstances, but now... Hardly a film is produced without a good sprinkling of that word. I still find it offensive, but I accept it has, over the last decade or so, lost its power to shock and offend. Now, it is just another word. And words do not have to be swear words or rude to offend. A carefully worded put-down, designed to hurt, can cause much offence. And shouting at someone when there is no need to shout can likewise be offensive.

"One can be offensive in other ways. Obviously, any form of violence against another person is offensive, but so too is the threat of violence. And body language can cause offence too. A shake of the fist. The raising of the middle finger. The British V-sign, despite its innocuous origins. Spitting, growling, raising of the forearm while slapping the bicep. Interrupting someone while they are talking."

Ben let Asba continue.

"And the final complication is that behaviour which is inoffensive to one gender may be offensive to another. Now, for gender, substitute race, colour, creed or age-group, and you can see it is a minefield."

"Wow! That's some list! But how can any society police offensive behaviour? It must be well-nigh impossible."

"You are right. Which, dear Wice, is why your world – particularly your western world – has so much trouble. For a start, most people cannot understand why words cause distress or hurt to someone else. Most of the time those causing offence do not do it deliberately. Yet offending people can be the prelude – if not the cause – of much human conflict, between individuals, families, tribes and nations.

"Now, to answer your question, how can it be policed. Your societies make laws to try to stop people saying or doing certain things which might cause offence. In theory, breaches of those laws are reported, and suspects are arrested and tried, and those found guilty are punished. In practice, it is not so straightforward. For a start, those laws are competing with the concept of freedom of speech. Secondly, it is difficult to prove *mens rae* – guilt in the mind of the accused – so often the case is dropped.

"Thirdly, it can be hard to secure a conviction, as it is not a black-and-white matter; there is every shade of grey in between. Where does the boundary lie between guilt and innocence? If you steal something, you have either taken possession of it, or you have not. If you murder someone, you have either killed them, or you have not.

"And finally, because such laws are so difficult to apply, they rarely command the respect of the population, and the enthusiasm to enforce them is lacking."

"So, oh learning servant! How does Gorith determine what is right and wrong? Don't tell me he can judge what's offensive and what is not."

"I was about to tell you that. But you are the master; I am the servant. I will obey your command. I will not tell you."

25

The days slipped by. In the mornings, Ben enjoyed himself exploring the island and in particular the coastline, identifying possible landing sites for the rib. But he'd had no success with the other part of his mission – the main part, the reason for his being there – of locating Anna. He wondered if she was actually on the island.

He'd noted three look-out points, all above the tree line around the crater, from which he could survey the whole ocean around the island. Gaston had confirmed to him that in each case the horizon was at least thirty kilometres away, giving Ben something like 3000 square kilometres of sea he could keep a watchful eye on. He was confident he would spy *Juli-Emma* should she enter those waters, visibility permitting.

Naturally, he took his camera with him on all his expeditions, and he would photograph anything of interest: plants, birds and insects, and any topographical features which he might later wish to study. While his new-found hobby started as a cover, he soon found it was becoming a passion.

Gaston helped him identify the subjects of his photos, and he would willingly share his pictures with other enthusiasts on the island. He would happily hand his camera around a group of them so they could see photos on the tilting screen, or in some cases he would invite friends back to Villa Rosalind to view them on the big screen. In short, he became a bit of an authority on the island's flora and fauna.

He worked hard at his job in the main dining hall, and the ever-increasing number of clicks he received showed him he was making good progress. Not that there was much progress to be made in clearing away dishes, but he undertook other things, like placing a pretty stone or a shell on each table, or a fresh flower in an egg cup. He made his customers feel welcome and looked after them. He would answer their questions, chat about the weather, and advise them on the food, and indeed on any other matter they might wish to discuss with him. He became an unofficial *maître d'*.

Thursday mornings remained special for him. It was his time with Asba. While they could share a laugh and a joke, tease each other and talk about anything, the one thing Ben dared not mention was 'the mission'.

It had irritated Ben that Asba had refused to tell him how Gorith knew if someone had been offensive, but it was a lesson for Ben. By pretending to take it as a command from his master, Asba had demonstrated how careful one has to be with words.

Ben did get his answer, but he had to wait a whole week for it.

"So, oh mighty servant, how does our artificially intelligent overlord decide if a Gorithian has offended another?"

"Simple, Wice – if you have the technology. Offence is

taken, rather than given. It upsets the receiver, and their body responds in a physical manner which can be detected by the monitoring functions of our smartwatches. Remember, they can count your steps, record how many flights of stairs you have climbed and how many calories you have burned, so it should not surprise you that they can sense emotion.

"We talk about our heart skipping a beat, or racing, or thumping in our chest. We hold our breath, we sigh, we gasp. Our watches can detect all of that. Furthermore, Gaston has been programmed to wake up, not only if he hears his name, but also if he hears any words or phrases which are potentially aggressive or offensive. That information is analysed together with similar information from the people you are with, allowing Gorith to judge if a transgression has occurred."

"And the guilty party gets a rap?"

"No. If no violence is involved, the 'three strikes and you're out' law applies. After that, a rap goes on your record, and it remains there until you go to Gorith."

"And if violence is involved?" Ben had to ask the question.

"It becomes a very serious matter, and the Council decides on the punishment."

It was the end of June before Ben ventured to ask Asba about Anna. Having thought about it for weeks, he came up with a way of bringing her into the conversation.

"A question for you, Asba."

They were sitting on Ben's veranda drinking a cup of coffee, recovering from a hike up to the crater. "Fire away, master!"

"What brought you to this island?" Ben had tried

previously to find out more about Asba, but whenever he'd tried, his servant would turn the question back on him.

"We all have a reason for being here. Tell me, Wice. What is yours?"

"Well, I heard about the Gorith Foundation from, er, a friend – indirectly – and I made some inquiries, and the concept of what the Foundation was trying to achieve appealed to me. You know, peace and tolerance and freedom and all that. So I thought I'd give it a go. I think my friend might still be here. I think she came about two years ago."

"That's interesting, as Gorith does not encourage students to reveal details of their studies here, as it might attract unwelcome guests. Gorith likes to choose who comes here."

Ben didn't want Anna to get into any trouble. "She didn't reveal anything. I found an advert, in a magazine of hers, and I responded, and here I am...

"Actually, it would be quite fun to meet up, if she's still here. To let her know I've made it – that I'd followed in her footsteps. I haven't seen her for, ooh, let me see, it must be ten years or so."

Asba smiled. "Let me see what I can do. I do not suppose you know her Gorithian name, do you?"

"No. But I think I might have a photograph of her, come to think of it. Among some old ones. From uni days. I'll go and have a look."

Ben jumped up and went inside the villa. He returned a few seconds later clutching a small head-and-shoulder shot of a blonde girl, smiling. Her long wavy hair hung around her shoulders and looked as if it were moving. Her eyes were wide and as blue as the Pacific Ocean. The photograph was creased and had rounded corners as if it had been removed from its resting place and returned many times. He handed it to Asba.

"Wice. She is very beautiful."

"Oh, really? I suppose she is, in a way." Ben could feel his heart bumping and wondered if Gaston was listening in.

"I think I have seen her," said Asba, stroking his beard. "I think I know who she is. But if I am right, she is not on the island."

Ben's heart came to a sudden stop. Well, blow me, he thought. What the merry hell am I going to tell Donnie and Sash, and Anna's parents, for God's sake?

He tried to sound disinterested. "Oh, it was just a thought... Doesn't matter at all..."

"Sorry, Wice. She must have left a month or two ago – if your friend is whom I have in mind."

"No need to be sorry, Asba. Not your fault!" Ben forced out a chuckle. "Just for interest, though, do you know where she went? Not that I've got any intention of following her. No way! I'm pefectly happy here."

"Again, Wice, I am sorry I cannot be more helpful. I have no idea where she went."

"Fine, Asba. No worries!"

"And I'm not sure when she will be back."

Ben wanted to hug Asba but did a stage yawn instead. "Back? So she's coming back?"

"Of course. Why would she not? Someone said she had gone into hospital, for some procedure, a female thing. As you know, our medical centre here can handle most things, but sometimes more specialised care is required. Medicine is not a field of mine, so I cannot give you further details, but she will be in good hands, I can assure you of that. Gorith takes great care of all of us."

Good news and bad news, Ben thought. I hope to God – or rather to Gorith – that she's okay. No point in worrying about it. But he needed something to take his mind off Anna.

"Thanks, Asba. Maybe I'll bump into her once she gets back. Who knows, eh? Now, Asba. Do tell me about that crucifix you're wearing. It looks kind of special."

"Yes. It is special. But it is not a crucifix. Note that it has a stem and seven points. These represent the cardinal virtues of antiquity: prudence, justice, temperance and fortitude, with the theological virtues of faith, hope and charity."

"So, where did it come from?"

"I was given it by Gorith about a year ago. Apart from the miniature camera in the middle, it is solid silver, hand cast. Here. Take a closer look." Asba lifted the chain over his head and handed the cross over.

Ben felt the smooth highly polished metal and admired the intricacy of the casting. He turned it over and read the inscription on the back. 'To Ash Banyan. With many thanks. Bless you, Gorith'.

"Cool! So what did you do to earn that?"

"I made a donation to the Foundation."

"Ah!" said Ben. "So that's what keeps the Gorith world spinning on its axis. I must admit I'd been wondering about that. I mean, kiles aren't going to get us very far. I know the Japs did a lot of work here, but just maintaining the place and paying the running costs must cost a bomb."

He didn't like to ask how much Asba had donated, but he wondered if everyone on the island was expected to throw something into the pot. It would have to be a big pot, he thought, and some pretty big donations would have to be thrown into it.

He reckoned Asba had read his mind, because he replied, "Donations are optional, and they don't have to be monetary. Take you, for example, you are a member, donating your efforts."

"What? Clearing away dishes and wiping tables? How many decades would I have to do that for, to be presented with one of those crosses?"

"My cross is silver. But Gorithians are also presented with wooden ones, bronze ones and gold ones. Solid gold. It depends on the nature of the donation. Tell me, Wice. Have you ever made a donation? Any sort of donation, at any time in your life?"

"The other day I donated my book to the library. And some months ago, before I came out here, I gave twenty pounds to a guy in the street, in London. At uni I once gave blood. A lot of us did, in my college. I think we were given a free pint of beer."

"Wice. How did you feel about that?"

"Great! A free drink when you're an impoverished student..."

"I meant about giving blood."

"Well, it was only blood. I've got about eight pints of the stuff and they only took one. I soon felt fine."

"Any other feeling?"

"I think I felt good about it, that I might be helping someone, maybe even saving a life. Yeah. Come to think about it; I had a feeling of... pride perhaps? More like self-respect."

"Would you do it again?"

"Sure. Why not?"

"Wice. It could be arranged, if you wanted. Here on

the island. If you did it on a regular basis, Gorith might present you with a wooden cross, as a symbol of his thanks."

"Hey! I'd like that. I'd wear it all the time. And everyone would see that I'd contributed. That I wasn't a complete freeloader."

For Ben, it was an exciting thought, of earning a cross on a chain. A symbol, not of something you have, but of something you have given. Not an item to be coveted, but a sign which would earn respect and admiration for its wearer. So at his next meeting with Asba, he brought the subject up. They were on their way to visit the island's farm, some twenty minutes walk away.

"Asba, I've been thinking about giving blood. I'd like to go ahead. But tell me, do others give blood? I've noticed a few wooden crosses, and a couple of bronze ones."

"Gorithians donate whatever they wish, when they want, and Gorith decides whether to give them a cross. Look ahead of you. The man coming towards us. He's wearing a wooden cross. He does nothing on the island. He is not a member, he takes no part in any committees nor meetings of the Council, but every month he donates plasma."

"Plasma?"

"Think of it as blood without the red cells... And look to your left, there through the trees. That woman over there. See the bronze cross she's wearing? She donates ova – eggs, which would otherwise be wasted. If you gave blood, you might save a life. That woman's gift could create one. Thousands of women throughout the world yearn to have children but cannot. Think of what her gift could do for some of them."

Ben thought of Ling and her inability to have children. But he was anxious to know about Asba's cross. "So what does the silver one signify? For example, what did you donate to be awarded yours?"

"A kidney. It was no loss to me. I'm fit and healthy, and I do not need two. The procedure only took a few hours from start to finish, and within a week I had fully recovered."

"But who did you give it to? Normally it's a relation, isn't it? Or a close friend?"

"I gave it to Gorith. Not that he used it himself, but he made sure it went to save a life or improve one somewhere in the world."

"You're not suggesting he sold it, are you?"

"No. I am not suggesting that. I know he did."

"But that's terrible. It's morally repugnant! Most of the civilised world has made trafficking in organs illegal. In any civilised country, you would be breaking the law by selling your kidney. It exploits the poor, the underprivileged, who through no fault of their own value the money more than their own body."

"I did not sell it. I donated it."

"Well, Gorith sold it!" Ben said, his voice slightly raised.

"But it didn't come from his body." Asba remained perfectly calm.

"And I suppose you are going to tell me Gorith sold it on the black market for as much money as he could get for it!"

"Wice. You are a good student and your learning has progressed well. The matter we are discussing does not usually arise until a student's third year. By then, it is hoped that they have become un-doctrinated and are able to handle alternative views to those imposed on them by authoritarian sources of their home countries – teachers, media and parents. I am happy to continue this discussion, but not if it upsets you."

Ben sighed. He was upset by the very thought of someone selling body parts. Like in the film *The Island* which he saw when he was in his teens. Or the other one, *Clonus*, which he saw at uni, although it was made before he was born.

Both were horror films; and having watched them, Ben shuddered at the very thought of anything to do with human cloning, surrogate motherhood or the harvesting of body parts. Then he remembered that *The Island* was set in 2019. At least Gorith's island was nothing like the one in the film.

He wondered if Asba had a point. That he, Ben Bellamy had been conditioned since birth to view the world in a certain way, to accept a certain set of ethics dating back hundreds of years, a framework of values which hadn't moved with the times.

"Okay, Asba. I'm bracing myself. So, do tell me. Did Gorith sell your kidney for as much money as he could?"

"Why should he not?"

"Because he would be exploiting the buyer! Profiteering from their medical condition!"

"Wice. Let us look at another example. The Gorith Foundation gets all sorts of donations. Obviously money, but sometimes investments, jewellery, works of art, classic cars, real estate, patents and copyrights – and sometimes donors bequeath their entire estate. How would you feel, Wice, if you donated something valuable to a charity and they failed to secure the best price for it?"

"I'd feel pissed off... But if he sells a kidney to the highest bidder, only the rich people can afford it."

"Not so. Many organs and other body parts are bought by hospitals, insurance companies, and charities. The money may come from governments, philanthropists, crowdfunding or sponsored events. And there are, out there in the real world, wealthy people who have so much money they do not know what to do with it and are only too pleased to find a good cause they can support. So my kidney did not necessarily go to a rich person."

"Hmm," was all Ben could muster by way of a response.

Asba smiled.

26

By early August, Ben had perfected his escape plan. It had two phases.

Phase One was to search his 3000 square miles of ocean every morning from mid-August onwards, from his carefully reconnoitred observation posts. If he spotted a sailing ship, he'd use his camera to zoom in on her and try to establish if it was *Juli-Emma*. If the ship was too far away, he'd take a photo and view it on the screen using the digital zoom. He would only signal if he was sure it was them, in order not to alert someone else to his presence. He'd keep the beam on them until they flashed back and contact was made.

If for any reason contact hadn't been established by 7th September, he'd revert to Donnie's original plan and wait for his evening flares, to be fired one hour after sunset from the west. Fortunately, Ben's dining hall was on the western side of the island, and despite the vegetation between it and the coast, he believed he'd see a flare at a height of 300 metres.

Sunset would be apparent, as its dying rays would strike the tops of the trees around him, and he'd set the timer on his watch for one hour. If he saw a flare, he'd get himself into a position at noon the day following where he could operate his improvised heliograph.

Phase Two was the pick-up. He had selected a landing site for the rib on the western side of the island but north of the dining hall by a few hundred metres and about half that from Villa Rosalind. It was a promontory, almost a sandbar, that jutted out into the ocean. While it was on the open sea and subject to rollers and surf, it was out of sight of any villas or other buildings.

On the night agreed, at precisely 11.00 pm, he would set up his camera with its flash up, on its mini-tripod, and in the time-lapse mode at an exposure every five seconds. Anna would be waiting in his villa, unaware of the plan. He'd go back to her and break the news to her, and the two of them together would run down to the pickup point. He'd change the time setting on the camera to one-second intervals to indicate they were ready.

Donnie would come steaming in on the rib, pick them both up and head back to *Juli-Emma* before anyone on the island had the chance to respond. All he needed to do was to communicate the plan to his two friends. But that was the purpose of Phase One. The only snag was that he had yet to find Anna.

At his next meeting with Asba, he would grasp the bull by the horns. They had walked up to the edge of the crater and were sitting down on some rocks. It was one of Ben's observation posts.

"Asba. I know about the graduate course, the one I'm on, but can you tell me about the others. I've noticed there are some elderly people on the island and I wonder if they are here to learn."

"No. We call them The Sunset Set and they normally spend a few weeks here."

"Wow! A long way to come just to see a sunset. I know they're marvellous, but-"

"For the sunset of their lives, Wice."

Ben was anxious to bring the subject around to Anna. "And the learning courses. Is there just the graduate course, like the one I'm on?"

"Yes, but it is rolling. There is no start or finish date. Students come, students go, when their learning servant advises them that they are ready."

"I see. I was just thinking about that girl I knew. Is she on a graduate course, too, do you happen to know by any chance?"

"Do you mean the one in the photograph you showed me?"

"Yeah, just wondered. I just thought it might be a good idea to exchange notes, when she gets back from her medical thing you mentioned. You know, discuss things. I mean, I know I can discuss anything with you. But maybe I could help her along a bit. If she had any questions-"

"Her name is Azalea Orchid. She's back, working on our coral reef conservation project at the research centre, on the far side of the island."

Ben had to stop himself leaping to his feet with excitement. *Play it cool, sunshine.* "So her procedure, or whatever it was, it went well?" he asked, through a carefully timed yawn.

"Yes. I know her learning servant. He said it all went well. Would you like me to suggest to him that Azor might like to dine in the main dining hall this week?"

"Could do, I suppose. The food's good, very good in

fact. And I would make her feel welcome – as I do all visitors."

"I am sure you would, Wice."

They sat in silence for a few minutes, enjoying the breeze and the incredible view. Ben didn't want to press Asba further on Anna. The wheels in Ben's head started to turn. "Asba?"

"Yes, master?" The submissive reply had become a bit of a joke, and it always made Ben smile.

"You said the Sunset Set came here for the sunset of their lives. That can mean-"

"It does. Are you ready for some further third-year learning? It's up to you, but it might upset you."

Ben remembered getting hot under the collar when Asba had told him he'd donated a kidney to Gorith who'd sold it. "Okay, Asba. I'm ready. Go for it."

His learning servant took a deep breath. "In your world, the end of life is not handled very well. For a start, it is often prolonged by the medical profession to the point where the suffering is almost unbearable, not only for the subject but for their family and loved ones."

"Surely, though, in this day and age doctors can control pain," said Ben. "The patient doesn't have to suffer."

"Wice. It is not just physical suffering. Often the subject is taken from his home into a hospital, hospice or old people's home or some such unfamiliar environment. While some of these establishments are very good, the subject can become distressed and disorientated, and lose control, not only over bodily functions but over their destiny. They become powerless; they lose their dignity. They can feel dreadfully humiliated.

"When the end does finally come, it can be traumatic

for all concerned. Close family can be left with horrific memories of their loved one's last days and final moments. For many subjects, their last hours and minutes can be the most horrific of their lives as they struggle to escape the fires of eternal damnation in an imaginary hell, because they are not sure their god has forgiven them for their sins.

"But it is worse. The subject knows – if they still have the faculty of cognisance – that when they die, their body will be buried in the ground to rot, or burnt in a furnace. The procedure tells the subject their body has no value; that it is worthless; dead meat."

He paused and looked at Ben. "Wice. You may think Gorith was wrong to sell my kidney. You may feel he exploited me. But let me tell you this. If I were to face death tomorrow, no matter what manner it may take, I will at least know that a small part of me, somewhere in the world, would live on, prolonging another life. It is a good feeling."

"So, do you encourage your sunset seekers to donate their organs, before it's too late?"

"No. We suggest they donate their organs after they have died. Their earthly remains; their entire bodies. If they die on the island, we have the facilities to take care of their remains and ensure they are put to beneficial use. They know – if they die on the island – that parts of them, many parts, will live on, helping other lives – perhaps saving lives.

"Do you know that the organs from a single human can save up to nine lives? And those sunset seekers know that their donation to Gorith will enable his foundation to continue its work of making human organs available for the benefit of humanity."

"I think I get that," said Ben. "I guess I would like that,

too, knowing my body had a purpose, a noble one. Bad luck, though, for those sun-setters who don't die on the island!"

He suddenly stood up. He recalled that creepy film, *The Island*. "You don't, er, you know…"

Asba smiled at Ben. "Wice. Please sit down. No, we do not. I will explain later."

When Ben returned after lunch to Villa Rosalind for his siesta, he could not take his mind off the possibility that sometime in the next week Anna would walk into his dining hall. As it was Thursday already, he assumed – or rather hoped – it would be Friday, Saturday or Sunday. Perhaps Saturday, if she's working hard on her project during the week.

For each of those days, he made a special effort in his appearance, treating himself to a freshly washed djellaba each evening and trimming his dark brown beard. He made even more of a special effort to make his dining hall welcoming and appealing, but it was not 'likes' he was after, at least not the ones which made his watch click.

The plan was simple. He would let her eat her starter and main course in peace, then join her at her table with a wonderful dessert of tropical fruit ice-cream with mango syrup and real cream in a jug made of seashells, a special for two.

Afterwards, he would suggest a walk in the moonlight followed by a coffee at Villa Rosalind, and he would tell her the plan and do what he should have done ten years previously. He just hoped she wasn't beyond redemption on the brainwashing side of things, although he had to admit that so far, Asba hadn't tried anything of that sort on him. Perhaps the pressure came later.

Saturday turned out to be the night. Heads turned when this beautiful woman walked into the main dining room shortly after eight o'clock. She glided through the entrance, her pale blue djellaba flowing lazily around her. She was wearing a garland of jasmine in her ash blonde hair which shone in the soft candlelight.

Her eyes twinkled as she looked around the room, and the laughter lines creased up as she smiled as she noticed the little posies of wild flowers on the tables, and the different coloured stones and white shells carefully arranged around each one. Around her neck, she wore a silver chain, on the end of which was a cross, cast in silver with a glass bead in its centre.

Ben was completely taken aback, firstly by her beauty. The girl of his university days had blossomed into the most wonderful example of womanhood he could imagine.

The second thing which knocked him for six was the tall, slim figure at her side. Probably twice her age, Ben thought. He had long grey hair curling around his shoulders, bushy black eyebrows on a strong masculine brow. His hooded eyes were the colour of Lapis Lazuli, dark and mysterious, and Ben felt them boring into him. His Svengali stare wasn't softened by a smile, but the corners of his full lips suggested a smirk was lurking there somewhere. Around his sinewy neck hung a chain, and on the end of it was a bronze cross.

Poor Anna, Ben thought, guessing the man was her learning servant. It made him realise how lucky he was with Asba. He approached them both but only had eyes for Anna. He held out his arms and smiled.

"For two, please," she said.

"Anna!" he replied.
"Excuse me?"
"It's me! Ben. Ben Bellamy!"
"Who?"
"From uni?"
"Not Benny, surely?"
"It's me. How absolutely won-"
"What on earth are you doing here?" She turned to her partner. "Seja, this is Benny. From my uni days. Isn't it amazing?"

Ben leaned awkwardly towards Anna and kissed her on both cheeks. He then held out his hand towards her escort. Seja just stared at him.

"Well, er..." She looked at her watch. "Wice! Where did the 'n 'get to? Good to meet you. We must talk over old times sometime. Can we take any table?"

"Of course," said Ben.

Had it not been for the body cams and Gaston's eavesdropping, Ben reckoned he would have floored Seja there and then.

But sometimes in life, he conceded, Lady Luck does shine her little light on one, even at the darkest moments. Seja obviously had not got long-range tanks fitted, and after the main course, he got to his feet and with his nose in the air he minced to the gentlemen's. Ben seized his chance and raced across to Anna.

"Anna! Azor, I mean. Listen! I must talk to you. Can we meet? Tomorrow morning, perhaps? Just the two of us? I have a message from your parents."

"Mum and Dad?" her face lit up, but then the smile faded and she frowned. "How are they?"

"They're fine. Sort of. I'll tell you more tomorrow morning. Villa Rosalind. For coffee. Please?"

"OK. What time?"

"Elevenish?" His heart was thumping. He shot a glance at the door to the gents'.

"Yeah. I can make it by then. See you."

Seconds later, Seja returned and pushed past Ben to get to his seat. Ben didn't mind. He'd got his date. It wasn't exactly the walk in the moonlight he had imagined, but it was a start.

27

The special effort Ben was making with his turnout and personal grooming continued, and by the time his virtual doorbell rang that Sunday morning he felt presentable enough to host his very special visitor.

"Wow! You look great! Come in! Coffee? Tea?" he said.

"Hi, Benny." Anna looked him up and down. "You don't look so bad yourself. Not sure about the beard, though. Coffee please, black no sugar... Sorry, would you prefer me to call you Wice?"

"I'd like you to call me Benny, like in the old days. You're the only person who calls me that."

Anna asked him what he'd been up to since leaving Cambridge, and he explained about the job and the sabbatical. He told her he'd seen her parents and that her dad had broken the sad news. He stumbled over the condolences and tried to console her by implying it was wicked of the Council not to have gritted the road, that Highways should have put up a barrier and George should have been collecting the twins, and it was just one of those unfortunate things.

She stopped him. "Benny, it was my fault. I'd had a few drinks. I was driving too quickly. I braked too hard. It wasn't George's fault, although he beat himself up about it... When we separated, all our friends thought it was because we blamed each other. It wasn't. In my case, I just couldn't imagine that George could ever love me again – having killed his children. He adored them.

"I had counselling, and my therapist tried to persuade me it wasn't my fault, and that if George had done what he said he was going to do, my girls would be alive. It was stupid advice because I made George feel even more guilty, and it did nothing to help me feel less guilty...

"And my parents. They were so upset. In some respects they were wonderful, but sometimes I would catch them looking at me, the killer of their little darlings; they were dotty about them...

"I think they thought that me coming home was going to be like having their child back. Little Anna! When I went to uni I *was* a child. When I married George, I was still a child in some ways. Having twins and being a mum was hard work, and I started to grow up. Then after the accident, I think I became a different person. The child in me had gone.

"I know it was terrible of me to leave. To disappear like that, but I couldn't bear it any longer. Mum and Dad were... It's difficult to put this into words... They were so nice to me. Bearing in mind what I'd done, they were too nice. It wasn't until I came here that I started to improve. Gradually I became stronger. The guilt didn't go away – I still feel it – but now I'm able to bear it. Seja's been a great help. And this island. It's magical! It grows on you... And I've kind of grown on it, I suppose!"

Anna smiled and sipped her coffee.

Ben took his chance to lighten the mood. "I gather

you're working at the research station. What's the project?"

"Ocean acidification, actually, the 'evil twin' of global warming. It causes all sorts of problems from coral bleaching to killing fish stocks. It's complicated, but what we're trying to do is genetically engineer a coral species which can withstand higher acidity levels. Hybrid, actually, half organism half nano-robot."

"To replace the dying coral and rebuild the coral reefs?"

"Yes, Benny. But here's the clever thing. If our new species works, it will extract carbon dioxide out of the oceans which in turn will reduce the acidity of the oceans and allow natural corals to regrow. They, in turn, will build up their exoskeletons of calcium carbonate, thus gobbling up CO_2 already dissolved in the oceans making them even less acidic. It's a virtuous circle. We prime the pump with our new species, and Mother Nature does the rest!"

"Wowsers! That is exciting!"

"Ah! But it doesn't stop there, Benny. You see, if all the sea-creatures which make shells or exoskeletons out of calcium carbonate are able to gobble up more CO_2, the oceans will be able to absorb more CO_2 from the atmosphere. Less atmospheric CO_2 means less global warming and less rise in sea levels."

"My God, Anna. That's amazing."

"Early days, Benny. Lots of hurdles. It's not as simple as it sounds."

"Sure, I appreciate that, but it must be satisfying working on something so important."

"I'm a small cog in a slightly bigger wheel, and my humble contribution to the project comes to an end early next year."

"Anna, is that what you got your silver cross for? Does

your contribution to the project count as a donation to Gorith?"

"No. I hope my project work will be a donation to humanity as a whole, or should I say the world. We sometimes forget that it's not just we humans who will be affected by climate change. This cross thing was for something else. I've only had it a few weeks. Before that, it was a wooden one."

"And a gold one next?"

"Dream on!"

Ben had to ask the question. "Anna. I would be interested to know what you got the crosses for. My learning servant got his silver one for donating a kidney. I'm not sure I approve of that."

"Benny. You of all people must approve. Your learning servant might have told you this, but in the United States alone there are over 100,000 people who need a kidney. In each year about 40,000 more are added to the list, but only 20,000 will receive one. Every year 4,000 will die because they cannot have one. Do you know what a single kidney is worth?"

"I haven't a clue."

"I'll tell you. Not far short of half a million US dollars. Although some years ago one was auctioned on E-Bay and the bidding reached $5.7 million before it was pulled.

"Jesus! How do you know about these things?"

Anna paused. Ben noticed she was frowning. He sensed she was about to say something, so he kept quiet.

"The girls, Benny. My girls. The organ transplant people at the hospital wanted to take their organs – heart, eyes, spleen, liver; you name it. I said no. The organs from those two little people could have saved up to eighteen lives.

And by preventing it, I was responsible for the death of up to eighteen people."

"Anna! That's not true. So soon after the accident. How could you make such a decision?"

"Actually, I didn't know they had died. Not at that stage. And I prayed to God to spare them. I knew if I prayed hard enough 'He' would. But he didn't... "

Anna stood up, finished her coffee and said, "Come on, Benny, show me your side of the island."

Ben enjoyed strolling along the paths with Anna. He felt proud of her, a woman of presence, one who would turn heads. He pointed out the special trees, showed her where he went swimming each morning and pretended to be a fashion photographer, asking her to wet the lips whenever he felt like including her in a shot. When he heard a bird singing, he would stop and listen. She would do the same, and they would share their thoughts on what it could be.

He didn't like to press her on how she got her crosses, but he wanted to find out if she had made over Uplands to the Foundation. He thought he would have one last try.

"You said you had a wooden cross initially. May I ask what it was for?"

"Sure Benny. I was quite proud of it at the time. I wanted to donate something, and my learning servant – Seja – went through the options. Apart from money or valuables, you could become a blood donor, or give plasma, platelets or something like that. Sperm would have been tricky, but in the end, I decided on eggs – every month. I didn't need them, and it was a shame for them to go to waste. Over $10,000 a time."

"Good God!" said Ben.

"I thought you'd be impressed, being an economist!

And for me it was wonderful. I can't see myself having any more children, not after last time – and I don't deserve to be a proper mum."

Not part of the master plan, thought Ben.

"But it's nice to think I'm giving other women in the world the possibility of motherhood that they wouldn't otherwise have. And if Gorith gets money for my eggs, good luck to him."

"So what was the silver job for?"

"That was something special. It's all very well donating eggs, but it can be a hit and miss affair, and for the recipient, it does require medical intervention each time. As a seasoned egg donator, they asked me if I'd take part in a research project which involved donating an ovary, and I agreed."

"But I thought you couldn't transplant ovaries. Something about tissue matching?"

"You're right. They transplanted the skin of one of my ovaries, the part which holds all the eggs. It's never been done before. At least not successfully, not from one woman to another. It involved surgery but I was happy to help. Anyway, it's all robotics, these days. Perfectly safe. A few years ago, real people would operate the robots, but now robots operate the robots! I was untouched by human hand!

"So, I'm limping along on one cylinder at the moment. Not that I feel any different. They looked after me really well. And I've got my silver! And I haven't done my two years, yet!"

Ben was not too impressed. All this talk about organ transplants made him feel slightly squeamish, especially the women's bits. It reminded him of his conversation on the boat with Sasha, about Ling, and he realised just how valuable it could be for someone like her to benefit from an organ donation. He wondered about mentining Ling's predicament to Anna, but decided not to.

He was pleased Anna seemed happy, despite her being lumbered with that streak of piss for a learning servant, Seja. On the way back he answered her many questions about her parents and passed on their love. He was careful not to admit to his mission, of taking her back to them, in case she confided in Seja. But Ben did ask if they could meet again. She said she'd see him at The Gathering the following Saturday.

As Ben's villa came in sight, he saw one of the rescue quad bikes parked outside. He wondered if someone had fallen over and broken an ankle. He knew about the fall alarms on Apple watches and assumed that the Gorith version had a similar app. When they got nearer, he saw Seja sitting astride the machine in a rather proprietorial fashion, making a thing about looking at his watch.

Anna ran up to the man and gave him a peck on the cheek, and he smirked at Ben. She hitched up her djellaba and climbed aboard behind him. And, with her arms around his waist, the two of them departed.

Seja had said nothing. He'd just glared. Perhaps, thought Ben, it was the Gorithian way of warning someone off.

Ben went inside and summoned Gaston. The big screen came on, and he asked Gaston to show him how much body parts from a healthy adult were worth. He discovered that the theoretical total was close to a staggering $50 million. That could not be right, he thought, but it put him off the idea of cremation. He had no wish for his organs to be burnt. How could a fund manager possibly contemplate $50 million going up in smoke?

As he drifted off on his bed after lunch, he did the sums. Ten super-yachts, twenty Lamborghinis, a pad on The Peak, a penthouse in St Katharine Docks. What he really wanted in life was to settle down and be happily married to Anna.

As it was always meant to be.

28

Being with Anna for a couple of hours had been wonderful for Ben. While he would have loved to have taken her in his arms, just being by her side had made him feel alive. When he was with her, the sky was bluer, the trees greener, the whole island was more vivid. And when the quad bike disappeared out of sight with her aboard, it was as if a grey pall had descended over the place.

In some ways, it seemed to him that they had never been apart. Ten years was a long time, but the two years they'd had together in an intimate relationship while at uni allowed them to skip all the small-talk, the chat-up, the courtship, the chase and the final conquest. And the opposing polarity of their spirits drew them together. Although in other ways, Ben felt they were poles apart.

He guessed Anna might still feel uneasy with him about the way he left her to go to Hong Kong, as he did about the 'Dear John' letter she had sent him returning the air ticket. But he acknowledged they'd grown up since those early days, and he hoped she could look back on his mistake without resentment.

However, Ben had two little niggles. The first was the extent to which Anna had succumbed to any form of mental pressure or persuasion during her time on the island. The second was her learning servant. He couldn't imagine Anna falling for such a drip, but he did wonder if Seja's intentions were honourable, as they used to say, and whether he was gradually wearing her down.

Ben was close to Asba – they were good friends – and he'd only known him a few months. He appreciated Anna and her learning servant were probably good friends too, but he hoped their relationship hadn't developed further. While he was consoled by the fact that Anna Black was a strong character and no push-over when it came to sex, he knew it was imperative to get her off the island before any lasting damage could be done.

Once on board *Juli-Emma*, he was confident that in the company of Donnie and Sasha, and with his help, she'd make a full recovery; by the time they arrived in Hong Kong, she'd be back to normal. Whether that meant they would slide back into a relationship with him was another matter entirely.

He was pleased to see Asba the following Thursday. Not only did he want to find out more about The Gathering, but he knew his days with him were limited if all went to plan. He wondered whether he'd have the chance to say goodbye, or if he'd be able to leave a farewell message. The trouble was that he couldn't risk divulging his secret, not even to his trusty learning servant.

"Asba! Do come in! Coffee this morning? Or a fruit juice?"

"Thank you, Wice. A fruit juice, if I may."

The two of them sat down on either side of the coffee table. The big screen was on.

"Wice. I see you have been talking to Gaston. Is he treating you well?"

"You make him sound like he's a person."

"Ah! The word 'person' is perhaps underestimating his abilities. I trust you are getting to know him?"

"Hmm. As well as you can get to know an interface program. I mean, isn't he – it – just a link to Gorith?"

"Perhaps Gaston is more artificially intelligent than you think. If you consider him to be a person residing in your watch, he is actually quite clever. As you are aware, he monitors your geographical position, your heart rate, blood pressure, amount of exercise and all those other bodily functions. And since you first put him on your wrist, he has been learning all about you.

"For example, he now recognises your heart rhythm. You may think that we all have similar ones, but each is unique, like a finger print. He knows every little murmur, and how your body responds to stress and pleasure. He can tell when you are asleep, and when you are merely resting on your bed, and when you laugh – or cough for that matter. He knows when you take him off your wrist, and certainly, he would be very upset if he ever found himself on somebody else's wrist."

"Er, does he mind if I don't wear him?" Ben smiled. It seemed such a silly conversation.

"Yes. He is happy if you take him off for a short time, here, inside Villa Rosalind for example to take a shower, but at any other time he would get upset and worry about you. You see, he wouldn't know where you were, and he would report it to Emergency and Rescue Service who hopefully would be able to find you by sending out a search party. And if you were lying injured, at the bottom of a cliff, say, they would take you straight to the Medical Centre."

"Wow! He's like a big sister. Doesn't let you out of his sight!"

"That tends to be the way he operates, yes."

"Batteries, Asba. I used to charge my phone each night, but my watch didn't come with a charger. How long is it before they have to be replaced?"

"About eighty years," said Asba. "But after sixty it can start to lose its performance. It runs on nuclear power-"

"What? Is it safe?"

"Most certainly. It gains its power from radioactive decay, rather from a nuclear chain reaction. They are used in heart pacemakers and spacecraft."

"How reliable are they? I mean, do they ever stop working or fail completely?"

"No. They are reliable. Some years ago the whole system went down, after a lightning strike on one of the masts. The watches were not affected, but it took two days to repair the mast."

"Do Gorithians ever go walkabout? I mean, do they ever get lost, or disappear, or leave the island?" Careful, Ben told himself.

"Not to my knowledge. We have had the occasional scare, but the subject has always been found – alive I am glad to say. Most people who leave the island go after a good send-off, so there are no safety issues there."

"Asba. This send-off. Is that what The Gathering is all about? The one on Saturday?"

"Exactly that. A farewell party. A celebration. Are you going along? You know you are now entitled to attend."

"Yes. That girl. Azor. She came to my dining hall on Saturday evening, with someone called Seja. Then she dropped in here for coffee the following morning. Said she would see me at The Gathering. What's the form?"

"They always commence at 3.00pm, and they last a few hours depending on how many guests are departing. Not everybody goes to every one, but you can expect a gathering of about four hundred. If you are walking from here, I would allow yourself at least half-an-hour. Our Gathering Hall is in the Great Crater, on the main floor. There is an underground passage to it, accessed from just outside the hub. It was built by the Japanese-"

"Thanks. But what actually happens during a Gathering?"

"That, my friend, you will find out on Saturday. But what I will tell you is that all our departing guests go on a trip some days before The Gathering."

"Around the island? Or do they visit other islands?"

"A sort of mystery tour, if you like. It is the highlight of their stay. A trip to end all trips. Everyone is allowed one before they depart."

"Does that include me?"

"Most certainly."

Ben fancied a trip. Although he enjoyed walking around the island, he thought a break and change of scenery might do him good. But his time on the island was limited. He was anxious to spot *Juli-Emma* as soon as she arrived in the area.

"When would it be possible for me to fit it in?"

"Today, if you want."

"Really? But would I be back for Saturday? I don't want to miss The Gathering."

"Yes. You would be back long before then."

"So, could we go, umm, now?"

"Yes. Remember this. You have only the one opportunity."

"Fine... Just had a thought, Asba. The Dining Hall."

"Your assistants can cope. Let's go!"

It was the trip of a lifetime. A wild, whistle-stop adventure visiting all the places in the world he'd always wanted to go to – and those very special places to which he had yearned to return. He was able to call into Cape Town and see his parents, and on his way through Hong Kong, he met Ling for a session in the Oriental Spa at the Landmark Mandarin Hotel.

He swam with the dolphins off Kaikoura in New Zealand and stroked the grey whales off Baha and watched the humpbacks breaching in the Sea of Cortez. He hiked up a mountain on the Antarctic Peninsula and skied across the Alps from Chamonix in France to Zermatt in Switzerland.

It was an exhilarating but exhausting tour, and on the journey back he'd fallen into a deep sleep, only to be woken by Asba gently shaking his shoulder.

"God, Asba!... I'm so sorry!... I didn't know I'd be away for so long."

Ben was worried about his job in the dining hall. And he remembered about meeting Anna at The Gathering. She wouldn't have liked that, he thought, being stood up. Christ, he said to himself, when he recalled the mission – and he had visions of Donnie running out of flares, waiting for him to show up on the island when he was, in fact, swanning around the world having a whale of a time. What would he tell Anna's parents? And if Donnie and Sasha had called off the rescue plan, how would he get back to England?

"Wice. It was just under seven minutes."

"What on earth are you talking about?"

"Your trip." Asba took it slowly, allowing Ben to wake up fully.

"What do you mean?"

"Your... holiday. It was a dream."

"Asba, I promise you I really did... it was so real."

"Look at your watch."

Ben did so. It was Thursday, 13th August 2020. His first thought was that he had not missed Donnie and Sasha and that he could, after all, achieve his mission. His second thought was he had not stood up Anna, and he would see her at The Gathering. Finally, he thought that something very peculiar had happened to him.

"Asba. Have I been drugged?"

"Yes. You have been administered an opioid analgesic comprising fentanyl and an analogue of it called carfentanil. It was a carefully controlled dose taking into account your body mass and other physiological factors. You won't remember coming here, but we are in the Medical Centre. There will be no lasting after-effects except the good memories. When you are ready, I will walk with you back to your villa."

Ben sat up. "I'm fine. I'm ready now."

The two of them walked slowly back to Villa Rosalind. Despite his protestations to the contrary, Ben felt a bit unsteady and was glad Asba wasn't interrogating him about his strange experience. Eventually, his curiosity overcame his wooziness.

"Why, Asba?"

"Why what, oh master?"

"Why do you do that to people? Drug them?"

"Did you not enjoy it?"

"Enjoy it? It was amazing. Euphoric. A wonderful thing. It was like going on a fantastic holiday and coming back with the memories. I'll never forget it. If it was a dream, it was the best one I've ever had."

"There is your answer!"

"Come on! There's more to it, isn't there?"

Asba let out one of his big sighs and smiled. "Wice. Are you prepared to brace yourself again, for a further uncomfortable revelation?"

"Er, I think I know what it is... The Sunset Set. Do they come here to die?"

"Some do. Some don't. They are given the choice – and the knowledge that if they make the decision here on Gorith Island, their organs will be used to help others.

"Of course, most of us have a preservation instinct, and in your world, this is fortified by an induced fear of both the act of dying and what will happen to them afterwards. Some worry that it might be painful. Others fear the indignity of it all, while those with loved ones and families will be concerned about the grief their passing might cause.

"If a person here does decide to 'go to Gorith', as we say, we try to allay those fears. One of the ways of achieving this is to explain the process."

"You mean how you kill them?"

"I mean how we fulfil their wishes. Some people wish to die. In your country, one in fifteen makes a suicide attempt at some time during their lives. Over five thousand each year are successful. It is the most common cause of death for men aged between twenty and fifty years."

Ben was stunned. If only they knew, he thought, that their bodies were worth so much, perhaps they wouldn't do it.

"In your world, it is not acceptable for someone to wish to die. Until 1963, suicide was classed as a crime, and it is still a crime to help someone die. It is usually deemed to have happened 'while the balance of the mind was disturbed'. In some cases this might be true; in others, the subject may have carefully weighed up the factors and made a reasoned decision.

"But all suicides are tragic. Messy things, prone to failure, traumatic for those who become involved – people like police and paramedics – and normally the sad news comes as a terrible shock, not only to family and friends but also to acquaintances who might feel, rightly or wrongly, that there was something they could have or should have done – or should not have done – which might have prevented the tragedy.

"For those who have made up their minds, having rationally considered all the factors, we offer a less sordid alternative to the train-tracks, the noose, the overdose or the leap off the balcony or bridge. Firstly, we do not only explain the process, but we allow them to try it in advance; just once as you did this morning.

"We show them there is nothing to fear and no pain. Quite the opposite. When the time comes, the dose is increased to just above the lethal limit for them, and the dream goes on for ever.

"Secondly, there is no funeral service during which the dead body is lowered into the ground to rot or pushed into a fiery furnace to burn. Their loved ones can instead gather to celebrate a life which has ended with dignity and purpose."

"Yeah. I get it. It all makes sense. But if they don't want to die?"

"It is simple. We would send them home."

"Thanks, Asba."

They reached the little path leading to Villa Rosalind.

"Wice. Would you like me to come in with you?" Ben heard the concern in his voice.

"No thanks, Asba. I'll be fine. Just a question, though. That guy Seja. Can you tell me about him?"

"He is Azor's learning servant, and he is a member of the Emergency and Rescue Service."

"Ah!" said Ben. "He collected Azor from here last Sunday, and he was riding one of those quad things. Is he allowed to do that?"

Asba looked at Ben and sighed. Ben got the message. "He is allowed to do whatever he thinks is right. He has been here longer than I have. You will see him again on Saturday. He is conducting The Gathering. It is his turn to be the master of ceremonies."

"What did he get his bronze cross for?"

"I believe it was for sperm donation."

29

Ben was grateful to Asba for the briefing about The Gathering. Without it, he would have been shocked to find out on the day its true purpose. It was one thing to have a memorial service in celebration of a life gone by, but quite a different matter to celebrate it with the person present, alive and kicking. Hopefully not kicking, he thought, remembering Asba had assured him only those willing were allowed to go to Gorith.

It was the day of The Gathering and another chance to be with Anna. And it was Donnie's 'not before' date, Saturday, 15th August, when Ben would start his daily scanning of the seas for the rescue ship.

He was pleased Gaston had found him a Morse translator and put it up on his big screen. Using the pick-a-letter facility on his watch, he would write a message into the text box and press 'translate'. In the box below would appear the message in code. He would then share this with his watch so that when the time came, he would have on his wrist all the dots and dashes. He now had at least twenty Morse code messages stored on his watch which might come in handy when contact was made.

Gaston had also helped by showing him a video on his

big screen of how a heliograph worked. To operate it properly, he had to make a small hole in the silvering on the back of his mirror, in the centre. Also, he needed a small strip of white plastic in which he could make a hole, and by lining up the shadow of the hole in his mirror with the hole in the white plastic, he could direct the rays from the sun onto his target. He thought it was a sad indictment of what Man was doing to the planet that he was able to find a suitable piece of plastic on the beach.

When he was walking about the island alone, he'd take his shaving mirror and have a bit of a practice. What had made it easier for him was having the sun almost vertically above, at least in the middle of the day. What had made it difficult was trying to keep the beam steady on a target when it was a long way away. He'd found it helped to crouch down behind a large rock and rest his hands on the top of it.

An aspect of the plan he had not yet nailed was his nerves. He knew lots of things could go wrong and he wasn't sure what he could do if they did. He tried to persuade himself that the uncomfortable feeling in his stomach whenever he thought about the mission was a good thing; it was his body preparing him for his forthcoming flight to freedom. Freedom, he thought. How ironic. You can't get more free than you are on Gorith island; perhaps he was escaping *from* freedom.

After breakfast, armed with his camera and shaving mirror, he made his way up to his eastern observation post, as that was the direction he expected *Juli-Emma* to come from. He'd done the walk many times, but he guessed this was the first of many when there would be a chance of him sighting her.

Sadly, it was not a perfect day for it, as the early sea fog reduced his visibility to no more than a kilometre or two. Not only did it prevent him from sighting the ship, but also from using his heliograph should his saviours suddenly appear out of the mist.

Time was on his side, though. While he was anxious to be in his dining hall to greet lunchtime guests, his assistants would make sure the dishes and juice jugs were set out in good time and refilled when required. Mid-day came and went, and he started to make his way down, knowing it would take at least half an hour. The descent was relatively effortless, but he took care to watch his footfalls on the rocky path, as a sprained ankle or a twisted knee could scupper his mission.

That's why he hadn't noticed the mist was beginning to clear. He stopped before descending into the trees and made a final scan. A tiny, ghostly silhouette of a yacht appeared on the limit of his vision, seemingly floating between sea and sky. He readied his camera and zoomed in. The craft seemed to be stationary, although the faint image came and went as the density of the sea fog varied.

Through the electronic viewfinder he could make out the rig, and the profile of a rib stowed on board amidships. But he had to be sure before he started signalling. He took half a dozen shots centred on the bows, and by zooming in on the screen, he was able to see the name. But it was not clear enough to read.

He remembered Donnie's briefing at the Royal Yacht Squadron. He raised his camera again and took some more shots, this time of the stern. He studied the screen moving from one shot to another. There was no doubt about it. The yacht was flying the White Ensign of the Royal Navy signifying that her owner was a member of the Royal Yacht Squadron based in Cowes.

The mist swirled above his head giving him tantalising glimpses of vivid blue sky. He felt the heat of the sun, rising from the east. He saw its white disc, shining brightly through the light-grey haze. With trembling hands, he extracted his heliograph and aimed it at the ship as best as he could using the diffused rays of the sun. And he waited.

When the sun burst forth for a brief moment, he struggled to keep the device on target because his hands were shaking. He did not try to signal, just to keep the beam roughly in the right direction. He was kneeling so he could rest his trembling forearms on his thighs. Sharp stones were cutting into his knees. "Come on, sun! Come ON, for God's sake!" He said it out loud.

He watched as the mists came and went, and when the ship finally disappeared from his vision, it reminded him of the story of the Flying Dutchman, the ghost ship captained by Van der Decken, who tried to steer his vessel through the bad weather around the Cape of Good Hope but failed.

Ben was reflecting on his own failure, his naive stupidity to think that a shaving mirror could play such a vital part in his ill-conceived rescue plan. Then he heard, from a long way off, what sounded like a rifle shot. A few seconds later he heard another, then another. He watched the three bright red dots hanging in the sky below their invisible parachutes.

His first instinct was to race back to his observation post, but then common sense told him to remain where he was. Five minutes later he was signalling them:-

".– .... .- – / -.- . .-. – / -.- – ..-" What kept you.

".... .- ... .. -. –. / ..-. ..- -." Having fun.

".—. — / - — -. / .. ..-.." Ten toni?

Ben thought that would give him plenty of time to brief Anna and get her to the pick-up point. With any luck, he could persuade her to remain at the hub after The Gathering and join him for dinner.

".— .... .-. . / -... — ... ..- -. /" Where, Bosun?

"- — ... - / .- . ... - / .-. — .. -. - / — ..-. / .. ... .-.. .- -. -.."
Most west point of island.

"—.. —.." Ben had to say Donnie's reply to himself to recognise what it meant. Dah dah dah dit dit, dah dah dah dit dit: Morse code shorthand for love and kisses. He then signalled to Donnie and Sasha about the camera flashes. From 9.00 pm, intervals of five seconds to mark the spot. Intervals of one second meant we're there waiting.

Despite the slow transmission speed of the messages, it all went well. Contact had been established and pick-up time and place confirmed. He didn't want to let them go, but he had his work to do, and some detailed planning. He sent his closing message:-

"-.-. / ..-" Simply the two letters, C and U.

He watched *Juli-Emma* through his camera viewfinder as the huge genoa unrolled and the vessel heeled over and surged forward, trailing a streamer of white surf which sparkled in the sunshine. At least the wind has picked up, he thought. They'll be round there in no time.

He set off from his dining hall at 2.15 pm so he would be sure of not missing Anna. He waited for her at the entrance to the tunnel, and after twenty minutes she showed up. Much to Ben's delight, there was no sign of Seja, and the two of them joined the string of Gorithians who in their ones and twos were making their way to The Gathering Hall.

"Tell me, Anna, what-"

"It's Azor. Gorith prefers us to use our Gorithian names when in public."

"Sorry. Just wondered what to expect. Whether I have to do anything?"

"Your first time? Of course it is. You've only been here four months."

"So how often are these things?"

"Depends. Every couple of months."

"Azor, I understand people go to Gorith during these gatherings. I mean, what sort of numbers are we talking about here?"

"About half-a-dozen, normally. People apply to go to Gorith, but nobody knows who has been invited until the day. It's quite exciting, really. Of course, for those who are selected it's fantastic – like winning the lottery – but inevitably there are some who are disappointed. They usually succeed second time around, so it's never a sad occasion."

"Do I have to do anything?"

"No, not really. Just follow my lead. Enjoy yourself."

"Anna – I mean Azor – afterwards, I'd like you to dine with me. It's very important. There's something I want to ask you."

"Can't you ask me now?"

"No, not with all these people around. It's about your parents – and the future of Uplands. We need to discuss it. I have a proposal to put to you."

"Could do, I suppose. Seja's tied up with the ceremony preparations. And afterwards. He's going to give me a lift back to the station when he's finished. About nine-ish. If we eat straight afterwards, it should be fine."

The tunnel widened as it opened out into a hall the size

of a tennis court with a high ceiling supported on steel columns. Around the sides of the room were tables on which lots of glasses had been laid. At the end of the hall were double doors which reached the ceiling.

"Wow, what a room!" said Ben.

"Come on. Let's get a drink. If you think this room's impressive, wait to you see the main hall."

Ben and Anna made their way through the gathering crowd to one of the help-yourself drinks stations. In the middle of the table was a large punch bowl full of what looked like fruit juice with lots of ice cubes floating in it. Ben grabbed one of the ladles and filled two glasses.

"So, what do we do now?" asked Ben. "Mmm, this is good. What's in it?"

"Sssh. We drink our fruit punch and circulate until the call. Then we go through those two doors and the fun begins. Look! There's Mafi! Come and meet him."

Ben looked at his watch as they approached him. Maple Fir, eh? As she introduced him, Anna explained to Ben that Mafi worked with her at the station.

"Really? It must be fascinating work," Ben said to him. "I gather you are trying to reduce the acidity of seawater?" The question was was a mistake.

"That's right! It is absolutely fascinating!" replied Mafi. "You see, in seawater carbon dioxide exists in two forms, as carbonic acid and as a dissolved gas."

Fizzy water, thought Ben. He nodded and took a sip of his drink.

It was a sign to Mafi to continue. "Theoretical calculations show that a single molecule of water can catalyse the decomposition of a gas-phase carbonic acid molecule to carbon dioxide and water. In the absence of water, the dissociation of gaseous carbonic acid has been predicted to be very slow, with a half-life of 180,000 years."

"Wowsers!" said Ben. "That's a long time!"

Just like any other drinks party, he thought. Anna came to the rescue and dragged him off to meet her villa-mate, Bula. Buttercup Larch, he noted from his watch, trying not to let his eyebrows give away his surprise. I don't mind, he thought, as long as I can join in.

As Ben listened patiently to Bula describing her painting technique, he spotted Bero and Roma across the room. When Bula paused to talk to Anna, he took the opportunity of sliding away and went over to see them.

"Hi, all good?" said Ben.

"Yes, thanks, Wice," said Roma. "We're a bit nervous, but we're hoping, aren't we, love?"

"Yes, dear," said Bero, and he put his arm around Roma's shoulders and turned to Ben. "Our learning servant said we have a good chance, but there is an element of luck so we mustn't be disappointed if we don't make it. It's our first time."

Ben wished them luck and looked around the room. There was no sign of Anna. He noticed that people were starting to move towards the big double doors at the end of the room, but thought he would wait until Anna appeared before joining the throng. He decided to top up his glass.

A fanfare of trumpets sounded from invisible loudspeakers, and the huge double doors opened to reveal a vast hall the size of an aircraft hangar. At the far end opposite the doors, there was a raised stage at the centre of which was a large lectern – or small pulpit. Concealed lighting illuminated the seven-point cross on the front of it, the emblem which Ben had come to realise was the logo, for want of a better term, of the Gorith Foundation.

In front of the stage, rows of chairs radiated out from it with aisles splitting them up into sections, reminding Ben of a Roman amphitheatre. On either side of the stage were steps leading up to it.

The fanfare gave way to loud music. Ben recognised the theme tune from the film *Chariots of Fire*. The crowd in front of him surged forward, urgent to get seats as close to the stage as possible. Ben was happy to tag on at the back, hoping that Anna would wait for him.

As people began to take their seats, the music faded and was replaced by a softer melody which reminded Ben of *Elysium* from the old film *The Gladiator*. The mood in the hall was one of quiet excitement, somewhere between that in a cathedral before a service, and in an opera house before a performance of *La Traviata*. The audience – or was it a congregation – were whispering to each other and looking around them in wide-eyed wonderment.

Ben took his seat in the back row, the one Anna had kept for him next to her. She signalled to him with her hand. Five minutes to go.

30

The music faded out and an expectant hush filled The Gathering Hall. The house-lights dimmed to nothing, leaving the audience in total darkness. You could hear a pin drop. A disembodied female voice broke the silence.

"Ladies and Gentlemen! A warm welcome from Gorith to all of you! He sends his love to each one of you here today, and he gives you all his blessings!"

Everyone in the room clapped, including Ben. Well, he thought, it's nice to be loved.

"And now, without further ado, I would like to introduce to you, your host and master of ceremonies today..."

At that moment, the footlights came on and a dozen spotlights shone on the lectern. At the back of the empty stage was a curtain of theatrical fog, lit by concealed lights constantly changing colour.

"Sequoia... Jacaranda!"

Seja appeared through the stage fog and strode up to the lectern. He acknowledged the roar of applause by stretching his hands upwards and outwards, palms facing the audience as he slowly scanned the room. Suddenly, he brought his arms down, which was a signal for the applause to stop.

He surveyed the scene in front of him, his eyes boring down into the audience. Somehow it made Ben feel guilty. It reminded him of his headmaster in school assembly, having announced that if the marble bust of the school's founder was not returned to its plinth in the quad by midnight, the culprits would be thrashed.

Seja's deep voice boomed out over several loudspeakers: "Let the show... begin!"

All the lights went out, and there was a pitter-pattering of feet on the stage as the first act took up its positions in the darkness. The female voice announced it was the Gorith Island Barbershop Quartet.

"What the hell is a barbershop quartet," whispered Ben to Anna.

"Barbershop vocal harmony," she whispered back. She took a deep breath. "It's a style of a cappella close harmony characterised by consonant four-part chords for every melody note in a predominantly homophonic texture."

"How d'you know all that?"

"Gaston just told me." Ben could just make out her cheeky smile. It was like the old days.

The spotlights came on and the singers began their programme with *Hello my Baby*. Next up was a classical guitar player followed by a magician who did card tricks. It made Ben realise why there was a rush for the front seats. Then came a husband-and-wife duet who sang country folk songs followed by a fire-eater. Ben was relieved when finally Seja reappeared behind the lectern. The audience fell quiet.

"This, my fellow Gorithians, is the moment you have all

been waiting for. It's time for me to announced the names of those of you here today who have been called by Gorith to join him." Seja paused. It was a signal to the audience to applaud.

When it died down he continued. "Let me remind you. It is a great honour to be invited. Many apply for the privilege, but few are chosen. It is an accolade unsurpassed in the world, a reward of the greatest value."

There were random shouts of 'hear hear' from across the hall, and one man shouted out 'God bless Gorith'.

Seja continued. "It is the ONLY..." Seja scanned the audience. "THE ONLY!" he repeated, lifting his forearm and pointed his forefinger at the ceiling. "The only way to rid yourselves of your raps!"

Anna whispered in Ben's ear reminding him what a rap was. Over the knuckles, he remembered — a black mark.

The sermon continued. "And NO-ONE... No-one can go to Gorith with a rap on their conscience."

After a while, Ben got bored and his mind started to drift. He was pleased he and Anna were in the back row, as it would allow them to get ahead of the crowd and back to the hub at the end of the proceedings; he was getting hungry.

He was looking forward to joining Donnie and Sasha that evening, although he still was not quite sure how he and Anna would reach the pick-up point without being seen – or rather without the system tracking them through the GPS on their watches.

Simply removing them wasn't the answer, as it alerted the Emergency and Rescue Services who may not be very pleased to be called out, not for an emergency but because a couple of Gorithians were trying to leave the island. He wondered if the phrase 'students are not encouraged to leave the island...' meant that students were actively discouraged from leaving to the point where they were physically prevented from doing so.

"And so, Gorithians, we come to the first name!" The crowd fell silent. Ben breathed a sigh of relief.

"It is... Oak... Birch!"

A loud cheer from the audience and the automated spotlights swung round and picked up an elderly man in the fourth row. He leapt to his feet, and with a big smile on his face, he made his way to the nearest aisle, acknowledging the congratulations and the back-slapping. He ran to the steps and climbed them two at a time, vitalised by some hidden source of energy.

Oabi waved his arms above his head as if in triumph, and the crowd clapped and cheered as he approached the lectern. Seja took a step towards him and presented him with a gift-wrapped parcel the size of a pack of playing cards. Oabi bowed his head in submission, accepted the gift, shook Seja by the hand and walked off through the screen of brightly lit fog at the back of the stage, his frail figure silhouetted against the ever-changing colours, becoming fainter until he finally disappeared out of sight.

The next names Seja read out were – with the dramatic pauses included – those of Bero and Roma. They jumped up and clapped their hands above their heads, and the audience joined them. Bero's bald forehead gleamed in the beams from the spotlights. Hands stretched out to give them a well-deserved pat on the back – or just to touch them in the hope that their newly acquired god-like status might somehow rub off on them. They received their presents graciously then danced together through the fog, with the audience cheering them on until they could be seen no more.

Ben leaned towards Anna. "Why give them a prezzie when they're going somewhere where they don't need it?"

"Goes to their next of kin," she whispered, "along with their effects and goodbye letters."

"What is it? A bar of Dairy-Milk?"

Anna jabbed him with her elbow.

"A mobile phone?"

"Don't be stupid."

"Ah! A little red book *The Thoughts of Chairman Gorith*?"

"Just shut up and listen."

Two more couples were called, and then three single names. Some of them had to be helped. They all behaved as if they had won a great prize, and each time the roars of approval and admiration for them became louder and was sustained for longer. Ben found himself joining them, clapping furiously and stamping his feet at the right moments, cheering and whistling as each person received their gift, and waving goodbye when the curtain of fog closed behind them.

Ben was feeling slightly strange and wondered if he was overdoing all the shouting, but he was enjoying himself, and he was pleased for Bero and Roma and all the others who had been gathered, knowing what a wonderful thing they were doing for humanity. They should be proud, he thought.

The next name Seja read out brought Ben out of his day-dreaming. It was Willow. Not that he associated it with himself much, because nobody ever called him that. There must be a few of those here today, he thought.

After the usual pause, Seja read out the other half. It was Cedar. A mistake, thought Ben. The system doesn't allow duplicate names. The automated spotlight beams wheeled through the hall and stopped on him, blinding him.

The cheering around him was deafening. He couldn't see anything. Helping hands were trying to lift him to his feet. Congratulating voices were urging him towards the aisle. He wanted to shout and cheer, that he, Ben Bellamy had been chosen by Gorith. He wanted to stand on that stage and receive his gift, to walk through the coloured fog and join the others, and then to fly forever.

He tried to stand up, but a pair of unseen hands were on his shoulders holding him down, pressing him into his seat. Anna was shouting something. Down further he went until he slid off the seat and into the cramped floor space between the rows. His eyes started to recover. He saw confusion on the faces around him.

He looked up and saw a figure standing behind the back of his seat. The strong arms which had held him down were folded across a broad chest. Ben caught sight of the silver cross above them, glinting in the beams from the spotlights. The house lights went up. The man's eyes were fixed on the master of ceremonies, standing on the stage. Seja glared back, his neck taut with rage.

The audience didn't seem to take it in. Those in the front rows continued to clap and cheer. Those nearest to Ben seemed puzzled, not sure whether to scowl their disapproval at Ben, still kneeling on the floor in front of his seat, or lend him a helping hand.

He looked up at the man behind his seat. For the first time, he saw fire in those kind eyes. Seja continued to glare back from behind his lectern. Neither man blinked. The spell was broken when *Chariots of Fire* suddenly boomed out over the public address system. People clapped and smiled as if everything was back to normal — just a slight hiccup.

The house lights went off, the spotlights swung back onto the stage, and the Barbershop Quartet hurriedly regained their positions. *Chariots of Fire* was abruptly turned off and the crooners started singing. *Hello my baby, hello my honey, hello my ragtime girl.* This time the audience joined in, glad to have a distraction from what was happening at the back of the hall.

Strong arms hauled Ben to his feet. "Wice! You must run, like the wind. Now!"

It was an order. Ben grabbed Anna by the hand, and the two of them ran for the doors, through the room where the drinks had been served, and down the tunnel. He knew they were being tracked, and he wondered how much time they had before they were caught. The only safe place he could think of was Villa Rosalind.

As they reached the end of the tunnel, they felt the wind on their faces, and Ben feared a storm was on the way. It was dark outside, but ground-level lights lit their way to the hub. They walked when they got there in order not to attract attention, and it gave them a chance to get their breath back. Most people, those not on essential duty, were still at the Gathering Hall, and Ben reckoned that they had managed to achieve a good start.

They walked along the path to Ben's villa and noticed the palm trees rustling above their heads as the wind tugged at the fronds. They had to raise their voices to be heard.

"My God, Anna. I nearly went! They would have had

my body! Sold it to the highest bidder! The whole thing's a con! They lull you into a false sense of security. It's mass hypnosis!"

"Rubbish, Benny. Absolute tosh. Surely you've been here long enough to know how things work on the island? They *apply* to go to Gorith. He only invites them if there is a sound reason. They had a choice. You had a choice.

"And they DON'T sell to the highest bidder. Read the accounts, for Christ's sake. The Gorith Foundation is what they call a NON-PROFIT-MAKING organisation. Surely you've heard about those. But I forgot. You're a hedge-fund salesman. Profit is the only word you know. Just because you are obsessed with making money, it doesn't mean everybody else is. And how many glasses did you have to drink? If it was anybody's fault, it was yours!"

"Look. How the fuck-"

"Don't you swear at me like that!"

"Okay. How did that creep – your learning servant for God's sake! How did he put my name on his list? Tell me that! It was attempted murder!"

"Oh for God's sake, Benny. Grow up! It was a mistake. There are lots of Willows and lots of Cedars. The names got muddled up. There's probably some poor soul left in the Gathering Hall wondering why Gorith hadn't gathered him. It'll be all sorted out and everyone will be happy."

"I won't," said Ben.

Anna put her arm in his. "Yes you will, Benny. Once you've sobered up! Now, what's this proposal you want to put to me?"

Ben was relieved his watch still worked on the door, and they entered the villa. Rations in Villa Rosalind were meagre, and Ben wished he'd taken the offer of a self-catering package. But he was able to put his hands on a couple of brown bread rolls and some processed cheese and make two sandwiches. He guessed Donnie and Sasha would have some food ready for them when they reached the boat.

The two of them felt cosy in the villa, as the wind continued to get stronger and whistle through the trees. It also felt safe. Ben remembered his first night when he was trapped inside, and how it felt like a prison. He thought if it's hard to get out without the right watch, it will be hard to get in.

Anna had managed to calm Ben down, but for him, things had changed. He was pleased they were leaving – and getting away from that awful creature, Seja. He wondered if he'd been seduced by the island, its culture, its economic system and the way it encouraged and rewarded human virtue.

He was happy with the donation of blood and plasma, eggs and sperm to help others, and even the donation of body parts. He accepted the idea of taking organs from the dead. And he accepted the concept of assisted dying. But he couldn't get his head around putting those two together.

After the sandwiches, they polished off what was left of the fresh fruit, and Ben made them both a coffee. He looked at his watch. It was 8.40 pm. He needed to set his camera up at the pick-up point, so Donnie could take a bearing to follow. Ben had no idea how far out *Juli-Emma* would be, but he assumed Donnie would take it steady in the rib to preserve secrecy. But if the sea state out there was not good, he'd have no choice.

Ben reckoned he had ten minutes before he had to run to the pick-up point and set up his camera. He went to his wardrobe and extracted the little box from his cabin bag. He knelt in front of Anna.

"Benny, what the hell are you doing? Get up and drink your coffee."

"Anna, will you..." The words stuck in his throat. He was putting right the mistake he had made ten years previously. At last, he thought. He opened the box and passed it to Anna.

She gasped. "Oh, Benny!... It's... Beautiful."

31

"Don't say anything!" Ben implored her. "Think about it!" He got up and kissed her on the forehead. He went into the bathroom and changed into his swimmers. He took off his watch and grabbed his camera.

"Benny, what on earth are you doing?"

"I'll be back in five minutes. Just got to do something."

"You can't do this, Benny. Your watch keeps you safe-"

"Trust me, Anna. Just give me five minutes, then I'll be back. I'll bang on the door, and you can use my watch to let me in. If I'm not back in ten, make your way back to the hub and wait for Seja.

Before Anna could react, Ben opened the door with his watch then tossed it onto the sofa. He dashed out into the darkness, and the door to Villa Rosalind automatically closed behind him.

He sprinted along the path towards the beach. By the time he got there, his legs were already feeling heavy. Running along the soft sand was almost impossible. An invisible force was dragging him back, sapping his strength, almost willing him to stop. Thank God I'm not wearing my djellaba, he thought.

With chest heaving and legs crying out for mercy, he

made it. The wind had died down, but when he looked up he could see no stars. Thank goodness this darn thing is waterproof, he thought, as he set up his camera on the tripod. His fingers trembled as he switched it on and selected time-lapse. He remembered not to look at the flash when he tested it.

As he ran back, relieved that he managed to achieve his first task of the evening, he felt the rain and heard the large drops splattering on the compacted earth of the path. He'd nearly made it when he found himself caught in the headlights of a quad bike, humming its way to the villa from the opposite direction.

He was only a few metres away from where the little path branched off when he heard a shout. He recognised the deep tones of Seja. By cutting off the corner and racing through the prickly undergrowth, he made it in time.

He banged on the door with both fists and – almost unbearably slowly – it opened, and he dived in, letting it close behind him.

"My God, Benny! Where have you been? It's pouring with rain. You're soaked. And your legs! They're all scratched."

He was completely out of breath.

"What on earth have you been doing? Come here. Come and sit down and I'll get you a glass of water."

He collapsed on the sofa.

"Here you are... And the answer to your question is yes! A big yes!"

Ben saw the diamond twinkling on her finger. The news sent a surge of energy through his body and he struggled to stand up.

"I think we'll be very happy together," said Anna. "This time, it just feels right. You and me, on this wonderful island. I'm sure Bula would be happy to move out. She could come here, and you could take her place in my villa, and I could continue with my work at the station-"

The banging on the door interrupted her and alerted Ben to the danger outside.

"Open this door!" shouted Seja. "In the name of Gorith, OPEN THIS DOOR! Now!"

The banging continued for a few minutes then changed. Rather than the thump of a fist, it sounded more like the crashing of rock. Anna let out a muffled scream. Seja continued his frenzied yelling.

"Gaston! Lights off!" Ben felt he had to do something. "Gaston! Shutters up!...Stop!"

A two-inch slit allowed them to peer out into the darkness. Ben could just make out the lights of the hub in the distance, through the trees. They could hear the constant hiss of the rain and Ben wondered if Donnie and Sasha were able to see his camera flashes.

Anna and Ben, newly engaged, held each other in a tight embrace, trapped and helpless, waiting for whatever was going to happen next.

A strange orange glow crept its way into the dark interior of Villa Rosalind through the space below the shutters. It was coming from the hub. The glow got brighter and flickered. A siren sounded.

"My God, that's the fire alarm," said Anna. She lowered her head and squinted. "Benny! It's the hub. It's on fire! Oh no! No!"

Ben looked for himself. "Bloody hell!" He remembered the little candles he put on each table, one of his improvements which had earned him several 'likes'. But then he realised that by now dinner would be over and cleared away and nobody would be there. How very strange, he thought, that a fire should start in heavy rain.

The banging on the door stopped, and Ben just caught sight of Seja's quad heading at speed towards the hub.

"Anna! He's gone to the hub. Quick! Give me your hand!"

Ben opened the door to Villa Rosalinda for the last time and threw his watch back inside. He dragged a startled Anna outside and they ran down the path to the beach. The heavy rain made the going along the sand even more difficult, but they eventually reached the pick-up point. Ben was relieved to see his trusty camera, dripping with water but still flashing. He adjusted the time-lapse and set it off, flashing every second.

"Benny, what *are* you doing? What's going on?"

"Anna! We're going home!" Ben could hardly contain his excitement.

"But this *is* home. This is *my* home."

"No no. I'm taking you back to England! To a proper home!"

Being treated like some chattel jolted Anna out of the romantic dream she'd been living for the last twenty minutes. She was sodden. Her wet blonde hair clung to her neck, forming a conduit for the rainwater to run down inside the back of her djellaba.

"This *is* a proper home. *My* proper home!"

"Anna, don't you see? This is nothing more than a commune, a cult. Where they seduce you into making donations to pay for it all. Tell me, have you given them Uplands as well as your eggs?"

"UPLANDS? OF COURSE I BLOODY WELL HAVEN'T, YOU IDIOT!"

Ben was taken aback by the shouting. "Okay, okay.

That's good. I was concerned about your parents, that's all."

"Don't you think *I'm* concerned about them? Don't you realise that I think about them EVERY DAY! I worry about them. I worry about what I've done to them. I feel terrible about walking out on them."

"But Anna. We are going home to see them. They are waiting for you. A ship's coming here soon; tonight, to take us off this... effing island and in a few weeks we'll be in England! You'll be home!"

"This *is* my home, Ben. How many times do I have to say it to you? Gorith is like a father to me. He provides me with food and shelter. He looks after me. He watches over me. Not a sparrow shall fall, not a hair of my head-"

"Father? Watching over you? You don't get it, do you? Don't think father. Think BIG FUCKING BROTHER! Spying on you every moment of the day, listening to your every word, monitoring you, checking up on where you are, what you do, what you eat. And stealing bits of you to sell. Is that the sort of life you want? Is that the sort of father you'd rather have?"

"YES HE IS!"

Ben was stunned.

Anna continued. "You've got it wrong, Benny. Totally and UTTERLY wrong. You've been here a few weeks, and you think you've sussed it all. Well, you haven't! Gorith gives us freedom, more freedom than you'll ever get in your lifetime. Nobody tried to murder you. There's no mass hypnosis, no brainwashing. Gorith gives us everything we need, and we willing give to him."

Ben had no idea how long he'd got. The camera was still flashing, every second. He wondered if he could bear to stay, make this his home – but he knew he had to get back, at least to report to Anna's parents. And there was Seja.

"I love him," said Anna.

Ben could hardly hear her over the sound of the rain. "Who? That bastard who tried to trick me? That low-life of a learning servant, that streak of-"

"No, you fool! Seja? You must be insane. I mean Gorith. I love Gorith. And he loves me."

"He? He? Have you ever stopped to think WHAT Gorith is? 'He' doesn't exist! 'He' is a nothing. 'He' is an it! I'll tell you what he is. Listen up, Anna. The name! The clue is the name, for fucks sake! He's an ALGORITHM!"

"I don't care if he's an algorithm. I still love him and he loves me."

Ben sighed. He wondered if he had misjudged everything. "Anna, do you love me?"

"Yes. I always have. And I always will."

"Do you want to spend the rest of your life with me?"

"Yes. But on this island. I have my work. It is my contribution to the world. I cannot give it up. Ben, if you really loved me, you'd understand."

Ben was lost for words.

"Well?" said Anna. "Do you love me?"

"Of course I do. I've crossed seas to find you and to rescue you, and take you back. To your parents and as my wife, as we had planned it."

"No, Ben. Our plan was to have a family together, remember? I've been there, done that, and I'm NOT going to go through all that again. I can't."

"Anna, for God's sake! I don't mind that. I just want you, more than ever. To share my life with you." He held out his arms, and she moved towards him. The rain beat down. Their wet bodies clung to each other. Ben struggled to find a solution.

The crackle of the fire at the hub had died down, leaving the dull red glow of dying embers just visible through the rain. Neither Ben nor Anna had anything further to say to each other. Both were soaked to the skin, yet they continued to hug each other. Ben was relieved that the rain was masking his tears, and part of him wished that *Juli-Emma* was indeed like the Flying Dutchman, a figment of his imagination, an illusion.

He wanted to be trapped on the island if it was with Anna. How could he possibly tear her away from this place, and from her work? Trust Anna! He smiled at the thought. At uni she had a reputation for trampling out forest fires; now she is saving the oceans.

The distant sound of twin Evinrudes on full throttle brought him back to his senses, a deep roar which now and then screamed into a whine as the rib bounced over the swell and the props raced in thin air. The searchlight in the bows bathed the beach in jerks of white light. Ben realised time was running out.

"Anna. I know your work is important. I accept that. But your parents. I promised them-"

"Benny. Go back. Tell them I love them very much and that I miss them dreadfully. Tell them to come and see me, here, on the island. I'll fix it this end. They can stay as long as they like. I'll look after them. I'll do what a daughter's meant to do."

"Anna. I can't leave without you."

"Yes, you CAN. And you must. For me. Be strong!" She struggled to get the ring off.

"No, Anna. Keep it! Wear it for me!"

The roar of the engines died to a bubbling sound as Donnie took the rib off the plane to negoitate the surf. Once through, he gave her a burst towards the shore before throttling back. As the bows ran up the sandy beach, he cut the engines and jabbed the elevator button. Ben heard the hum of a quad bike getting nearer. He looked at Anna, as if he was waiting for her to say something.

"Come on guys!" shouted Donnie. "Give the bows a push and jump in!"

"Anna!" yelled Ben, "Come on!"

"Hurry!" shouted Donnie, as the stern of the boat began to swing towards the shore. The sound of the quad bike was getting louder.

Ben ran down to the water's edge and tried to swing the rib to keep the stern clear of the beach. Not getting enough leverage, he ran into the water and gave the stern a mighty shove.

Donnie dropped the engines. "Get in!" he shouted and reached his arm across the rubber gunwale to give Ben a hand.

"No! Wait!" cried Ben. "Give me two secs!" He waded back to the beach and ran to Anna. All he could say was her name.

"Go, Ben!" shouted Anna. "You go. Go ON, for God's sake!"

Ben hesitated. He saw the profile of the quad bike silhouetted against the glow from the hub. He ran to the rib, gave it an almighty shove and threw himself into the bows.

"Change of plan Donnie. Anna's staying," yelled Ben through the rain.

Donnie fired up the engines and selected reverse.

"HIDE, Anna," shouted Ben. "It's Seja! He's in a rage. RUN!"

She stood there looking at Ben. "Give Mum and Dad my love. Get them here. I love you."

"Will do!" shouted Ben, "I promise!" as the rib began to turn. He heard the clunk as Donnie changed to forward gear. "I love you, too. And give mine to Asba. Thank him for everything. Now RUN!"

Anna waved, turned and ran into the scrub-land behind the beach.

Ben watched her go, and by the time the quad arrived there was no sign of her. "Time to go, Donnie!"

The Evinrudes roared as Donnie aimed the rib at the surf. It climbed it with ease and whooshed down into the trough, ready for the next one. Ben heard a boom from the quad bike and a hiss overhead.

"What's up, Bosun?" yelled Donnie.

Ben guessed he hadn't noticed Seja on the shore with his quad equipped for emergencies and rescue.

"Dunno," Ben yelled back, just as the invisible Kevlar wire zinged between them, dragged at speed by whatever Seja had fired at them. Two seconds later, they found out what it was, as the sharp stainless-steel teeth of the grappling hook bit into the rubber gunwale. There was a hiss of escaping air. The rib swung violently to port as the wire tightened, and the boys had a job to remain aboard their craft.

Donnie throttled back. Ben swung the bow light around so they could inspect the damage. One arm of the grappling hook had ripped a four-inch tear in the gunwale and had caught on a reinforced seam. Ben tried to free it.

"You'll have to go back to slacken the wire," said Ben.

"That quad on the shore. The bastard's after us!" He shone the spotlight on the beach so Donnie could see the problem. Seja was standing on the quad, smirking, obviously pleased with his direct hit.

"Okay-sy. Let's have some fun," said Donnie, and he performed a one-eighty, feeding the slack wire carefully around the towing cleat on the transom plate. "Ready?"

"Go for it!" Ben had sussed the plan and held the spotlight ready.

Donnie pointed the bows due west and gunned it. The props dug deep as the water churned around them. Suddenly, the wire went taut. Ben heard the scream above the roar of the engines. He swung the light towards the beach just in time to see the figure of Seja being cartwheeled into the air as the quad was yanked into the sea.

It was no match for the 300 horse-power of the twin Evinrudes as they laboured at full throttle, towing their catch out to sea. The going got slower as the quad sank into the deeper waters off shore until finally the wire snapped allowing the vehicle to sink to the seabed.

Ben was able to extract the grappling hook and assess the tear. It would have to wait. Fortunately, only one compartment had gone down and the craft remained operational. Donnie freed the Kevlar and set his course. With its load released, the rib was up on the plane and gaining speed. Ben's presence in the bow helped to keep the nose down, and the distant red flare put up by Sasha helped Donnie keep on course.

Ben smiled when he heard Sasha's voice over the VHF, and he had to admit it had one over his home-made heliograph. Donnie told her about the punctured gunwale and Sasha agreed she'd come and meet them, reducing Donnie's distance of travel by a few kilometres.

Ben guessed that no-one on the island – except him – had been aware of *Juli-Emma*, the mother-ship, waiting well off shore, ready to pluck one of their number from under their noses. And his shipmates hadn't a clue what sort of day it had been for him.

He hoped Anna would be safe. Perhaps with him out of the way her learning servant might calm down, although Ben guessed he would not be very pleased about losing the quad bike. As the rib raced across the dark ocean, Ben realised she'd made the right choice. He knew she would be happier remaining on the island, and the knowledge numbed his pain.

32

"Where's Anna?" said Sasha, as the rib eased up alongside the *Juli-Emma*. "My God, the gunwale! That looks bad. What happened? Where is she?"

Ben heaved himself aboard leaving Donnie to recover the rib. "It's okay, Sash. Anna's not coming."

"She's what? She's not hurt, is she?"

"No. She's fine. She decided to stay."

"Oh, Ben! You poor boy. You must be very upset. Come inside. Let me get you something."

Two minutes later, there were three steaming mugs of hot chocolate on the saloon table. Donnie soon joined them, and his big grin lightened the mood. "Well, that was a game and a half. You should've seen us!"

He related to Sasha the events of the evening. Clearly, he was delighted he'd got one over on the man who'd punctured the rib. "And no great harm done. Just the one rip. I'll repair it in the morning... Hey, Bosun, it worked!" The two men high-fived it.

While Donnie was delighted the plan had gone well, Ben felt awkward he'd put him and Sasha to such trouble yet hadn't got Anna, the whole purpose of his mission. He was sad he'd lost her – for the second time – but he felt relieved she hadn't turned him down flat. He crashed out on his bunk without a heavy blanket of rejection weighing him down.

Although finding himself in his cabin the following morning did little to console him, he was relieved to be reunited with his two suitcases containing most of his worldly goods – or at least those he'd brought with him when he started his sabbatical.

Or most of them, he thought, making a mental inventory of those items he'd abandoned on Gorith Island, like his trusty camera with all the pictures he'd taken, his wallet with his bankers' cards and photo of Anna, his Rolex watch, his shaving mirror – along with his sponge bag and sundry clothes – and his passport. And his mobile phone. At least his iPad was in one of the cases.

After breakfast, while Donnie was repairing the rib, Sasha told Ben her news. She was pregnant.

"Hey Sash, that's fantastic! Congratulations!"

"Thanks, Ben. We're going to go public with it at the party on 3rd October. I'm so sorry there won't be your engagement to announce as well."

"Just one of those crazy things." Ben sang the words to pretend it was a triviality.

Sasha continued. "You know, I'm so lucky. Take Ling, for instance. She would love to have a family, but there isn't much hope. Perhaps the procedure might have worked... But it's a long shot."

"D'you know the sex of it?" asked Ben.

Sasha laughed. "No, Ben. We don't have an ultrasound on board – other than the depth-finder, and I'm not going to swim underneath the boat, er, I mean ship. So I'm really looking forward to getting to Hong Hong and finding out. I was hoping to quiz Anna on lots of things... Donnie's already signed him up for Rugbytots. He's hopeless!"

"Well, it's nice to hear I'm not *completely* hopeless!" said Donnie entering the saloon. "And guess what. I've repaired the gash. Made it obvious, though, like a duelling scar, evidence of the Battle of the Beach, where the trusty crew of *Juli-Emma* fought off the natives on a desert island to rescue an English gentleman from their evil clutches!"

"Don't worry, Ben," said Sasha. "He'll improve on it before we reach Hong Kong."

During the days following, Ben kept his friends enthralled by relating the account of his visit to Gorith Island, from after their phone conversation in Honolulu until he clambered aboard the rib on that dark rainy night. Donnie had advised the crew that they had thirty days sailing ahead of them, all being well, so Ben didn't feel the need to cut his stories short. And he was happy to answer the many questions his ship-mates fired at him during his narration.

Sasha listened eagerly when Ben told them about Anna's egg donations. He remembered she was a bit of a whiz on all that stuff. And now she was expecting, he was mightily impressed she seemed to know all there was to know about ovaries, eggs, embryos, foetuses and neonates. He went on to tell Sasha that Anna had taken it one stage further in that she had donated an ovary, which was why she wasn't around when he'd arrived on the island.

Donnie told Ben how brilliantly *Juli-Emma* had handled the storm in the Atlantic, and Sasha related the story of how 'Donald' got legless on dark rum in Antigua, and she had to carry him back – in her delicate state. They were pleased with the two ocean passages, and Sasha told Ben they could have reached his island a week earlier. Ben was relieved to hear that they'd had fun on the way and that the voyage hadn't just been one mad rush to reach him.

Naturally, Ben was anxious to get back and break the news to Anna's parents. The good news she was alive and well, the bad news she was staying on the island. But then there was the good news she'd invited them to join her. He knew they weren't expecting him back until December, so he hoped it would not be too much of a disappointment she wouldn't be with him. He reckoned they could reach Gorith Island in time to spend Christmas with their daughter.

Sasha and Donnie had begged him to stay for the party, and he thought he should accept their kind invitation. Donnie said they would easily be in Hongkers by mid-September, having effected the rescue so early. Ben thought it would give him time to drop into the office and see a few friends, then go back to Anna's parents straight after the celebration.

Unless the weather turned nasty, making passage aboard a super-yacht was a pleasant, relaxing experience, and in the company of others, it nurtured conversation of all sorts, from light banter through to reforming the world. And indeed, this had been the case for the last leg of *Juli-Emma*'s maiden voyage.

Both Sasha and Donnie were amazed to hear about Anna's work at the research station, and although neither were chemists, they were aware of how the seas were becoming more acidic and the knock-on effects. The term 'evil twin of climate change' was new to them, and hearing

Ben describing oceanic acidification in such a way provoked a heated discussion about global warming.

On 4th September they sighted the island of Guam and passed from the Pacific Ocean into the Philippine Sea. Donnie announced that they had only 2000 miles to go and to celebrate the occasion he had a treat for them.

"Lady and gentleman. Today, we are going to visit a world-famous national monument, indeed the largest national monument in the world." He waited for the flurry of questions.

Sasha teased him with a mock yawn and disappeared below. Ben was intrigued but went along with the tease and said nothing.

A few minutes later Sasha returned. "Gentlemen, soon we will be passing over the Mariana Trench, a crescent-shaped trough in the Earth's crust averaging 2,550 km long and 69 km wide."

"Wowsers!" said Ben. "How deep is it?"

"My friend Wiki says that if you dropped Mount Everest into it at its deepest point, the top of it would still be over a mile underwater."

"Why would anyone want to do that?" said Donnie.

"And why in Heaven's name is it a national monument?" added Ben.

Both questions provoked mirth but went unanswered. Sasha said she was going to wear her life jacket when passing over the trench, as she would be well out of her depth.

For Ben, it wasn't all fun. There were the quiet moments, when he was alone, on watch up on deck or lying awake in his cabin, when he would reflect on what had happened. Sometimes he would descend into his own ocean trench of depression, loving Anna for being Anna and hating her staying on the island, for causing his despair.

At other times he would be almost euphoric, proud that he'd respected her choice and pleased she would be able to continue with her work. He wondered if that, by leaving her there, he had in some way made a small contribution to saving the planet.

The euphoria would not last long. The truth was clear: he'd abandoned her, just as he'd done ten years ago. He'd ratted out on her, dumped her, left her at the mercy of that dreadful Svengali character. He could have pushed the bows of the rib out and left it at that; he didn't have to jump aboard. Donnie would have understood.

On the other hand, he'd made a promise to her parents. If he had disappeared off the face of the earth in the same way their only daughter had, he would have aggravated their grief rather than alleviated it.

Who's to say, he would ask himself, what might have happened if he hadn't climbed aboard that rib? Would there have been room on that small island for both him and Seja? Perhaps Anna would have been caught in the cross-fire of a feud which could have only ended in one way. Asba's words would come back to him: physical violence on Gorith Island was a mortal sin. The victor would not be permitted to win.

Sometimes, Ben couldn't help feeling a degree of sympathy for the man. Anna was a very attractive girl; appealing, alluring even. And maybe she enthralled him, perhaps unconsciously — La Belle Dame Sans Merci.

Did he have a right to blame Seja if she had? Ben wanted

to punch George when he heard he'd muscled in on Anna. Was Seja simply overcome by jealousy?

Ben had to admit that the creep hadn't forced him to 'go to Gorith'. Nobody was forced. He had seen with his own eyes that all those who had been gathered went up on that stage willingly. They knew what they were doing. They knew what to expect. All Gorith was doing was to make a difficult decision easier. Ben conceded that merely adding someone's name to a list did not constitute an attempt on his life.

Although his run-in with that arse-hole had made him question the true nature of the Gorith Foundation, he nevertheless felt a loyalty towards the algorithm and its followers. And, of course, to his dear learning servant, Asba. As for that other L-word, he told himself it was impossible to love artificial intelligence, wasn't it? At least Asba was a real person.

He had to admit that the concept of harvesting organs from dead people and selling them was, on the face of it, macabre and grotesque – the stuff of horror movies and nightmares. Indeed, Asba had warned Ben to brace himself before explaining it all, pointing out that the concept was not normally covered so early in a student's learning journey. And having had a chance to reflect on that aspect of Gorithian culture, Ben was now beginning to accept that the practice did have its merits; huge ones, for both receivers and donors.

Another matter for reflection was the constant surveillance on Gorith Island. Was it Big Brother spying on you? Or Gorith keeping a fatherly eye on everyone?

Christians the world over are quite happy for their god to be watching over them all the time. There, listening, just as Alexa or Siri or Gaston might be. All you need to do is to say the name: Our Father, Lord God, Heavenly Father, Almighty God. You don't have to wear a watch, but on the other hand, you can never be sure you've been heard; and if your prayer is answered, it can be in mysterious ways.

It was an emotional moment when, on 20th September 2020, they sailed into Hong Kong Harbour. All hands worked hard to present *Juli-Emma* in ship-shape condition, although Donnie was adamant the mother-to-be shouldn't undertake any strenuous work. He'd radioed ahead to his father, and a joyous welcoming party awaited them on the quayside. It had been an epic voyage of over 20,000 nautical miles, and Donnie was confident that it would earn its rightful place in the long and illustrious history of the company.

For Ben, five weeks on the yacht and 6,000 nautical miles had put sufficient time and distance between him and his island for the healing process to begin. While he would never forget Anna, Asba and his visit to their world, he was able to relive the memories without too much emotional upheaval.

His problems on arrival were of a more practical nature. They began shortly after the handshakes, the pats on the back and introductions were over, when he gave himself up to Hong Kong Border Clearance. It was a tricky moment, especially as the Chinese officials insisted on speaking Chinese and pretending they did not understand a word of English.

Eventually, Ben twigged what they were saying: until someone from the British Consulate could come and vouch for him, he would have to remain in detention. It was not part of his plan.

Fortunately, Ben had briefed Donnie on his predicament, and Donnie had promised to talk to his father about it. He still held sway in such matters and was able to persuade the authorities that perhaps a photocopy of Ben's passport might suffice until the Consulate could provide him with a replacement.

Producing a photocopy without the original had stumped them, but then Donnie had suggested that Ben's hotel in London might have kept a copy. A great idea, but none of them had the slightest idea where he'd stayed. Sasha saved the day by suggesting Ling would know because that's where those two had met.

33

For the second time in six weeks, Donnie and Sasha had sprung Ben from captivity, this time merely by providing the border authorities with a copy of his passport. He was able to visit the British Consulate in person, and they assured him his replacement would be ready in a few days. Donnie suggested he stayed at his place until then, as booking into a hotel might be awkward without a passport, especially if you didn't have any plastic either.

On the second night, they decided to dine at The Jockey Club, and Donnie invited his sister to make up the four. Ben was able to thank Ling in person for sweet-talking the manager of the airport hotel into emailing the passport copy. After the meal, Ben offered to walk her home; and being the hospitable person she was, Ling asked him in for a nightcap.

Two days later Ling asked if Donnie and Sasha would like to come round to her place for a kitchen supper and to bring Ben along too if he wasn't otherwise engaged. The meal was exquisite; Ben had never tasted such wonderful food. The four of them got on splendidly, and Ling was fascinated to hear more stories of their mighty voyage around to the far side of the world and the dramatic rescue.

At the end of the meal, Donnie said he ought to get Sasha back as she was feeling a bit tired, and Ling insisted they did not lift a finger to help clear away the dishes. Ben agreed and said he would stay and help Ling.

He told Ling about his silly dream, about bumping into her at the Oriental Spa at Landmark Mandarin Hotel, and he asked her if she'd ever been there. No, she said, but I've always wanted to. He had to go and pick up his new credit cards from the bank next door to the hotel the following day and wondered if Ling would like to drop into the Spa with him and give it a go. Yes, she said. She could fit it in between appointments, just.

Later in the week, Ling told him she was going dinghy sailing at the club, but she imagined the last thing he would want to do was to get in a boat with her after all those weeks on *Juli-Emma*. On the contrary, he protested, he was really looking forward to doing just that.

By the day before the great party, they'd seen quite a bit of each other. Ben had brought her up to speed on the mission, and having been involved from the very beginning, she'd shown great interest in how it had all panned out. And finding a sympathetic ear, Ben shared with her his thoughts and feelings about Anna. She listened and made a good job of helping him come to terms with it all. But when the opportunity arose, she took his mind off Anna completely.

For his part, he asked about how she was feeling following her stay in hospital after her brother's wedding. She said that the robotic surgery had gone well, and only time would tell if the procedure had worked. He was impressed that the scar was so small.

On that Friday, Ben's world was thrown upside down. He had decided to clock into 'the orifice', aka the Head Office of Standard Chartered, to bring himself up to date on matters corporate. He bumped into Warren, a colleague.

"Bengy, my old mate! How *are* you? How's the sabbatical going, then? And I'm just sooo sorry you're not coming back. We will miss you!" Warren had frowned, trying to show sympathy but his eyes were dancing with delight. "So, what are you going to do?"

"Oh, a bit of this and that," said Ben. Like hot-footing it *right now* to HR, he thought.

HR went through the standard script, cherry-picking the relevant clauses. Ben's mind was in a whirl, but he heard the words 'letting you go' and 'good for your career'. And what a wonderful job he'd done over the – they paused to consult their notes – past ten years.

The surprise was that he was being posted to their international headquarters in London, *on promotion*, and as he was on leave, would he mind awfully getting his arse over there right now as the position was vacant.

Didn't he get the email? He bloody well didn't.

'Now' didn't mean 'now'. Tomorrow would do. He said he'd fly on Sunday and report on Wednesday, giving him a couple of days to get over the jet-lag. He got the HR smile.

It slowly dawned on Ben that after the party he wouldn't be seeing much of Ling. He couldn't identify the precise moment, but he sensed that their relationship as friends, mates, and pals had already finished – and been replaced by something much deeper. He wondered if she would feel the same. When he broke the news to her about the job, she was devastated – and the declarations of undying love were made as they held each other tightly. He said she must come and visit him in England, and she implored him to come back to Hong Kong as often as possible.

The party for Sasha and Donnie was a lavish affair. It had to be. Otherwise, the share price of Jason Mardine would have taken a hit. The news of Sasha's pregnancy added a buzz to the proceedings, and both Ben and Ling put on a brave face and pretended they were enjoying the celebrations, rather than drowning their sorrows over Ben's imminent return to London. Bearing in mind he was flying back the following day, they sneaked away early and hoped nobody had noticed. In the morning, Ling brought him breakfast in bed.

Ben was pleased he had time at Chek Lap Kok Airport to load his address book from his iPad onto his new phone, and he thought he'd try ringing Uplands. Arthur and Linda were having breakfast.

"Ben! My goodness. Where are you?"

"Hong Kong, Arthur, about to get on a flight to Heathrow."

"What? Any news?"

"Yes. Lots." Ben took a deep breath. "She's safe and well." Ben let it sink in. He heard a muffled cry.

"Sorry, Ben. Do you mean Anna? What did you say?"

"Yes, Arthur. Anna. She's alive and well."

"But, that's wonderful! Have you seen her?"

"Yes, I have seen her – and talked to her. She's fine. Physically and mentally. She sends her love. Look, any chance of coming down and seeing you tomorrow? I can report progress then."

"Yes of course. Any time. Do you want to stay the night?"

"Love to, that would be kind." Ben could hear Linda in the background. "Around ten thirty?"

"Perfect. And Ben. Linda's just reminded me, there's a parcel here for you."

Many time-zones later, Ben found himself on the same train as six months previously, rumbling out of Charing Cross on its way to Staplehurst. This time he had all his luggage with him. Worth the hassle, he thought, as it saved him checking into a hotel. Unusually, he had slept well on the plane, all the way, not having had much sleep the night before.

A warm welcome and a cup of coffee awaited him at Uplands. Arthur had lost weight, but Linda was positively sprightly. The three of them sat around the kitchen table, and Ben noticed the parcel on the floor by the dresser. Surely not, he thought. He was itching to open it, but decided he would first present his carefully sanitised report to Anna's anxious parents.

They were thrilled she was alive, and that she had found peace and happiness on the island. They were proud she was working at a research station, on something so important, and when Ben told them Anna would remain there, they both agreed it was the right thing for her to do.

It was a good lead-in to the next bit of his speech. "She wants you to visit her, on the island."

Linda's eyes opened wide and she smiled at Arthur.

He frowned and stroked his chin. "Ben, I'm not sure I can make it. The journey, I mean. It's an awfully long way for someone in my condition."

"Yes, you can, dear! I'll look after you!" said Linda.

Ben let them discuss the matter and went over to the parcel. He ripped off the brown paper and unzipped his old cabin bag. The first thing he took out was a battered camera. It was the one he'd bought at Heathrow six months previously. He flipped up the flash, and some grains of fine sand fell onto the table. Nothing happened when he switched it on, and the manual zoom wouldn't rotate, but he was able to extract the SD card.

Next, he went to one of his suitcases in the hall and took out his iPad. Having wiped the sand off the card, he fitted it into the SD slot and returned to the kitchen.

Linda cried when she saw the photographs of Anna. Ben was no Litchfield, but she looked stunning, a picture of perfection, happiness radiating from her bright blue eyes. Ben moved onto the shots of the island and the villas, Ben's dining hall and the lagoon. Arthur gasped at the colours of the birds and wild flowers and was intrigued by the crater.

"It's like paradise!" said Linda.

Ben smiled and felt a lump in his throat. They asked all the obvious questions, when could they go, how would they get there, and who would look after Uplands when they were away. Ben said he'd be happy to house-sit, and assured them he would handle all the arrangements and go with them to Heathrow. Anna would meet them when they arrived on the island. He advised them to travel light and reassured them the journey would be fine – first class most of the way – and that, all being well, they could be there for Christmas.

"Ben, how long could we stay?"

"Entirely up to you, Linda."

"You mean as long as we like? Arthur! We could emigrate! Like the Nortons did, going to join their daughter in Australia, remember? You'd only have to do the one journey!"

"Do they have doctors there," said Arthur, "who could handle the, er-"

"Yes, Arthur, they certainly do. A fully equipped medical centre."

That evening, in the privacy of the Uplands guest room, Ben unpacked the rest of his cabin bag, the old one which had seen service in the Pacific. Both djellabas had been washed, ironed and neatly folded into a clear plastic bag. He checked his wallet and found all the credit and debit cards were there, as was the picture of Anna plus a few business cards he'd collected.

His old mobile was dead, but his Rolex was still ticking away, albeit on Honolulu time. He felt that familiar feeling, the pain behind the eyes. *Stop it, you fool.* Wondering what to do with his old passport served as a distraction.

His new job turned out to be much better than he'd expected, well supported by good staff and with a large luxury office on the nineteenth floor overlooking the Thames. He was stunned by the generosity of his entertainment allowance. His PA explained it was to keep up with the Chinese. And with his connections to the House of Jason Mardine, he was expected to pull in some good deals.

Uplands Farmhouse was lovely to come home to, a retreat far from the buzz of Canary Wharf – and compared with Hong Kong, it was a different world. Linda mothered him, and Arthur treated him as an equal, and together they would talk for hours, often over a beer, about politics, technology, religion or any other subject that might be in the news. He confided in Ben that his prostate wasn't as young as it used to be, but he didn't want Linda fussing about it.

Their application to visit Gorith Island had taken a few evenings to complete, but Ben eventually managed to get it off in good time for their planned departure in early November. It was accepted, and Ben spent some time with Linda and Arthur going through the documents.

Ben and Ling kept in touch using Facetime, but he missed the cuddles and the closeness which technology had yet to replicate. While Ben's job prevented him from flitting over to Hong Kong, he had no trouble at all in persuading Ling to join him at Uplands for Christmas. After Anna's parents had departed on their saga, he found Uplands lonely, and he looked forward very much to Ling coming to stay.

It struck Ben that the Arrivals Hall at Heathrow was not the most romantic location, but the reunion was truly wonderful. He thought Ling looked radiant, fit and well, and with a glow to rival that of any film star, including Yang Mi. When Ben's chauffeur dropped them at Uplands, Ling could hardly believe they were only fifty kilometres from London, and she immediately fell in love with the house, the garden and the surrounding Kent countryside.

Ben had asked Linda's daily to have a fire going for their arrival, and the crackle of the logs and the Christmas decorations set the perfect scene for Ling to tell Ben about the present she was going to give him.

"Hang on, Ling. Shouldn't it wait for Christmas day? Surely it should be a surprise?"

"Yes, Ben. It will be a surprise, a big one!"

"So why tell me now?"

"Because I can't give you the present until after Christmas."

Ben had guessed, and he could hardly contain his smile. But he would fake surprise when she told him.

"Okay, then. Surprise me."

"Have a guess first!"

"You're not going to, er, have a baby, are you?" Ben shook his head as if it were the last thing in the world she would do.

"No." She was beaming.

Ben tried to hide his disappointment. It would be awful if he let on. Sasha had told him about the op, and that it was a long shot, and he hadn't given the possibility the slightest thought until he saw her at Heathrow; somehow, she just looked different. He kicked himself for mentioning it and thought he should apologise for being so insensitive. But she was giggling. Then he got it.

He couldn't believe it. He was in utter shock. Talk about surprises, he thought. That was a haymaker, and I didn't see it coming. He consoled himself for being half right and decided to open the champagne there and then, rather than serve it as an aperitif before the candlelit dinner he'd arranged for that evening. Ling allowed herself one sip, but no more. Ben gulped down his first glass. He needed to.

"Ling, I can't tell you how pleased I am. It's the most wonderful news, for you – and for us. And I have something I'd like to ask-"

"STOP!... Ben. It *is* wonderful, for both of us. I'm thrilled. To be having them, and that they are yours. I cannot think of any man I would rather have as the father of my children. And I hope we can be good parents together. But-"

"What is it, Ling? We love each other, don't we?"

"Yes. We do. But my answer has to be 'no'. I know you love Anna and she loves you. I realise that. I also understand she decided to stay on the island. But what if she came back? Supposing she finished her work on that island and returned? Perhaps not tomorrow, but next year? Or in five, ten or fifteen years? Think of the complications. The practicalities. For a start, this is her house. We are only looking after it for her and her parents. And if you two did want to get together, I would... I'd hate it. But another part of me says she has a right to you. I would just be in the way. I'd have to stand aside.

"Remember, Ben. You proposed to her on that island, and she accepted. The contract was sealed. Just four months ago. And you and Anna were together long before you and I met. You and she go back a long way, thirteen years is it? You can't rewrite history. You can't undo what you've done, can you?... Ben?"

"But-"

"No buts, Ben. Let's just carry on as we are. Live for the moment. Love each other. Love our kids. Love life, have fun... Come on... Don't be silly!... Come here."

There were many celebratory toasts that festive season, at Sasha's parents on Christmas day with Donnie and Sash who had flown over for four days, with Donnie's best man and his new wife on New Year's Eve, and at the very informal party his PA had arranged after the holiday. His boss crowed at the news and welcomed Ling into the fold with a fatherly arm around her shoulders, happy that the great tai-pan's only daughter was partnered to a member of his own tribe.

Nobody was concerned that Ling and Ben were not

rushing down the aisle. All their friends and family appreciate that in 2021 the lock in holy wedlock had long gone, and it had become quite acceptable for parents not to make that commitment for life, but to break it if and when it suited either or both the parties.

Ben understood and accepted Ling's feelings on the matter, and he did everything possible to make her feel she was not second best, not a stand-in when the star of the show failed to turn up, not a substitute hauled onto the rugby field when another player – a better one – got carried off with a torn ligament.

34

The flurry of Christmas and New Year soon passed. Ben had persuaded Ling to remain at Uplands as he was keen for her to be attended by a Harley Street gynaecologist renowned for his specialism in multiple pregnancies. All was going well on that front. Ben was pleased Ling and Sasha had become good friends, now that Donnie was back at the London office.

There was no news from Anna or her parents, and Ben assumed all was well. He did wonder about Arthur, but he knew they were both in good hands medically. Linda had asked Ben if there were any retirement homes on the island, and he wondered if they might prolong their stay. He'd got the impression she was worried about something. He wasn't sure if it was for herself or Arthur.

All was also going well on the job front. It seemed that his association with Jason's was opening doors for him, and he soon realised that he was above the level of the daily grind. No longer in the engine room but on the bridge. He even had staff to steer the ship, leaving him free to work out where the next port of call was going to be. Late nights in the office were rare, but when they did occur, his driver was only too pleased to whizz him in the Mercedes down to Uplands.

On one such late night in early March, he was dropped off at home having dozed for most of the way in the back of the Merc. Ling was fast asleep in bed. Before joining her, he decided to have a cup of tea. On the kitchen table was a package about the size of a small shoe box, addressed to him. Removing the outer wrapping revealed a smart wooden box, on the top of which was sellotaped an envelope with his name on it. Inside was a single sheet of A4 covered on both sides in close typescript.

> Hi, Benny, it's me, Anna. I'm dictating this to Gaston, so if there are any spelling mistakes, it's his fault. But if I stumble a bit, it'll be mine. Anyway here goes. News from Gorith Island!
>
> The first thing is we're all OK. Very well in my case and Dad's hanging on in there. Mum's not so hot, but she's loving it here. Both of them have joined in well; Mum's painting and Dad's learnt to fish. Both are having a great time and have met lots of people and made some good friends.
>
> They love their new names. Mum's is Lida and Dad is now Apol. We had a lot of laughs about that, but you soon get used to them. But I still call them Mum and Dad.
>
> Oh, and they send you their love, and they're enormously thankful to you for the help you gave them, and for taking care of the house. And they want to thank you for, er, finding me – I can't think why, but that's parents for you. And I want to thank you for, well, for everything... Sorry... I'm going all silly...
>
> You'll be glad to know your dining hall is back up and

running – and they still put those little candle thingies on the tables each evening. The council investigated the fire and found they were not the cause. They returned an open verdict, but we all know who did it. Coincidences like that don't just happen.

He sends his love, by the way. He really means it, you know. He was very fond of you. And he knew you were planning to leave the island. God knows how. Or should that be Gorith knows how?

And – and and and – he became my learning servant! I've had seven months with him. He's a wonderful man. Seja got stripped of his cross after firing his harpoon at you, but he's trying to earn it back by siring even more offspring throughout the world. And he's started giving blood, which might just cool his ardour. It's funny, but I didn't find him at all attractive. Just not my type.

Talking of the attack on the beach, did you realise I was watching? I ran into the trees and then stopped. I crouched down so Seja wouldn't see me, but I could see everything – except when that light shone right at me. Made my eyes go funny. I'm surprised the man in the boat didn't notice me.

I'd changed my mind, by the way – about joining you – but I had to wait for the right moment. Seja was there, between me and the boat, and then you pushed off. He fired that thingamajig, and I thought the boat was turning round to come back to the shore.

I thought you were coming back to pick me up. Then you suddenly shot off again, out to sea. The quad bike followed you, but Seja fell off the thing and was lying on the sand moaning about his back. I grabbed my chance and ran to the water's edge. I was screaming my head off, but you obviously didn't hear me above the engines.

I watched you. I kept shouting. And I saw a red flare go up, far out to sea. I assumed it was a ship of some sort. The noise of the engines got fainter and fainter, and I realised there was no way you were going to hear me. Anyway, I'd lost my voice by then. I waited until the boat had gone completely... Sorry... Slight sniffle there... Then I walked home, on my own, in the dark to the other side of the island.

I kept thinking you had done all that for me, gone to all that trouble, finding me in the first place, and coming here, and laying on the rescue ship. And the ring!... All that, just for me! You made me feel I was worth something...

Work's going well. The development contract's been signed, and we hand over on Friday, the day before The Gathering. Mila and I have done our bit, the recording of data and the basic research. It's now up to the Koreans to make the stuff. It'll be a few years before it's in production, but I'm pleased I was part of the project in the early days.

And I'm pleased I made those donations. I feel I've made up for, you know, not allowing my little girls to give their organs, for all those lives I could have saved just by giving my agreement. And perhaps I've made up for being such a bad mum by enabling others to become mums.

Now we come to the tricky bit, so hold on to your potatoes. Mum and Dad have decided to go to Gorith on Saturday. They are terribly excited about it. Really. They know exactly what's it about and think it is fantastic. I have talked it through with them, and honestly, Benny, they're really up for it. It solves all their worries.

Dad says they're at the age when they take one day at a time... you know, not being sure how long they've got. And Mum's worst fear is going before Dad and leaving him to cope on his own which he couldn't.

Do you remember my grandmother? Mum's mum?

Anyway, she had Alzheimer's. It was so sad. Dreadful. The person you know, the person you love, dies before your eyes, slowly. Honestly, Benny, it was heartbreaking. Mum thinks she's got it, too. I reckon in her case it's just old-age dementia, but she's terrified it's going to get worse.

It would be awful for Dad, to lose her in that cruel way. Imagine what he would feel. What a way to end it all!... It puts me off religion. If there is a god up there, he's a cruel god, if you ask me... But then you're not asking me. Back to parents, before I get cross.

They're very excited about the prospect of helping others, saving lives, even. They know they're old and decrepit, but they hope Gorith will be able to salvage something. Apparently, a kidney has a clock-life of about 140 years, so they should be in luck. And I'll be there at The Gathering with them, cheering them on! It'll be fun. So, Benny, no sadness please! See the positive!

Er, just thinking if there's anything else... Yes, Uplands. All fixed. Gaston helped, and the documents have gone off to London. It's yours – or soon will be. Hope you got the parcel. I cleaned the camera off as best I could, but it had been lying in the sand for a couple of days. Asba put the things together, bless him. I don't think I could have handled it...

Well, all the best!... Sorry... I'm hopeless at goodbyes."

Ben sighed. He looked inside the box. Wrapped in lots of tissue paper, there were three smaller boxes, each the size of a pack of playing cards crafted in polished hardwood with a brass catch. And a much smaller one which he recognised; she was returning the ring. He went to the study and put it in the left-hand draw of Arthur's desk. As for the other boxes, he hesitated. They were quite heavy. He guessed what they were, but couldn't understand why there were three of them. He thought he'd leave it till morning.

As usual, he woke up early and crept down to make a cup of tea, Earl Gray for him and green tea for her ladyship. She was beginning to regain consciousness when he returned.

"Here we are, then, your grace!" he said.

"And a very good morning to you, Ben."

"Sorry. I said good morning earlier, but you were out of it. Sleep well?"

"Sort of. And you? Thanks for the tea. By the way, what's that parcel doing in my kitchen with your name on it?"

"Oh, that," said Ben. "I'll get it."

Two minutes later he returned with the wooden box and the A4 sheet. "You'd better read that first, then we can go through the box together."

Ben watched her. Her face was a mixture of smiles and frowns. He waited until she had finished.

"The names, Ben. That's weird! Apol and Lida?"

"Well, their names were Arthur and Linda, so at least they didn't have to change their first initial. Anna's is Azor, so she kept hers, too."

"You say Arthur and Linda's names 'were'. Does that mean...?"

"I'm afraid so. No, not afraid. That's the wrong word. I'm pleased. It's a good way to go. It suited them, at their age." He tipped the contents of the wooden box onto the bed. "Here, take one," and he handed Ling one of the three smaller boxes. "I'll open one and you open one."

He watched Ling's face as she lifted the catched, raised the lid and lifted the cross out of his dark blue velvet bed. She gasped.

"My God, Ben. It's beautiful. It's so heavy."

"Turn it over."

"There's an inscription on the back. It says, '*In loving memory of Lily Dahlia, who gave life to so many. Bless you. Gorith.*' So she's gone. That's so sad."

Ben opened his. "This one reads '*In loving memory of Apple Olive, who gave life to so many. Bless you. Gorith.*' He was such a lovely guy. We were close."

Ling rummaged around the discarded tissue paper and found the third box. She held it out to Ben.

"No, Ling. Your turn."

She opened the box and extracted the cross. Ben watched.

She felt the weight of it in her hands and smiled at Ben. "Must be solid gold!" She ran the tips of her long slender fingers over the intricate pattern cast in the higly polished metal. Then she turned it over and read the inscription on the back. She frowned.

"Ling. Read it out."

"Sure. Same as the others, except the name of course. '*In loving memory of Azalea Orchid, who gave life to so many. Bless you. Gorith.*' Azalea Orchid – what a lovely name!... What is it, Ben? Why are you looking at me like that?... Ben?"

He opened his mouth to speak.

"No, wait! Let me see if I can get it. Two flowers, therefore a woman. Short name must be..." Ben watched as Ling's jaw dropped, dragging down the corners of her mouth. She dropped the cross on the duvet cover as if it were red hot. The smooth skin between her eyebrows crumpled, and she burst into tears. His flood-gates opened, too.

The tea in both cups – untouched – was stone cold by the time the sobbing had stopped.

That evening after work, Ben and Ling were sitting in the farmhouse drawing room on either side of the log fire. They talked about Anna, and about the island. Ben said that when he waved goodbye to her, he had a feeling he would never see her again. He told Ling about how he had proposed to Anna in the villa and presented her with a ring before rushing off to set up the camera. He related how Anna was wearing it when he returned, but when the boat arrived to pick them up she had urged him to leave the island without her. And he explained to Ling that in the large box, along with the gold crosses, was the ring he had given her.

He went to the study and returned with the ring box, saying that Ling might as well have it, as a small memento of the part she had played in the adventure. There was nobody else in his life who would want it. It wasn't as if he had a sister or a daughter to give the thing to.

He passed the box over and went to the drinks cabinet to pour himself a whisky. He turned around to see Ling standing up, back to the fire. He was pleased to see she was smiling having been so upset that morning. Strange, he'd thought at the time, considering she'd never met Anna. But then, they were a right old pair, Anna giving her eggs away, and Ling suffering from anovulation – at least until her ovary graft.

He returned and flopped down in his fireside armchair. Ling remained standing. He noticed she was wearing the ring. "Glad to see it fits," he said.

"It sure does! And, Ben. It's a yes. A big yes!" She giggled, and Ben rapidly struggled to his feet.

The twins arrived in June. Ben was thrilled to have two girls, and laughed when Donnie offered him his commiserations. Just what I wanted, Ben told him, and I'm ahead in numbers.

Ling and Ben tied the knot the following spring, at the In and Out Club, London. The families remained close and grew up together. Jack was a tough little bugger and was the spitting image of Donnie with his ginger hair and dark eyes. Ben's two girls had curly blonde hair, large blue eyes and loved to dance. Ben knew how lucky he was. Things had turned out well. Like they were 'always meant to be', as his old nan used to say.

THE END

'Coincidence may be described as the chance encounter of two unrelated causal chains which — miraculously, it seems — merge into a significant event.'
Arthur Koestler 1905-1983.

Printed in Great Britain
by Amazon